The Fleischer Menace

By Brett Hoskins

Copyright © 2024 Brett Hoskins

This book is a work of fiction. All names and characters are fictitious and any resemblance to actual persons, living or dead, or real events is coincidental.

Published by Treacle Moon

Cover illustrations by Katy Cambridge

All rights reserved. No part of this publication may be re-sold, reproduced, distributed or transmitted in any form or by any means, including photocopying, recording or other electronic or mechanical methods, without the prior written permission of the author, except in the case of brief quotations embodied in critical reviews and certain other non-commercial uses permitted by copyright law.

ISBN: 9798320144191

Chapter One

Brighton, England - 2054 BST Saturday 14th July

    McCabe was still tuning his guitar when they walked into Reinhardt's Bar and one of them shot Bronek in the chest, two rounds tap tap. Two men, one tall and broad, the other short and stocky, both wearing black balaclava style ski masks and blue boiler suits. The short one held a Franchi SPAS-12 shotgun which he pointed at the audience to keep them under control, the other had a silenced 9mm Glock 17 handgun. The shooter, the one with the Glock, gave Bronek a third shot in the head as he dropped from his chair and lay contorted and silent on the oak boards. Fifty eight witnesses sat in stunned silence for a few moments and then the screaming started as the gunmen calmly walked out into the street. No gig tonight.

    By the time the police arrived and contained the scene the audience had fled, which left Jimmy the barman, Julia who owned Reinhardt's, and the four surviving members of the Reinhardt's Bar Allstars as the only remaining witnesses. Mario the chef, who had been in the kitchen when the shooting took place, had seen nothing and was refusing to come out; instead he was carrying on with his work as if everything was normal. Genna and Emily, the Sussex University student part time waitresses, had run shrieking through the kitchen and out of the back door as soon as the shots were fired and hadn't returned. In time, most of the audience would be tracked down by the police who would trace some from their table reservation details and others because they were known to the staff of Reinhardt's, but their statements wouldn't be of much use.

McCabe, having moved away from the body, was sitting on a barstool and steadily emptying the bottle of Chablis which Jimmy always set up for him when he played at Reinhardt's. Julia and Jimmy had disappeared into the little back room behind the bar and were drinking brandy and chain smoking. Andy, George and Stewart, the other members of the band, were sitting at a table with their backs to and as far away as they could get from Bronek's body and they were not speaking.

The paramedics, who arrived shortly after the police, had confirmed that Bronek was dead and the police had begun their murder enquiry with well practiced efficiency. A forensic pathologist was contacted and asked to examine the body and a uniformed constable took the names and addresses of the remaining witnesses while he waited for the pathologist to arrive. To ensure continuity of evidence the same constable would remain with Bronek's body until it was removed from the scene and delivered to a mortuary for a post mortem examination. Two detectives, who had been standing on the pavement outside while they were politely and quietly briefed by a uniformed sergeant, stepped through the front door and into the room to have a look at Bronek's corpse. Then they began the process of collecting evidence.

Eventually, over two hours after the shooting, the detective who was clearly in charge approached McCabe and sat on the stool next to him. She was tall, slim, in her late twenties and attractive with short black hair expensively cut. Her clothes were stylish and gave the impression that she didn't have to rely on just her police salary. The Detective Sergeant who was with her looked tough and impassive as he stood to the side, and slightly behind her, with a notebook and pen at the ready. He projected the impression that he'd seen it all in his 23 years of police service and he wasn't going to believe anything that McCabe told them.

"No need to be too formal, is there?" she asked. "I'm Detective Inspector Laura Connor and I need to ask you some questions."

McCabe looked at her, still visibly shocked by seeing someone murdered six feet away from him.

"Can we make a note of your name, sir, and jot down some details?"

"McCabe."

"First name?"

"Chad - Chad McCabe"

"Did you see what happened, Mr McCabe?"

"We were tuning up, just about to start the gig. Two men walked in and one of them shot Bronek."

"Are you a friend of Mr Kowalski?"

"Kowalski?"

"The victim. That's the name we found on his bank card."

"Was that his name? Sorry, I only knew him as Bronek."

"Yes, his name is Bronek Kowalski. Do I take it that you were in this band together?"

"Yes. When we get together and play here we're called the Reinhardt's Bar Allstars. It's a pretty informal arrangement. We play Gypsy Jazz."

"I'm not familiar with that," replied the detective.

"You will have heard it," said McCabe. "Gypsy Jazz. In France they call it Jazz Manouche. It's a swing jazz style developed by Django Reinhardt and Stéphane Grappelli between the two world wars."

"Ah, yes. I've heard of Stéphane Grappelli," she replied.

"There you are then. You'll have heard him playing Gypsy Jazz. That's what we do. The five of us," he gestured to the three Allstars who were talking to other police officers. "The four of us now ..." he tailed off.

"Do you play together regularly?"

"When we're all available. I've been away for a while and this was my first gig with them for a year."

"But you didn't know Mr Kowalski's surname."

"Music's like that. We get together, do the gig and then go our separate ways. I play rhythm guitar. Bronek played rhythm guitar. George over there plays violin, Andy plays solo guitar and Stewart plays double bass. We don't need to get together to practice because we all know the numbers and play them regularly at other gigs, so we don't get to know each other much. I know Andy quite well but not the others, especially Bronek. He didn't talk much. Just turned up for the gigs and left immediately after. The others stay around for a drink afterwards. I know Bronek was married but that's about it."

On the other side of the room the pathologist had finished his preliminary examination of Bronek's body and a police photographer was recording the scene.

"You say you've been away for a while. Do you mind telling me where?"

"I've been in France. I took my boat down to the Med through the French canals."

"Alright for some," interrupted the Sergeant as he looked up from his note taking. "Holiday?"

"Sort of," answered McCabe. "Travelling, playing in bars, stuff like that."

The Sergeant wrote it down while muttering, "Alright for some," again.

"OK. I think that will do for now," said Connor. "We might want to ask you some more questions. Where can we get in touch with you if we do?"

"I live on my boat," replied McCabe. "I'm at Brighton Marina for a few days and then I'm moving the boat to St Katharine Docks in London."

McCabe opened his mobile phone cover and took a card out of one of its pockets and gave it to her.

"Here. That's my boat name, email address and phone number."

She read the boat name from the card, "Honeysuckle Rose. Pretty. Not planning to leave the country again, are you?"

"Not for a few weeks," replied McCabe.

"OK, thanks."

She turned away and then turned back again and stared directly into McCabe's eyes.

"Do you know why anyone would want to shoot Mr Kowalski?"

"It was a mistake," answered McCabe. "They were supposed to shoot me."

Chapter Two

Lower Shiplake - 0042 BST Sunday 15th July

The electric gates closed quietly and firmly behind the anonymous looking black Vauxhall Astra as it drove slowly along the wide gravel drive and stopped under the floodlights, in front of the imposing Thameside house. The two occupants, Ernst Kegel and Gunter Meise, got out of the car and Kegel the driver, who had shot Bronek, stretched his arms and shoulders while Meise went to the front and rear of the car and removed the magnetic false number plates. The two men had travelled the 87 miles from Brighton without speaking and had taken their time. The journey could have been quicker but, knowing that their Fiat escape car would be tracked by police ANPR cameras, they had first driven to Poynings, a small village behind Brighton on the northern side of the South Downs, where they had left the Vauxhall at the roadside an hour earlier. There Kegel and Meise had set fire to the Fiat, leaving the boiler suits and ski masks in it, to destroy any evidence. Taking their weapons with them, they had returned to the A23 in the Vauxhall and driven carefully and quietly to the house in Lower Shiplake.

Still without a word they entered the property together and then separated, Gunter to eat and Ernst to report to his boss Ulrich Fleischer.

Chapter Three

"That's why I've been away," continued McCabe. "There are people who want to kill me."

Laura Connor stared fixedly at him and said, "You'd better explain that."

"About a year ago I got caught up in a criminal operation which was smuggling drugs and people in a yacht from France to Brighton. I was the main reason that it got broken up."

"I remember that," said the detective. "A yacht called Tiger Fish."

"Right. I'm the reason that they got caught so I made a lot of enemies that day. Myself and my friend, Tricia Knight. We thought it would be a good idea to stay away for a while which is why we've been abroad for the past year."

"Who in particular do you think would want to harm you?"

"It could be any of them. There were a lot of people involved: the traffickers in France, a terrorist group, the people who were running the yacht, Ricky Bishop and his thugs who went to prison."

"Bishop, yes. A nasty bit of work." Laura Connor was thoughtful for a few moments, "So you think that you were the target and that they shot Mr Kowalski by mistake?"

"I think that's probable. We look similar. Tall, dark hair, both playing guitar in Reinhardt's tonight."

"In which case you're still in danger, so be careful. We'll follow up that line of enquiry. You say you're going to sail to London?"

"In a few days, yes. We're going to leave my boat near Tower Bridge and then borrow a cruiser and have a look at the upper Thames."

"This would be you and - did you say Tricia Knight?"

"Yes."

"Do you have a UK address?"

"No, as I said, I live on my boat. Any correspondence I need is done by email."

"OK. We've got your phone number so we know how to contact you if we need to." She gave McCabe a card, "Please call me if you think of anything that might help us."

"I will."

"Good. Thanks for your help. I'm sorry we've kept you here. You're free to leave."

"Is it OK if I take my guitar?" asked McCabe, pointing to it on the stage.

"Not tonight, I'm afraid," replied Connor. "At the moment it's evidence in a murder scene. Nothing can be removed from this room until our forensic people have finished examining it."

"How long will that take? I'll need it for gigs."

"Twenty four hours maybe. Perhaps longer. We'll deal with it as quickly as we can. Thanks again for your help."

They both stood and Laura Connor and her sergeant moved on to interview George Lee the violin player.

McCabe could have called for a taxi to collect him but he was eager to leave and he went without saying goodbye to the Allstars or the staff, glad to be away from the horror of Reinhardt's Bar still with Bronek's corpse lying by the stage. He walked the half a mile from Reinhardt's to the taxi rank in East Street, cautiously aware of every shadow in every shop doorway, and it was with a sense of relief that he settled on the back seat of the cab for the short drive to Brighton Marina.

McCabe always seemed to return to Brighton. He had a property there in Lewes Crescent and he turned to look at its white painted facade shining out of the darkness as the taxi travelled past on Marine Parade; a four storey, Grade 1 listed Georgian building in one of the city's prime locations. It was extremely valuable and now that he had moved out of the upper apartment and let it, the rent from that, coupled with the sale of the ground floor flat on a long lease, more than funded his lifestyle of sailing and playing music. He now had a considerable amount of cash and investments and a regular income from the rent.

It wasn't his property that brought him back to Brighton - a management company looked after that - it was the town itself. For more than thirty years since he first went to live there he had left many times but always, sooner or later, he was drawn back to the town which never seemed to change. Whatever monstrosities the planners and developers inflicted upon it, Brighton still maintained its character and atmosphere and was like a risqué old lady who would never stop having fun.

It wasn't the people who brought him back either. People came and went in McCabe's life and he didn't mourn them but just moved on. He had no family ties anymore and the only person who even remotely resembled anything like family was Tricia Knight. So much had happened in the last year, since they had escaped from the violence of Ricky Bishop, that the shared dangers and experiences had brought them closer together by the day.

After sailing from England to Fécamp in France to get away from the trouble that Brighton posed for them, they had become involved with the people smugglers that McCabe had referred to when he was interviewed by Laura Connor. They managed to survive that and decided to keep as far away as possible from England for a while. Next they had sailed along the French coast to Le Havre where Honeysuckle Rose's mast was taken down and laid along the deck. They had motored up the River Seine to Paris and worked their way through the French canal system to the Mediterranean and, after stepping the mast again, sailed along the coast to Nice. Stopping along the way for anything up to a month at a time, McCabe teamed up with other musicians and played guitar in cafes and restaurants when he could. Tricia worked behind bars when the opportunity presented itself, not that he required her to but because she liked to pay her way.

The taxi stopped at the drop off point at Brighton Marina's West Jetty. McCabe paid the driver then he walked to the security gates, passed through and continued along the length of the jetty to the visitor's pontoon. The air was still and warm and the prolonged spell of hot weather, that England was enjoying, meant that many of the boats in the marina had their owners staying on board for the weekend. Most of them were relaxing al fresco after dinner, drinking and talking and creating a steady hum of background noise which hung over the hundreds of boats moored there. Occasionally, raucous laughter broke out in different parts of the marina and then, just as quickly, subsided as the numerous boat parties turned up the music and knocked back the alcohol. When McCabe reached the visitors' pontoons, where his boat was moored, he noted that his neighbours were mainly French yachts moored together in groups made conspicuous by the red, white and blue tricolours hanging limply at their sterns. Most of the British boats had taken down their ensigns at sunset following tradition, but a small number were still in evidence, either because their owners were unaware of the custom or they just didn't care about it. The people on those boats tended to be the loudest and most riotous, and McCabe had wondered before whether there was a direct correlation between a lack of interest in boating tradition and general anti-social behaviour on the water. To the French though, it was important to show the flag because it was Bastille Day and they sat quietly in their cockpits talking and sipping at their wine in the polite way that the French do.

When he reached Honeysuckle Rose McCabe stopped for a moment and just looked at her as she sat motionless in the still water, illuminated by the dim pontoon lighting. Built in 1959 she was a Hillyard 12 Tonner, 36 foot, centre cockpit sailing sloop. Constructed with oak frames and a mahogany, cream painted hull, these days most owners would shy away from a boat like that because of the constant maintenance and repeated coats of paint and varnish required to keep her in good condition and seaworthy. Fibreglass or steel hulls were the modern way and McCabe could see the sense in it but, for him, nothing could compete with the feel of wood and tradition that Honeysuckle Rose provided. Light was streaming from her saloon windows and McCabe knew that he was home. He unzipped the sideflap of the canvas cockpit canopy, climbed aboard and zipped it up again. The door to the saloon slid open and Tricia stood there in the glow of the cabin lights, petite and pretty with the usual impish smile on her face.

Chapter Four

Tricia stood to one side as McCabe descended the hardwood steps into the saloon and sat down heavily at the polished mahogany dining table. She watched him anxiously.

"What's happened? Have you had an accident?"

"No. Not me."

"Well why have you got blood on your face and jacket then?"

Realising that he must have been spattered by Bronek's blood, McCabe peered down at his tan coloured jacket and saw the dark specks that had sprayed onto it. As he took the jacket off and threw it onto the floor he said wearily, "It's not mine, it's Bronek's. Somebody shot him."

She stared at him aghast.

"It's true. They just walked in and shot him as the gig was about to start."

"Is he OK?"

"No, he's dead."

Tricia sat down on the starboard settee berth and faced him across the table, horrified.

"Who would do such a thing? Why Bronek?"

"That's what the police asked me. I told them that I think they were after me. It's what we've been afraid of, isn't it? It could have been any one of a number of people. You remember what happened last year. Perhaps it was a mistake to come back to Brighton, Tricia."

"Well we can't stay away for ever."

"Maybe we'll have to."

"Chad, if they want to find us they'll track us down wherever we are. I'm not going to be frightened off by them and we have to come back here sometimes. I've got friends here. My sister lives here."

She looked at him defiantly.

"We need to leave, Tricia."

"Well I'm not going to."

Even though it was only a year, they had been together for long enough that McCabe knew that if she made up her mind, nothing that he could say would change it, but he tried once more.

"Let's leave Brighton in the morning and let things die down, Trish."

"No. I've got things to do here. People to see."

He looked at her in silence for a moment, studied her face, no longer impish but still pretty, as she frowned at him like a defiant child and he knew that he wasn't going to win. He tried another approach.

"OK. How long do you need?"

"Two weeks."

"We can't stay here for two weeks, Trish. We've agreed that we're going to take the boat to London and then go up the Thames."

"A week then."

Happy to have reached a sort of agreement and without really thinking about it he replied, "Alright, a week then," and immediately regretted it.

Straight away Tricia brightened but then, just as quickly, she frowned again.

"Tell me what happened."

McCabe described the shooting and told her about the police interview while she listened attentively. When he had finished they sat quietly for a few moments until she stood and moved around to his side of the table. She sat and put her arms around him, pulling him towards her until, with his head on her shoulder, she nuzzled her face into his hair.

"I'm sorry Chad. It must have been horrible for you."

"A bit of a shock," he replied.

"A good night's sleep will help. I don't want you to sit up drinking."

"Not tonight, Trish. I'm exhausted."

"OK. Let's go to bed."

She let go of him and they both stood.

"I'd like to see Bronek's wife but I don't know where she lives," said Tricia. "The poor woman must be distraught."

"You know her?"

"I met her at one of your gigs once."

"I'll call Andy in the morning and see if he knows her address."

"Andy?" asked Tricia.

"Guitarist who runs the Allstars."

"Oh, yes. Good idea. Now! Bedtime! Night night." She made it sound like an order.

McCabe went to his cabin in the forepeak at the bow and Tricia went to the larger cabin in the stern of the boat, which she had slept in and made her own for the past year. The two cabins were separated by the saloon and the centre cockpit. The forepeak was adequate for McCabe's simple needs and he undressed and climbed into the single bunk, immediately settling down and switching off the reading light above his head. He thought of Tricia lying in the double berth at the other end of the boat. A bond had formed between them that would prove to be unbreakable and their relationship, albeit a platonic one, was like that of a long married couple. When they met, McCabe was a hopeless binge drinker lacking any sense of direction and Tricia Knight had saved him and given him purpose. McCabe loved her but he didn't tell her because he was twenty three years her senior, which he saw as an insurmountable barrier between them. Tricia was twenty six years old. Chad McCabe had changed her life and she loved him but, because he had never shown any sign that he felt the same way, she believed that if she told him, their relationship would be spoiled for ever.

    McCabe turned onto his side and pulled the duvet tighter around him. A breeze was starting to develop outside and he listened to the gentle slap slap of small wavelets against the wooden hull as he drifted off to sleep, wondering whether they would both be shot tomorrow.

Chapter Five

Brading Road, Brighton - 1101 BST Tuesday 17th July

Bronek's house was a narrow, three storey, Victorian property in a terrace of identical houses rendered, painted white and built onto the side of a hill on the inland side of Brighton. Cars were parked on either side of the narrow street, which meant that the taxi which brought McCabe and Tricia had to stop in the middle of the road while McCabe paid the driver. They checked the numbers and identified the house and were standing at the bottom of a steep, straight flight of ten concrete steps which led up to the white uPVC front door. They climbed the steps to the small concrete landing at the top and McCabe pressed the white button screwed to the brickwork to his right, which rang two chimes in the hallway on the other side of the door. There was a long silence and then, above and to the left of them, a window was opened by a few inches and they heard a woman call out.

"What do you want?"

McCabe stepped back carefully to avoid falling down the steps and looked up at the still partly opened window, but couldn't see the woman who had spoken.

"It's Chad McCabe and Tricia Knight. I played with Bronek at Reinhardt's. We've come to make sure you're OK."

There was a pause until she replied, "I'm fine thank you. I don't need any visitors."

Tricia chipped in, "We'd like to come in for a few minutes, just to talk to you?"

There was another pause until the window was opened fully and the woman looked out and stared at them. After a full ten seconds she suddenly seemed to make up her mind.

"OK. Stay there. I'll come down."

They detected an Australian accent.

McCabe and Tricia waited patiently and a minute or so later they heard the woman removing a chain and unbolting the door. She stood to one side holding a small child on her left hip and they stepped past her into the hallway. She gestured with her free hand to the door at the end of the short hallway and they walked into a small kitchen in the middle of which was a cheap, modern pine table with six wooden chairs around it taking up most of the space in the room. Five of the chairs matched the table, the other was an old hardwood wheelback with curved arms and a cushion. What remained of the available floor space was littered with the child's toys. A Moka pot was quietly percolating on the gas stove and the room was filled with the smell of fresh coffee. They could hear the woman still in the hallway sliding bolts across the front door and refitting the chain in its place. Then she came into the room and put the child on the floor where it hurriedly crawled to a set of multi-coloured plastic building blocks and began to build a tower.

"Please," her voice was hard as she gestured with her right hand at the table. "Have a seat."

She sat opposite them leaving the wheelback chair at the head of the table empty. Bronek's chair?

"I know who you are," she said. "I saw you a couple of times when he was playing guitar."

"I'm afraid we were never introduced," replied McCabe, "so I don't know your name."

"Tushka, a Russian name. You thought I was Australian. I am. My parents are Russian but I was born in Sydney. What can I do for you?"

McCabe noted the attempt to answer questions before they are asked and a hint of impatience in her voice. He studied her carefully for a moment and took in her high cheekbones, piercing light blue eyes, dark eyebrows and lashes, and unnaturally white, rough cut blonde hair. She was attractive and he thought that she was probably in her late twenties. Tushka glared at them both with a look that defied them to pity her and he wondered how to start the conversation, deciding that the direct approach was best.

"We came to see if you're OK and to say how sorry we are about Bronek."

"Thank you. Were you with him when it happened?"

"Yes."

"Did he suffer?"

"No it was instant."

She looked relieved at that.

Tricia joined in the conversation, "It must have been a shock for you."

"Not at all, I've been expecting something like that to happen for a long time? Do you know what he did for a living?"

"No," replied McCabe, "he was a bit of a mystery."

"He was a fool with stupid ideas. At least he's made it simpler for me now. I was going to leave him anyway. Would you like some coffee? I always make too much so there's plenty for three."

Without waiting for a reply Tushka stood and took two white espresso cups with saucers from a cupboard above a small worktop and put them beside the cup and saucer which were already on the table next to a small bowl of sugar. She took the Moka from the stove and poured the coffee, Arabica very strong, into the three cups, put the Moka back on the cooker and turned out the flame underneath it. Tushka sat down again without bothering to ask them whether they wanted milk and continued the conversation.

"It's a treat to have someone to talk to, so I've got to thank you both for coming. Where was I? Oh yes, my husband the loser," she paused. "I told him so many times that if he carried on the way he did that someone would have a go at him and now they have."

McCabe reached for a cup of coffee and passed it to Tricia then took one himself. They both spooned in two sugars and stirred, waiting for Tushka to speak again but she had stopped and seemed to be holding back tears.

After a few moments Tricia spoke, "Do you think you're just reacting to the fact that he's gone and you're angry with him?"

Tushka's Australian accent became more pronounced as she snapped back "Too right I'm angry with him. It shouldn't have happened."

The tears came and McCabe was on the verge of telling her that the killers were really after him but he held back, fearing that her reaction would be violent.

Tushka continued, "I gave up everything to help him and I could see that it was going to happen but he wouldn't listen." She paused for a moment and looked at them both with tears streaming down both cheeks, "I hate him."

Tricia began, "I'm sure you …"

"I do," shouted Tushka, "I hate him." She sobbed quietly and then composed herself a little, "You probably think I'm horrible."

"Not horrible," replied McCabe. "Just upset."

Tushka sat up straight and assumed a dignified manner, "How did you know where we lived?"

"I've got Bronek's guitar. I picked it up from Reinhardt's when I went back for mine yesterday. Your address was on a label on the guitar case."

Which was just as well, thought McCabe, because even Andy hadn't known Bronek's address. He didn't tell Tushka that the reason that he hadn't brought the guitar with him was because he couldn't remove the blood stains from the case.

"Well you can keep it. I don't want it."

"But it's valuable …" started McCabe.

"I said I don't want it. You have it or give it away. It'll just remind me of what a mess it all became. We had everything going for us when we met, you know? That was what? Six years ago? We were both living in London. I'd been studying for years and I'd just completed a degree course. I was going to be a journalist and then I met Bronek. I admired his commitment to his cause and I gave up my own ambitions to help him."

She was silent again looking into the distance deep in thought.

"What was his cause?" asked Tricia.

"He was a student but he spent more time as a political activist. Anything that would bring about a change of government in his country: meetings, demonstrations outside the embassy, pamphlets, newsletters. I used to think that it was all very exciting and romantic, like he was a Che Guevara type figure.

That and the guitar playing. Evenings in student flats with people from his own country: jazz, white wine and political overthrow. Three years ago we got married and had Karolina," she gestured at the child playing happily with a toy tea set now, "and we moved to Brighton."

"Why Brighton?" asked McCabe.

"We live very hand to mouth and Bronek thought that it would be cheaper to live here and it's close enough to London to get there easily if he needed to. I don't think it's any cheaper and I don't know anybody here."

"What was Bronek's job," asked McCabe.

"He didn't have a job. Apart from what he got from playing gigs, which wasn't much. I don't know where the money came from. I haven't been working. He would go away for days and leave us here and then come back for a few days then go away again. We argued a lot. I'd had enough really. It was causing a lot of trouble between us. Perhaps you know more about him than I do?"

"I don't. I only met him at gigs and he kept himself to himself. We haven't been in Brighton much anyway for the past year or so. We're just passing through at the moment and we'll be gone in a few days."

Tricia sipped her coffee and listened.

"Where are you going?" asked Tushka.

"London," replied McCabe. "We're travelling on a boat."

"Can you do something for me?" asked Tushka.

"Sure, if we can," he answered.

"I've got a letter that Bronek was going to deliver. Would you mind taking it for me?"

"It might be quicker to post it," chipped in Tricia. "We're going to be a few days sailing around the coast and up the Thames."

"That's alright," said Tushka. "It can't be urgent or Bronek would have already taken it. He didn't trust the post so, where he could, he would always deliver letters by hand. He thought that his letters would be intercepted and read. Perhaps he was right or perhaps he just had paranoia. He thought he was being watched, as well."

"Who by?" asked Tricia.

"Who knows?" replied Tushka. "Whatever he was doing he thought it was very important but I don't suppose it was. He never seemed to achieve anything. I'll get the letter."

Tushka stood up and left the room and they heard her climb the stairs as they finished their coffee.

Tricia turned to McCabe and whispered, "Do you think we ought to get involved in this, Chad?"

"I'd like to help her and I'm intrigued. I'm curious to find out a bit more of what he was up to," he replied.

They heard Tushka descending the stairs and she came back into the room and handed McCabe a sealed, DL sized white envelope, with the name Shapiev written on it and a London address.

"If you could do that for Bronek I'd be really grateful," she said.

"Of course we will," said McCabe as he stood up and put the envelope in his jacket pocket. "We'd better be moving."

Tricia stood and they followed Tushka into the hallway. She opened the front door and stood to the side in the cramped space as they eased their way past her.

"Are you sure you're going to be OK?" asked Tricia.

"I'll be fine. I'll go back to Australia and get a job as a journalist before it's too late, and Karolina can start school and have a great future. Thanks for coming to see me."

McCabe, on impulse, said, "I'm going to come back later in the week and make sure you're alright."

"OK, but there's really no need," Tushka smiled at them both, "I'll be fine."

McCabe and Tricia raised their hands in a goodbye wave and turned down the steps as Tushka went back into the house. They walked down the hill to the corner with Elm Grove and McCabe took out his phone and called for a taxi.

The taxi arrived within five minutes, dropped McCabe off in the Old Steine and then turned left along the seafront to take Tricia back to Honeysuckle Rose at Brighton Marina. McCabe walked through The Lanes, busy with tourists in the sunshine, to The Cricketers pub in Black Lion Street, where he had arranged to meet Andy Mason for a beer.

Andy, dressed in his usual jeans, trainers, tee shirt and black Gypsy Jazz Club hoodie was already there, sitting on a high stool at the bar and sipping his second pint. He welcomed McCabe as he squeezed through the narrow front door, and ordered a pint of Harvey's bitter for him without needing to ask what he would have. McCabe sat on a stool next to him and they sipped their beers in silence while they considered what to say next. They had known each other for years but never mixed socially as the only thing that they had in common was their mutual love for Gypsy Jazz. The meeting at The Cricketers a few days after every gig was a regular routine that had been going on for years. The purpose of the meeting was for McCabe to be paid and an excuse for a beer or two in the plush, red velvety, brass and glass surroundings of their favourite pub.

"No money for Saturday's gig, I'm afraid," said Andy.

"I wasn't expecting any. We can't really expect Julia to cough up for a gig that didn't happen. Her business is going to suffer badly enough as it is."

"You'd think so, wouldn't you?" answered Andy. "The police finished at Reinhardt's on Sunday and she opened up, business as usual yesterday evening. The place was packed. They all want to look at the murder scene."

"How about you?" asked McCabe. "It was a bit of a shock, wasn't it?"

"I still can't believe it happened," said Andy shaking his head. "One minute we're sitting there ready to get started. Next minute Bronek's dead. Who would do that? Why?"

"I thought they were after me," said McCabe.

"Why would they be after you?"

"You remember the business last year with Ricky Bishop?"

"Ah yes," answered Andy. "I thought he went to prison."

"He did, but he's got a lot of reasons to hire people to have a go at me. That's why we stayed away for the last year. We left on the boat in a hurry and went to France just to get away from him."

"So you think he's trying to kill you?"

"I did until I saw Bronek's wife this morning. She seemed sure that they were after Bronek."

"I don't really know her," replied Andy. "I didn't know Bronek either, really. I met her once, unusual name."

"Tushka."

"That's it. Tushka. Very attractive."

"How did you recruit him into the Allstars?" asked McCabe.

"I met him jamming in a bar in London a few years ago and told him that if he was ever in Brighton I could get some gigs for him. I gave him my phone number, so when he moved to Brighton he got in touch with me. I didn't get to know him though. I just used to meet him at Reinhardt's and then meet him in here later in the week to pay him. He didn't stay for a drink even. Just came in, got his cash and left again. Why would anyone want to kill him?"

"Tushka said that he was a political activist trying to bring about a change of government in his home country."

"Wow!" Andy took a sip at his beer. "What was his country?"

"I don't know. I assumed he was Polish," McCabe answered.

"I don't think he was. Eastern Europe but not Polish."

"His wife said that she's Australian. He certainly wasn't that."

They drank their beers in silence for a few moments until McCabe spoke again, "She said that her parents were Russian."

"Was Bronek Russian?"

"No. Definitely not Russian."

"An enigma then," said Andy.

"Absolutely," replied McCabe. "I've told Tushka that I'll go back and check that she's OK in a couple of days. I'll ask her where Bronek was from then."

They sipped their beers and sat quietly, each deep in thought, until Andy asked, "Can you play at Reinhardt's next Sunday?"

"Sorry, won't be here. We're taking the boat around the coast to London and tying up in St Katharine Docks for a while."

"You could catch a train back for the gig. I'll pay the train fare."

"Can't. We'll probably be at sea next weekend."

"I've got a bit of a problem then," said Andy. "You can't make it and George Lee is playing violin at a gig in Rye. That just leaves me and Stewart the bass player." He stared glumly at his beer.

"All you need is a rhythm player, Andy. You can do the gig with a trio. Julia will understand. She'll be glad that you can keep things going."

Andy perked up, "You're right. Rhythm guitar, plus me on solo guitar and Stew on double bass. Good sound. I'll ring around and find someone who wants to do it."

"I'm sorry to let you down," replied McCabe.

"Don't worry about it. It's a constant headache trying to keep a quintet together. People are always off doing other bookings. George is the worst. He's in such demand that he travels and does gigs all over the place at short notice, so I can't ever rely on him being in Brighton at the right time even if he's already agreed to play. I can't blame him, he's a great violinist and he can get more money elsewhere. It's not as if any of us get paid much for playing at Reinhardt's."

McCabe kept quiet, aware that Andy, as organiser, made sure that he got paid twice as much as the rest of the band.

"Can I rely on you to play when you're back in Brighton, Chad?"

"Of course you can, but I'm not sure when that might be if one of the local villains is trying to kill me."

Chapter Six

Brading Road, Brighton - 1106 BST Thursday 19th July

Two days later the taxi dropped McCabe outside Bronek's house and he stood for a moment looking up at it. Struggling with his conscience, he wondered whether to walk away and not bother the angry mother and her child inside, but he had told her that he would visit so he must. He started up the flight of steps and when he reached the top he could see that the front door was slightly ajar. From inside the house, he could hear a slow, monotonous beating like the sound of a toy tin drum being hit with a stick. He pressed the button screwed onto the brickwork and heard the doorbell chime inside the house. The beating sound stopped. He waited and turned his back to the door looking out at the houses opposite, all at different levels but identical to Bronek's house as they descended the hill in a long white terraced line. He looked up at the blue of the sky, completely empty of clouds, and thought that he would rather be on his boat than visiting someone who probably didn't want to see him, but one of the rules he lived by was that he always did what he said he would. Sometimes it was a mistake.

The beating sound started again. McCabe turned and pressed the bell push. The chime sounded inside and the beating sound stopped. He rang the bell again and the chimes sounded. There was a pause for a few seconds before the noise started again: clang, clang, clang, clang and then it stopped. He pressed the bell push, the chimes sounded and the beating started again: clang, clang, clang, only three this time. McCabe waited and, after a few seconds, two beats sounded. He waited and the noise started again: clang, clang, clang, clang in a continuous slow monotone but still nobody answered the door. He pushed the door with his right hand and it swung open revealing the empty hallway. At the same time the beating became louder.

He stepped into the hallway and called out, "Hello?" as he advanced slowly along the passageway to the kitchen.

The noise grew louder: clang, clang, clang. McCabe reached for the door handle, pressed it down and slowly opened the door into the kitchen. Sitting on the kitchen floor surrounded by her toys, facing him and staring straight ahead as if into the distance was Bronek's daughter Karolina. She was dressed in yellow pyjamas, a faded red dressing gown and blue socks. On the floor in front of her was an upturned frying pan on which she was beating steadily and slowly with a wooden spoon. She did not look up or even seem to notice McCabe. Behind the little girl, seated in Bronek's wheelback chair and stripped to the waist, was her mother. Both of Tushka's hands were nailed palms down to the table in front of her and her severed thumbs were laid neatly side by side between them. On her bare arms and breasts were nineteen cigarette burns. Her face was hardly recognisable through a mass of blood, bruises and layers of cling film that had been wound around her head until she had slowly suffocated. Her head, mouth open as if still fighting for air, lolled back and her long blonde hair was stiff with blood which had run down it from a gash across her throat and formed a pool, now dry, on the floor behind the chair. The child continued to beat on the frying pan oblivious to his presence and McCabe backed slowly out of the room fighting the urge to throw up. In the hallway he turned, already reaching for his phone, stumbled to and through the still open front door and sat on the top step of the concrete flight leading down to the street. Still fighting the urge to be sick, head down, knees apart and breathing deeply he slowly regained his composure then, lifting his head, he dialled 999 and, when his call was answered almost immediately, he asked for the police. Inside the house, the child continued to beat repeatedly on the frying pan.

Three minutes later a police patrol car, blue lights flashing, came fast up the hill between the two lines of parked cars and stopped outside the house. Two uniformed police officers, a man and a woman, got out of the car in a hurry, putting on their hats as they did so and leaving the car, still with its blue lights flashing, blocking the road. McCabe stood and descended the steps to meet them as they came up the footpath.

"Was it you who made the 999 call, sir?" asked the man.

"Yes. Inside. In the kitchen. You'll find a woman and a young girl."

"OK. Just wait here, sir, if you would," said the other officer as she brushed past McCabe and started up the steps.

The policeman stayed with McCabe standing between him and the roadway as if blocking his means of escape. Neither of them spoke. In less than a minute the officer who had gone into the house came out again and, with an angry expression on her face, came down the steps.

"We're going to need a statement from you, sir," she said. "I'd like you to sit in the back of our car."

"Of course," replied McCabe and the three of them walked to the police car.

The woman opened the car's rear nearside door and put her hand on top of McCabe's head as he swung himself into the back seat. She closed the door firmly and McCabe was alone in the car watching the blue of the flashing lights reflecting from the windows of the parked cars, and trying to ignore the neighbours who were starting to gather and stare at him.

He watched as the police officer quickly briefed her colleague then, as the male officer stood on the pavement and talked into his radio, she went back into the house, came out again and took up station at the top of the steps. The policeman opened the driver's door of the police car and got in, twisting his body to talk to McCabe.

"Can I take your name, sir?"

"Chad McCabe."

The policeman spelled it as he wrote, "C h a d M c C a b e?"

"That's right."

"Do you have any ID on you?"

"I've got a debit card."

McCabe pulled the iPhone from his pocket, opened its protective brown leather case and pulled out the card which he handed to the officer.

The policeman looked at it, handed it back, wrote in his notebook again and said, "Can you tell me what happened here today?"

"I came to see Tushka Kowalski …"

The policeman interrupted, "Who is …?"

"The woman in the kitchen."

The policeman scribbled, "Go on."

"I came to see Tushka and I found her dead in the kitchen."

"Girlfriend was she?"

"No, nothing like that. I hardly knew her."

"I see. Well, if you'll wait here someone will be along to interview you."

"Any idea how long?"

"No idea sir. We're waiting for them to arrive but we'll be as quick as we can. You just sit tight if you would."

The policeman climbed out of the car and the door closed with a thud behind him. McCabe watched a steady stream of police arrive in a variety of vehicles and cordon off the street on either side of the house. They were followed by white suited technicians and people in civilian clothes who he took to be detectives. Among them he recognised Laura Connor who had interviewed him at Reinhardt's a few nights before.

After forty minutes of being ignored McCabe decided that he had sat there for long enough and tried to open the door, only to find out that it was locked. Ten minutes later his temper was rising and he hammered on the window to get the attention of the woman police officer, who was now standing by the front gate and monitoring who could go in and out. She came over to the car and opened the driver's door.

"Don't do that please, sir. You'll do some damage."

"I want to get out," shouted McCabe.

"Stay there if you would, sir. Someone will be along to speak to you soon," and she slammed the car door and resumed her position by the gate.

McCabe sat back, angry and helpless, and watched as a few minutes later a woman came out of the house carrying the little girl wrapped in a blanket and they were both driven away in a police car.

The front door of the car opened and Laura Connor slid into the driver's seat, leaving the door open. She turned to face him diagonally across the car.

"Mr McCabe, we meet again," she said cheerfully. "I need to ask you some questions. Like why are you here and how well did you know Tushka Kowalski?"

"I came here to see if she was OK. I don't know her at all. I was here the other day and I told her that I'd come back."

"When was that?"

"Two days ago. Tuesday."

"Had you met her before Tuesday?"

"No."

"So why were you so interested in her that you came back two days later?"

McCabe raised his voice, "Because her husband's just been murdered and I was concerned about her. What are you suggesting?"

"I'm not suggesting anything," continued Connor quietly, "but it looks a bit strange that you came to visit someone you don't know and the second time you visit she's dead. How did you get in?"

"The door was open."

"So you just walked in?" asked Connor.

"No, of course not," replied McCabe angrily. "I rang the bell, I waited and I could hear a banging noise from inside but nobody answered. I tried the bell a few times and then thought that I'd better check so I went in. The child was sitting on the floor in the kitchen and banging on a frying pan. Tushka was in the chair."

"What did you do then?" asked Connor.

"I came out of the house and called the police."

"So why did you leave the little girl where she was instead of bringing her out of the house?" asked Connor.

"Are you kidding?" replied McCabe angrily. "Not these days. A man of my age even touching a small child is likely to be accused of all sorts of things. She looked safe enough so I left her where she was. Your people were here in a few minutes anyway."

"OK," said Connor. "We might need to talk to you again, so don't go far."

"I told you the other night that I'm taking my boat to London. You've got my phone number if you want me."

"I'd rather you stayed in Brighton for the time being, Mr McCabe," answered Connor.

"Are you arresting me?"

"Not at the moment," she replied.

"Am I under suspicion?"

"It certainly looks suspicious, Mr McCabe, being present at the murder scene of two people, especially as they were husband and wife. Was anything going on between you and Tushka Kowalski?"

"Of course not. I didn't know her."

"Nevertheless, I'd like you to stay in Brighton," said Connor.

"Well I'm not going to. If you want me you know how to contact me."

She stared at him intently for a moment, "OK, Mr McCabe. You're free to go but don't leave the country." Laura Connor got out of the car, walked around it and opened McCabe's door. He got out and walked towards the cordon of police tape then heard a voice behind him call out.

"Chad!"

McCabe turned and saw Detective Sergeant Barnard walking towards him.

"You do get into some scrapes, Chad, don't you?" said Barnard holding out his hand and treating McCabe to a limp handshake.

Connor was behind McCabe and she addressed Barnard, "Do you know this man, sir?"

"Yes Inspector. We worked on a case together last year."

She looked at McCabe with renewed interest.

"OK," she said, "Perhaps I could have a word with you later?"

"Of course," replied Barnard, and he and McCabe waited until she had moved out of earshot.

"Well?" asked Barnard. "What is it this time? Some suspicion you've got or just coincidence that you're linked to two murder scenes?"

"I have no idea what's going on," replied McCabe. "A guy I play guitar with gets killed in front of me. I visit his wife and she's been tortured and had her throat cut. What's it got to do with me?"

"Don't you know?" asked Barnard.

"I thought they were after me and shot Bronek by mistake but now I'm not so sure."

"Well, you seem to have a talent for finding trouble, that's for sure," replied Barnard.

McCabe had last met Barnard in Fécamp in Normandy over a year ago and guessed that he was something to do with counter terrorism, although to what extent he wasn't sure. There was something different about him; still the same baggy grey suit with the stretched out of shape jacket pockets, a white shirt, still a light blue tie but without stains on it so it must be fairly new. What was it? He suddenly realised. Barnard had stopped sneezing, which prompted McCabe to say, "Your hay fever has cleared up."

"Indeed it has. A miracle drug called Mometasone nasal spray twice a day. Gone. Just like that!"

Barnard clicked his fingers and smiled in his benign, avuncular way. The smile didn't fool McCabe for a second. He knew that the man had a razor sharp mind and, judging by his actions in France last year, he seemed to wield an immense amount of influence.

"What are you doing here, Chad?"

"I've been sitting in that police car asking myself the same question," replied McCabe. "I thought I was doing a good deed but I seem to have got myself embroiled in a mess. Are you working on this case?"

"No, not officially. I'm interested in it because of another enquiry I'm conducting."

McCabe knew better than to ask Barnard what that was about because he knew that he wouldn't tell him.

"Your colleague told me not to leave the country. She obviously thinks that I had something to do with the Kowalskis' deaths."

"She's paid to think like that, Chad. They start by suspecting everyone and work inwards from there. You were at the scene of Bronek Kowalski's death the other day. In Inspector Connor's mind, because you are linked to both murders, you could have been having an affair with the wife so you had the husband bumped off, then you fell out with the wife and murdered her. What's probably confusing her is that Tushka Kowalski was horribly tortured before she was killed and the house was searched from top to bottom. Not the actions of an angry lover, unless he was completely deranged." He looked at McCabe thoughtfully, "I don't think you are."

"I thought I was the target when Bronek was murdered," said McCabe.

"No, you weren't the target. You're more likely to be targeted by Ricky Bishop and he's not responsible for this" replied Barnard. "I told you the last time we met that Bishop's memory and reach will be long and that you and Miss Knight should watch your backs. After what you did to him Bishop will want some sort of revenge, and just because he's in prison it doesn't mean that he can't organise something. People like that don't forget and they don't forgive."

"I'm not going to let somebody like him stop me from leading a normal life."

"Well just be careful," replied Barnard. "He could stop you leading any sort of life. You've got my number if you want me. Call me any time, day or night."

Barnard turned towards the house and McCabe, relieved to still be a free man, ducked under the police tape and walked down the hill to the corner. From there he phoned for a taxi. The police had closed the road and an angry driver, who wanted to get to his house, was arguing with an officer who was refusing to let him through. As McCabe waited for the taxi to arrive he checked his phone contacts and confirmed that Barnard's number was still there from when he had entered it into the phone the year before. He turned and looked up the hill at all the police activity outside the house. Something was bothering him. If Laura Connor was a Detective Inspector and Arthur Barnard was a Detective Sergeant, why had she called him sir, and why was Barnard interested in Bronek?

Chapter Seven

The taxi dropped him at Brighton Marina and, as he walked along the West Jetty to the visitors' pontoon and Honeysuckle Rose, McCabe remembered the letter that Tushka had asked him to deliver and wondered whether he should have told the police about it. It was probably innocent enough he thought, just a letter to a friend perhaps. He would deliver it for Bronek as Tushka had asked. At least it was something that he could do to help them. Maybe it would be the last kindness that anyone would do for them. He wondered again why Barnard had got involved. When they had last met, Barnard was chasing terrorists. What did that have to do with Bronek? Tushka had told him that Bronek had been a student activist protesting against his own government but that was common enough and didn't amount to terrorism. Nothing to do with you, he told himself. Keep out of it.

The sun was so hot that he could feel it reflecting back at him from the bleached wooden pontoon decking as he walked past row after row of moored yachts and motor cruisers, mostly unoccupied on this weekday. Their owners would be at work busily earning the money to pay for their boats and moorings. McCabe tried not to think of Tushka Kowalski and the little girl, but the horror of the scene in the kitchen kept reappearing to him. He needed an afternoon on Honeysuckle Rose, pottering about in the sunshine while he carried out some routine maintenance. Probably a few whiskies as well, to try to block out the image of poor Tushka tortured and killed.

As he reached Honeysuckle Rose McCabe saw that the canvas canopy was folded flat and Tricia was sitting in the cockpit enjoying the sunshine with a glass of white wine in her hand. She smiled and waved at him. Sitting opposite her, with her back to him, was a woman with long auburn hair which cascaded over her shoulders and he knew, unmistakably, that it was Tricia's sister Caz. This was a meeting that he had been both looking forward to and dreading.

He pulled himself up from the pontoon onto the side deck of the boat and Tricia raised her glass to him, smiling and excited, "Look who's come to see us."

Caz turned to face him, also smiling, and raised the glass of wine that she was holding as she spoke in the slightly husky voice that he remembered so well, "McCabe! We meet again," and her stunning, cat like green eyes burned into his.

Tricia jumped up. "I'll get another glass," she called as she descended the steps into the galley.

McCabe sat on the cushioned cockpit bench, next to where Tricia had been sitting, and looked across at Caz who was still watching him, confident and aware of the effect that she was having on him. He realised that he was blushing, an annoying habit that he'd had as a child, but something that hadn't happened since he was a teenager. Caz gazed back at him with a slight smile playing over her lips and eyes, and McCabe tried to maintain his poise and banish from his mind the erotic thoughts that he'd had about her so many times since their first meeting.

Tricia returned with a glass and poured some ice cold Chablis into it as she sat down next to him.

McCabe took a sip from the glass and spoke at last, "How nice to see you," he croaked nervously.

In his mind was the image of the only time that he had met her before, when he had let himself into her flat, on Tricia's instructions, to be confronted by a naked and furious Caz. That was over a year ago, when he had known Tricia for only a few hours and she had set him up to get some cash for her one quiet Brighton Sunday morning, only for him to find that he'd walked into Caz's adult film studio on her day off. She had made it clear to him that she was not pleased. For more than a year McCabe had resisted the temptation to surf the Internet and find some of her films, because he knew that if he watched her once he would become addicted.

"I told Caz that we were here," said Tricia, "and she's come to see us before we leave."

"I was just leaving myself," said Caz. "Another five minutes and you would have missed me."

"How have you been?" asked McCabe.

"Since we last met? Very busy," she replied, smiling again and drawing him in with her beautiful green eyes like a rabbit caught in headlights.

McCabe struggled to concentrate as he thought of Caz being busy in the film studio and he looked away blushing again. Always confident and sure of himself, this woman seemed to have the ability to turn him into a shy, awkward, idiot.

Caz quickly finished the last of her drink and stood up, "It's been lovely to see you, Trish."

McCabe and Tricia stood and the sisters kissed each other on both cheeks and agreed, as they always did, that they mustn't leave it for so long next time.

Caz stepped out of the cockpit and down onto the pontoon. As she looked up at them both she asked, "Would you walk me to the gate please, McCabe?"

"Of course," he replied and joined her on the pontoon.

She waved a farewell to Tricia and they walked past the moored boats and then turned along the concrete jetty towards the main gate. As Caz got slightly ahead of him he noted how gracefully she moved and how immaculately dressed she was in navy blue canvas yachting trousers, brown deck shoes and an expensive, white, Ralph Lauren polo shirt which contrasted vividly with her red hair. Over her right shoulder she carried a small, grey Gucci backpack that served as a handbag.

As he caught up and walked alongside her she spoke, "You seem to have made my sister very happy, but she says that there's nothing going on between you. Is that right?"

"Absolutely right," he replied.

"I find that rather strange. Two good looking people on a boat together for over a year and it's still platonic. Are you gay, McCabe?"

"No, definitely not," he replied with a nervous laugh.

"Well," said Caz as they reached the gate and McCabe unlocked it, "there's hope for me yet then."

She flashed a dazzling, faintly freckled smile at him and he noticed how wide her pupils were as the skin at the nape of his neck prickled with excitement.

Caz moved to go through the gate but stopped and became serious, "Look McCabe, I worry about my little sister sometimes. You will look after her, won't you?"

"I'll do my best but she's very headstrong."

"I know she is," replied Caz. "She was like that as a child, always getting into scrapes because she wouldn't listen to anyone. I've had to bail her out more than once."

"Then you'll know how stubborn she can be," said McCabe, "but she's a free agent and she does what she likes."

"Can I have your phone," asked Caz, "and I'll put my contact details into it?"

"Of course. Good idea."

He pulled his iPhone from the hip pocket of his cargo pants, found the Contacts section and handed it to her.

She rapidly entered her name, phone number and email address into it using just her thumbs. McCabe watched her delicate, beautifully manicured hands holding the phone and remembered how, when they had first met, those hands had been pointing a revolver at his chest.

"There," she said, and handed the phone back to him. "You will get in touch if you're worried about her, won't you?"

"I certainly will," promised McCabe.

Caz put her hands on his waist and leaned up and kissed him on the cheek, with a murmured, "Keep safe, both of you."

He felt the softness of her lips and smelled her faint perfume and, for a moment, the closeness of her body made him dizzy. She stepped through the gate and expensive, stylish and beautiful, with her hips swaying and her head held high she walked away from him along the dusty concrete ramp towards the road. McCabe gazed after her and, as she reached the restaurants at the top of the ramp, diners eating al fresco turned to watch her pass. Only when she had disappeared from his sight did he walk back to Honeysuckle Rose already aching to see her again.

Tricia was washing up the wine glasses when he got back to the boat and, as always, she smiled at him as he came down the steps from the cockpit to the saloon.

"Did you see Tushka?"

McCabe sat down heavily at the table, opened a locker behind the settee berth and took out a glass and a half empty bottle of Laphroaig whisky. He poured himself a generous shot and sat back as he quickly drank it. Then he poured himself another one.

"Get ready for a shock, Tricia."

Tea towel and glass in hand she sat opposite him at the saloon table and looked at him intently, "What is it?"

"She's dead, Tricia. I got there and the door was open. I couldn't get a reply so I went in. Tushka was dead in a kitchen chair and the little girl was sitting on the floor banging away on a frying pan in a kind of trance."

Tricia stared at him, eyes wide, "Dead? She looked OK the other day."

"Somebody murdered her," replied McCabe taking a slug of the whisky and pouring himself another.

"I can't take this in, Chad. Who would do such a thing?"

"I've been wondering that myself. All I can come up with is that the people who killed Bronek did it."

Tricia put the tea towel down and stood the wine glass on the table. Then she went to the refrigerator, opened it and took out the already opened bottle of Chablis and sat at the table again. She poured some wine into the glass and sat bolt upright as she sipped at it, "I can't believe it."

"It's true. I called the police when I found her. They were there straight away. I think they thought I'd killed her. Perhaps they still do." He sipped at his whisky.

"They can't do," said Tricia. "They wouldn't have let you go."

"They told me not to leave the country. It was the same police Inspector - the woman who interviewed me at Reinhardt's the other night. Then Arthur Barnard turned up. Remember him?"

"Barnard? He only works on national security, doesn't he? Why would he be involved?"

"I don't know Trish but he was there. He said he was interested because of another case that he's working on."

Tricia sat back deep in thought until, after a few moments, she said, "Did you tell him about the letter that Tushka asked you to deliver?"

"No. I didn't think of it at the time."

"Don't you think you should let him know about it?"

"It's only a letter. To be honest I don't really want to get involved in it all. I was already at the top of the list of suspects as Tushka's probable murderer this morning. They locked me in a police car, for Christ's sake. They must have given me the benefit of the doubt, otherwise I think I'd be at the police station by now and they'd be sweating a confession out of me."

"OK," replied Tricia. "If you're sure."

"I'm sure. I'll deliver Bronek's letter when we get to London and that'll be the end of it. As for going to London, I think the sooner we leave the better."

"Oh why? I've still got people to see."

"We ought to leave."

"Oh, please no. I haven't seen my friends for so long. Please Chad."

She looked so forlorn that he instantly gave in, as she knew that he would. After travelling together for over a year she understood how to get her way, mostly based on his desire to make sure that she was happy, which was something that she never abused but still used to her advantage.

"OK," he sighed, "but let's agree to leave in a couple of days. Barnard thinks that we might be targeted by Ricky Bishop."

"But he's in prison," exclaimed Tricia.

"That doesn't mean that he can't harm us. Barnard was quite serious that we should be on our guard. Brighton is where all Bishop's cronies are so it would be a good idea to move on. Let's go on Saturday. That gives you the rest of today and tomorrow to catch up with your friends. Is that enough time?"

"Not really but if we're in danger it will have to do. I've arranged to meet a couple of girlfriends this afternoon. In fact I'd better get a move on. Although I have to say, after hearing about Tushka, I'm not really in the mood."

"You should go," said McCabe. "It'll help to take your mind off of it."

"You're right," replied Tricia. "Will you be alright here on your own?"

"I'll be fine."

"OK, but don't sit there drinking whisky all day." She stood and grabbed her leather shoulder bag which was lying on the seat beside her, "Phone me if you want anything."

She kissed him on the cheek and then she was gone, disappearing up the saloon steps and over the side of the boat onto the pontoon. McCabe sat and listened to her footsteps receding on the wooden boards and poured himself another whisky, conscious of the fact that her kiss hadn't had the same effect on him as her sister's. He sat there quietly for the next ten minutes going through the events of the day in his mind and then, realising that he was becoming morose, he stood up, finished the whisky in his glass and put the glass on the table.

 McCabe went into the forward cabin where Bronek's light brown guitar case, which he had picked up from Reinhardt's Bar at the same time as he had collected his own, was leaning against the bunk. He laid it on top of the bunk and tried to ignore a dark blood stain still faintly visible on the front of the case despite his efforts to clean it. He opened the case for the first time and Bronek's Cigano GJ-15 Grand Bouche guitar lay there snug and secure until McCabe carefully lifted it out, revealing the usual small compartment underneath. He stepped into the saloon and placed the guitar carefully on the starboard settee berth. Going back to the guitar case he opened the lid of the compartment to reveal the bits and pieces that you might find in any Gypsy Jazz guitarist's equipment: two spare sets of number 10 Argentine strings, an Intellitouch PT10 guitar tuner and a couple of Wegen picks. Underneath those items was a small fabric case the size of a man's index finger, purpose made to contain a USB flash drive. He lifted the flap on the end of the small case, removed the drive and examined it. Handwritten on the black plastic in tiny white letters were the words "Licks and Tricks".

 McCabe put the items, including the flash drive, back into the compartment, replaced the guitar and closed and latched the lid of the guitar case. All serious musicians, but especially guitarists, have a small armoury of progressions, arpeggios and riffs, known as licks and tricks, which add colour to their playing and McCabe resolved to check out the flash drive at some time to see if he could learn something new. He went back into the saloon, grabbed the bottle of Laphroaig and the glass as he passed the table, went up the saloon steps and settled himself in the cockpit. As he sipped the whisky and gazed out, without really seeing, at the moored boats in the marina he thought of Tushka and Bronek and their little girl who would grow up without remembering them. Then, as the whisky took hold, he thought of Caz, unsure of his feelings and what he should do about them.

Chapter Eight

Ricky Bishop sat on his prison bed and stared with his remaining watery blue eye at the blank wall in front of him as he listened and talked on his mini phone. Sometimes known as a BOSS phone it was tiny - less than the length of a credit card and half the width - and it had been smuggled into the prison concealed in the rectum of a returning day release prisoner and delivered to him as arranged. BOSS stands for Body Orifice Security Scanner and is a system used by the Prison Service which, as the name suggests, is designed to detect hidden objects. The almost 100% plastic phone is designed to beat it and can be bought online very cheaply. The SIM card that went with the phone had been wrapped in a condom and swallowed by another returning prisoner and delivered to Bishop after it had been crapped out in a prison toilet. The USB charger for the phone was already in the prison and all Bishop had to do was pay for the hire of it when he needed to. Both items, the phone and the SIM card, which cost very little on the outside, had cost Bishop a great deal of money, but with them he could continue to run his criminal enterprise receiving information from outside and giving instructions to those who worked for him. At this moment he was talking to a man he had never met and only knew as Quietus, a killer he had hired several times before. Bishop had already given Quietus as much information as he knew about McCabe.

"I want him dealt with now. Your usual fee in advance." Bishop paused and listened, then he replied, "I know it's short notice but he's surfaced again in Brighton and I don't know how long he's going to be there for." He listened again, "Good. Just get on with it."

He stood and switched off the phone, put it into its protective case and returned it to its hiding place. Sitting on the bed again he raised his right hand to his once handsome face and ran it over his scarred features. He smiled grimly to himself. At last he would have his revenge and Chad McCabe was going to pay for disfiguring and half blinding him.

Chapter Nine

Brighton Marina - 1334 BST Saturday 21st July

Honeysuckle Rose had nosed her way between the breakwaters at Brighton Marina, turned to port and they were heading south east towards Beachy Head on a bright, clear afternoon in almost perfect visibility. The sea state was slight, the sun was high and the old Hillyard slipped easily through the sparkling water, pulled along by the cruising chute which McCabe had set and pushed by a full mainsail held back by a rope preventer to stop the boom from unexpectedly thrashing across the deck. The wind blew a steady force 3 from the west and Tricia, with her eyes closed and wearing only a black bikini bottom, was stretched out on her back on a long cushion on the foredeck while she took advantage of the hot sun to maintain her tan. McCabe sat contentedly at the wheel, maintaining a steady course a couple of miles offshore, and he mentally ticked off the familiar landmarks as they passed: Rottingdean, Newhaven, Seaford Head and Cuckmere Haven. Tricia took her turn at the wheel after two hours and McCabe sat quietly and watched the green Sussex Downs sloping gently down to the high chalk cliffs which were slowly sliding past on the port side. Now they were abeam of the dazzlingly white Seven Sisters Cliffs familiar to film and TV watchers as often used stand-ins for the white cliffs of Dover which were still 54 miles away. At Birling Gap, McCabe took the wheel again. After another hour, with the wind slowly fading, they passed the Beachy Head Lighthouse standing in the sea below the cliffs, its broad red and two white horizontal stripes unmistakable to any mariner making way along the Channel. Behind the lighthouse the soaring chalk cliffs seemed to slowly roll away from right to left as they sailed by until, suddenly, a huge expanse of sea began to open out on their port side. To McCabe this always seemed to be the sailing equivalent of flying out over the edge of the Grand Canyon. First the West Hill at Hastings seventeen miles away was visible then Bexhill and Normans Bay, Pevensey and finally the town of Eastbourne only four miles from them to the north. McCabe maintained the course that they were on to clear the Royal Sovereign Light with its great concrete helicopter platform standing over a hundred feet above the waves. As soon as they had it on the port beam, he set a course for the headland of Dungeness jutting out into the Channel from the Romney Marsh twenty seven miles to the north east.

Their passage plan was to sail to Queenborough near the mouth of the River Medway, expecting to arrive there after a couple of days at sea but, as with all sailing plans, the weather gods decided that was not to be. Now they found themselves becalmed when the wind died. McCabe snuffed the cruising chute and stowed it away, released the preventer from the boom and hauled up the mainsheet so that the mainsail was in line fore and aft, then he started the old BMC Commander diesel engine. Having sailed for thousands of miles together, their usual routine at sea during the night was a four hours on and four hours off rota, which might change as circumstances demanded, and Tricia, having dressed in warm clothes, was now at the helm. McCabe was seated at the saloon table studying Admiralty chart 2675 and referring to a BBC weather forecast on his mobile phone. The forecast told him that there would be very little wind for the next twenty four hours which meant that if they tried to sail they would just drift up and down the channel as the tide turned every six hours or so. He considered their options. They could keep the engine on and motor or they could go inshore and anchor until the tide turned in their favour again and the wind returned.

The tides in the English Channel are powerful and ebb and flow roughly east to west, west to east at a rate of knots. For a small boat, travelling with the tide is always a better option if you want to make progress, otherwise, even with the engine on, it is sometimes pointless to punch through water that is travelling in the opposite direction to the one that you want to go. If you are sailing for an hour to the east at four knots and the tide is pushing the boat west at, say, one knot, the boat will actually only make three nautical miles over the sea bed in an easterly direction. If there is no wind at all and the boat is not making any way forward, the tide will just push the boat backwards and, on any passage of more than six or seven hours, at some point it will turn against you. McCabe and Tricia discussed this and decided that rather than drift backwards they would continue with the engine on and make whatever progress they could. The neap tide which was flowing at the moment would mean, at its maximum, a current of less than a knot against them so, if they pushed on at six knots on the engine then they would make at least five knots of speed over the ground; five nautical miles in the right direction until the tide turned again and worked in their favour. As the wind dropped completely the sea settled into a smooth, glassy, flat calm and they motored on into the evening.

While Tricia steered, McCabe prepared an easy meal of ham sandwiches and mugs of tea and they sat happily in the cockpit watching the land in the distance on their port side and, on their starboard side, tankers and other commercial ships travelling in the opposite direction to them in the westbound shipping lane only three miles away. As the clock in front of them on Rose's bulkhead neared 2000 the sun slowly disappeared behind the Sussex Downs on their port quarter and the great shadow of Beachy Head darkened the sea around them. McCabe took over the steering from Tricia and she went below and switched on the navigation lights, red port, green starboard, a white stern light and a white steaming light on the mast facing forwards to show other vessels that they were motoring not sailing. It rapidly became dark although the visibility was clear for miles and they could see behind them the powerful beams from the Beachy Head and Royal Sovereign lighthouses sweeping the sea with great white flashes of light, twice every twenty seconds and once every twenty seconds respectively.

In front of and around them they could see the navigation lights of small fishing boats and the lights of the larger vessels in the shipping lane. What appears to be an empty sea in daylight often seems much busier at night when it is easier to see from the lights what is out there. Above them in the cloudless sky a mass of stars was slowly appearing and it was going to be a perfect night to be at sea until, twenty minutes later, the engine spluttered and died. Honeysuckle Rose slowed and then drifted gently to a stop. Twice McCabe turned the starter key but each time the engine failed to start.

Tricia, who had been dozing in the corner of the cockpit, sat up, "What's happened?"

"The engine's packed up. It's OK, I'll sort it."

McCabe stood and took a quick look around to make sure that there were no ships or boats anywhere near them and then went below and switched off the steaming light as they were a sailing boat again and not under power. He sat at the saloon table and plotted their position on the chart and satisfied himself that there were no hazards near them. Checking the tidal atlas, he saw that now, three hours after high water, there was hardly any tidal flow and he was happy to let the boat drift. He opened a locker under the saloon port berth and pulled out a small toolbox. Taking the toolbox with him and grabbing an inspection light from its bracket on the bulkhead by the steps, he went back into the cockpit where Tricia was keeping watch. She didn't need to ask what he was going to do because this wasn't the first time that the old engine had let them down and they both knew what the routine was.

McCabe lifted the wooden cockpit sole up and got down into the engine bay with the inspection light. The engine was hot and he took care not to burn himself on it in the confined space. He was familiar with the 59 year old engine's foibles and he knew what to look for - fuel starvation. He removed the water trap in the fuel line and tipped the contents into a small bucket. Water in the fuel, maybe. Dirty diesel clogging the filter, perhaps. He cleaned the water trap and then removed the fuel filter and cleaned that as well as he could by swilling it round in some clean diesel. After reinstalling the water trap and filter he bled the fuel system and tried to start the engine again. On the third attempt, it fired. McCabe ran it for a minute then pulled a toggle in the cockpit which decompressed the engine and stopped it. He got out of the engine compartment, replaced the cockpit sole and turned the key to switch off the electrics to the instrument panel.

"Water or dirt in the fuel lines, Trish. I need to service the engine, change the filters, and make sure that it's not going to let us down again before we go much further."

"Have you got all the spares you need for that?"

"I have but rather than take it apart out here we need to get into a port where I can do it without worrying that it's going to give up on us again."

"OK," replied Tricia. "Where shall we go?"

"Rye. We're nearly there anyway but we can't get in there until around high water which was three hours ago. We'll have to wait until tomorrow morning."

"What time?" asked Tricia.

"We can start going in at about six so I suggest we get some sleep. I'll take first watch and call you at two."

Tricia kissed him on the cheek and, with her usual, "Night, night," she went happily down the steps and into her cabin.

McCabe settled back and stared up into the sky as his boat drifted gently under the blackness, now pricked by a dense mass of stars which were spreading and deepening from the land to the north, above him and down to the southern horizon. The threat that they had left behind in Brighton seemed far away, but he didn't know that he was already being hunted by Bishop's hired killer, the man known only as Quietus.

Chapter Ten

Rye Bay - 0510 BST Sunday 22nd July

As the sun was appearing to the east of them, McCabe took a compass bearing on the Dungeness Light and another on the radio mast at Hastings which was shown on his chart. Going below and transferring the bearings to the chart gave him a rough fix placing them six miles to the south west of Rye Harbour entrance. He had fitted a GPS navigation system and chart plotter to Honeysuckle Rose while in France the previous year, but he still preferred to navigate using old fashioned dead reckoning and he used the satnav only to confirm that his calculations were correct. He checked and they were. The tide was turning in their favour again and McCabe went back to the cockpit where Tricia was sipping a mug of coffee which he had made for her after her three hours on watch. He turned over the engine, which started without problems, pushed the Morse throttle lever forward and, with the mainsail sheeted in hard and no foresail, they motor sailed as McCabe pointed Rose's bow to the north east. He began to look for the red and white fairway buoy two miles south south east of the harbour entrance. Passing that to seaward and then turning in would ensure a safe approach to the entrance, avoiding any hazards.

Tricia had called him at 0430 and he was feeling the fact that he'd only had two hours sleep, although the adrenalin started to work as they got closer to Rye. McCabe thought back to a time, over thirty years ago, when he knew very little about boats but had been playing his guitar in a bar in Hastings and was fortunate enough to meet a music enthusiast who was also a boat owner. He couldn't remember the man's name but what he did remember was the 26 foot Westerly which he owned and which was kept at Rye. McCabe crewed for him on the occasional Sunday when the tides and weather were right to take the boat out into Rye Bay and sail around for an hour or two, making sure that they got back into Rye before the channel dried out. If they had ever got the timing wrong, and they never did, it would mean that the small boat would have had to take the ground at low water, probably lying on its ear, and a wait of up to eight hours staring out at Camber Sands before the sea returned and lifted them off. It didn't teach him much about sailing but he learned a lot about tides.

Not speaking, McCabe and Tricia watched the approaching land as their boat sliced its way through the flat mirror calm of the sea and the sun slowly rose on what was going to be a hot, still day. By 0600 they had reached the Fairway Buoy and had turned towards the coast on a more northerly heading of 330 degrees true, although the compass wasn't necessary as they could see the red tripod beacon in the distance which marks the entrance to the harbour. Twenty minutes later and an hour before high water they motored past the beacon and through the entrance.

"There you are, Trish. We're in."

She looked at him in surprise and then at the entrance only forty metres wide, "This isn't a harbour. It's a river."

McCabe laughed, "You're right of course, but this is it, the seaward end of the River Rother. The entrance to Rye Harbour."

The river narrowed down even further and they motored on in a dead straight line for another half a mile, with featureless marshland on either side, until they reached the village of Rye Harbour on their left. The village stands isolated from the main town of Rye, a random collection of buildings started in the nineteenth century and planted on the shingle beach which was created by nature during a great storm in 1287. The storm redrew the coastline leaving the town of Rye itself two miles from the sea. On their right was the Harbour Master's office where they were required to stop and announce themselves.

While Tricia steered, McCabe lowered and flaked the mainsail, lashing it to the boom with half a dozen canvas sail ties. He returned to the cockpit and took over the wheel, turning Rose with her bow towards the sea facing into the tide which was flooding up the narrow river. They came alongside the Admiralty Jetty and while McCabe steered, neatly stemming the flow of water, Tricia secured the bow line to the jetty then took the stern line and secured that to the jetty as well. Satisfied that the boat was moored adequately enough for a temporary wait, McCabe switched off the engine. Leaving Tricia to look after Honeysuckle Rose he climbed one of the several ladders to the deck of the jetty and made the short walk to the small, modern, two storey Harbour Master's building standing alone and exposed to all weathers, a black and white lookout station keeping watch over the sea and marshes.

McCabe was surprised and pleased to find that the office was manned at this time of the morning and soon, after arranging a mooring at Strand Quay in the town of Rye itself and paying the surprisingly reasonable mooring fee, he was back on board Rose. Still with a mile and a half to go before they reached their mooring, they cast off, turned the boat and continued their way up river, motoring along the channel on a steadily rising tide which was gradually covering the foul smelling mud and slime on either side of them. They passed, moored out of the channel on both sides, small black fishing boats, with their distinctive RX registration numbers, still sitting on the mud and waiting patiently to lift off as the incoming sea swirled around them. After a mile they left the River Rother and turned to port to enter the Rock Channel and five minutes later they turned to starboard towards the Strand Quay. They identified the berth that the Harbour Master had allocated and tied up quickly and efficiently, neither of them talking, as they went through the well rehearsed routine of mooring which they had developed over the past year. Honeysuckle Rose's starboard side was secured to the high wall of the quay and they carefully allowed for the fact that their boat would rise and fall with the tide. Twice a day at low water when the channel dried out, she would be sitting with her keel in the mud.

Ahead and astern tied to the wall and secured to the wall on the other side of the narrow channel, was a varied collection of yachts and motorboats. Two of the yachts were flying Dutch ensigns and another flew a French ensign. High up their masts, under the starboard cross tree, each visitor from across the Channel flew a small red ensign as a courtesy flag which they would continue to fly until they left British waters.

By midday McCabe had given Rose's engine an oil change, new fuel and oil filters, and checked that the air filter was still reasonably clean. He had made sure that the stern gland, where the propellor shaft passed out of the boat, wasn't leaking and had given a turn to the old brass pump which forced more grease into it. He checked all the hoses for potential leaks, and didn't find any, checked that the bolts holding the engine bearings were tight and made sure that no electrical cables were fraying. Finally he bled the fuel system and ran the engine for an hour until he was satisfied that it was running smoothly and wouldn't give any more problems. Running the engine also had the added benefit of heating the boat's domestic water system and charging its leisure batteries which fed the boat's 12 volt lighting and electrical system. When he was convinced that all was working properly he switched off the engine, went below and stripped off to shower and shave in the forward heads. He came out of the shower twenty minutes later wearing a dark blue cotton dressing gown and towelling his hair to see Tricia busy in the galley preparing a brunch of sausage, fried egg, fried bread and baked beans.

"There you are, Chad. This is your reward for all your hard work," she called.

He grinned, "Wow, thank you."

McCabe being cooked a fry up was an ongoing joke between them as she refused to eat one herself for health reasons.

He went back into the cramped forward cabin and dressed quickly in jeans, a dark blue FatFace polo shirt and brown Henri Lloyd deck shoes. He studied his face in the small shaving mirror on the back of the cabin door as he combed his hair. Not given to vanity, nevertheless, he was pleased to see that with his jet black hair, kept short at the sides and long enough on the top to be combed back, and his rugged tanned features, he still looked good, although who might be interested in him he had no idea. He slipped his stainless steel Rolex watch onto his wrist as he came out of the cabin into the saloon, just at the right time to see Tricia dishing up the meal and that two neat places and a pot of coffee had been set on the saloon table. Before Tricia had joined him on Honeysuckle Rose, McCabe had fed himself adequately but with not much variety. She had changed all that by insisting that she would do all of the catering for them, not because she thought that it was a woman's place, but because she knew that she would be better at it. McCabe enjoyed that arrangement and he was eating more healthy and varied meals now than he had in his entire life before, notwithstanding the meal that he was about to eat. Tricia produced a fry up when she thought that he should be rewarded, so she must be pleased with him. They both sat at the table and ate. Tricia restricted herself to toast.

"What would you like to do today?" she asked and then, like an unsubtle child, immediately suggested, "Can we have a look at the town, Chad?"

"Certainly we can. I know Rye very well," he replied, "but I haven't been here for years."

"Let's do that then. I've never been here before so you can show me what it's like."

"With pleasure," he replied and he meant it.

They chatted while they ate and, together, they cleared the dishes. McCabe washed up while Tricia dried, happily humming a tune to herself. Both were unaware of the danger that they were in. Quietus had found them.

Chapter Eleven

The previous afternoon, using the information that Bishop had provided, Quietus had visited Brighton Marina and talked his way onto the Visitors' Pontoon where he expected to be able to walk past McCabe's boat and observe him, but the boat wasn't there. Explaining to another boat owner that he was Chad's friend and had come to visit him, he learned that McCabe and a woman had cast off at midday saying that they were going to sail around the coast to London. He also, with careful questioning, obtained a description of Honeysuckle Rose including her name. Quietus was a polymath but his knowledge of small boats was cursory. He knew enough about the subject to know that a boat of Honeysuckle Rose's size would take a few days to make that journey, so it was possible that they would put into harbours along the coast and perhaps he could find them.

Yesterday evening, Quietus had checked out Sovereign Harbour Marina, located between Pevensey Bay and Eastbourne on what used to be called The Crumbles when it was a shingle beach and a few bungalows. He had waited all evening until it was dark but McCabe's boat hadn't put in there. While he waited, Quietus amused himself with the knowledge that the marina had been built on the site of the famous Crumbles Murders both of which he had made a study of. The first in 1920 was the straightforward murder of a 17 year old girl by two men for the purposes of robbery, but the second, in 1924, of a 38 year old woman by her lover was of much more interest to him as it involved dismemberment, boiling, and the hiding of body parts in a trunk. As he mused over these murders again at the very place where they happened, he thought of the mistakes and stupidity of the murderers, who were all hanged. The study of cases like those was helpful to him and his modus operandi was guided by them. For that reason every killing that he committed appeared to be an accident, which was why he had never been caught or come to the attention of the police.

This morning he had driven to Rye and had stood on the viewing point near the Ypres Tower, the 14th century sandstone structure that stands high on the hill that is Rye. In front of him, in the distance, Quietus could see Honeysuckle Rose and he followed her slow progress as she approached the town along the River Rother. As she turned into the Rock Channel below him, Quietus knew that he had found his target, Chad McCabe.

He would seek out McCabe later and see what could be done about killing him. Accidents take time to arrange, but if an opportunity presented itself then he would take it. The yacht had slowly motored past until, that part of the channel being hidden by buildings, it passed out of his sight carrying the two friends who were oblivious to the fact that a killer had found them and was considering his next move. If it was going to look like an accident he might have to kill the girl as well.

Chapter Twelve

McCabe locked the boat up and he and Tricia climbed the wooden ladder that was fixed to the harbour wall adjacent to Rose's stern. He looked down at his boat, comfortably settled in the mud below him, and was satisfied that she was secure. On the quayside where they were standing a motorbike rally was forming up. Dozens of bikers from all over the South of England were arriving and parking their machines, every one of them gleaming in the strong sunshine and ready for inspection. It was going to be noisy so a good time to leave and go into town. In front of them a steady flow of vehicles slowly passed, skirting the edge of Rye on the narrow main road. On the other side of the road stood the distinctive black wooden clad buildings that this part of Rye was famous for.

After stopping for Tricia to buy an ice cream at the van parked on the quayside they took advantage of a short break in the traffic, crossed the road and walked into the town following a street known as The Deals. At the end of The Deals they continued into Mermaid Street, busy with tourists all gazing in awe at the long row of quaint mediaeval houses lining either side of the narrow road and disappearing up the steep hill into the distance, each house of a different shape and size. The occasional car slowly made its way up or down the street and the tourists, picking their way awkwardly over the uneven cobbles, reluctantly stood to one side as it passed and then stepped back into the street as if to deny any further vehicle access.

McCabe and Tricia turned right into Traders Passage and followed it up the increasingly steep hill to where it became Watchbell Lane and then to Watchbell

Street. There they stopped to look at the view. Below them and to their right they could see Honeysuckle Rose moored snugly by the quay. In the distance and ahead of them was the sea and they could see large commercial ships, fifteen miles away in the west-going shipping lane, appearing not to be moving but just hanging there on the horizon.

They turned left and continued slowly along Watchbell Street with Tricia admiring and commenting on the different types of architecture while McCabe, who had seen it so often before, tried to see the town with her eyes and regain the sense of awe that everyone experiences when they visit Rye for the first time. At the end of the street they reached the surprisingly large churchyard which, with its grass and graves, takes up much of the top of the hill on which the town is built.

They walked through the graveyard to the massive 12th century St Mary's Church which stands imposingly in the centre of Rye and can be seen from miles away in all directions across the marshes. The church's side door was open and small huddles of people stood about chatting to each other. McCabe walked up to the door and looked in. It was the wrong time of the day for a service but the church was full of people. A sign on the door read Jazz at the Church and he realised that there was live music on offer and they had arrived during an interval. Tricia, was reading an inscription on a nearby gravestone and he walked over to her.

"It looks as though there's a gig going on. Would you like to go in and listen?"

"Why not?" she smiled at him enthusiastically.

The small groups of people became one larger group as they started to file back into the church and, when the last person had gone in, McCabe and Tricia followed. As they entered, an attendant closed the door behind them and they turned left to the back of the church where there were two empty pews. Apart from those, the church was full to capacity with every seat occupied. At the front of the church, between the audience and the altar, a four piece group dressed identically in black long sleeved shirts, black trousers and black shoes was about to play and McCabe and Tricia both instantly recognised the violinist - George Lee from the Reinhardt's Bar Allstars. Of course! Andy had told McCabe that George was playing a gig in Rye today and this was it. Too late, he realised that it was a ticketed event and that he and Tricia had unwittingly slipped in without paying. Before he could dwell on that any further the band swung into a modern arrangement of Gershwin's Summertime and he gave himself up to the music and sat back in the coolness of the church to enjoy it.

   At the end of the performance, after the usual applause, whistling and shouts of encore, the charade of the band going off and coming back on, and the delivery of their best and final number, the musicians disappeared into the vestry and the audience started to drift away. McCabe and Tricia stayed where they were at the back of the church and, when most of the audience had left, they walked to the front where a young roadie wearing denim and long hair was busy putting music stands and chairs in their correct places ready for the evening performance.

   "Hi," said McCabe as they reached him. "Would you mind telling George Lee that we're here?"

   "I can't bother him, man. The gig's finished."

   "He won't mind."

"Does he know you?"

"Yes, we play together"

"Who shall I say?"

"Just say Chad."

"Stay there, man."

The roadie walked to the vestry and went in and, a few seconds later, came out again followed by George Lee. The roadie went back to his work not interested in anything else that was happening around him.

George came forward with his right hand extended all bonhomie and public school accent, "Chad, dear heart. What are you doing here? Hello Tricia."

He shook hands with McCabe and then went up to Tricia, towered over her, and held her firmly by the shoulders while he kissed her on both cheeks.

McCabe answered, "We came into Rye with the boat this morning and were doing the tourist bit and just wandered in."

"Well I'm so glad that you did, dear boy. Come and have a drink. I'm staying at The Mermaid. Meet me at the side door in five minutes. Good idea?"
McCabe looked at Tricia and she nodded.

"Great idea," he replied.

"Cool. I'll be right there," George called over his shoulder, already half way back to the vestry.

McCabe and Tricia walked out of the door that they had entered the church by and followed the path to the left around the building until, ahead of them, they saw a porch and assumed, correctly, that its door was the one that they were looking for. They waited, discreetly to one side, as band members and other people came out and, within a couple of minutes, George himself came through the door, tall, violin case under his left arm, stylish fedora, dark blue double breasted suit with turnups to the trousers, black shirt, white tie, black socks and highly polished black brogues. A leggy blonde was at his side wearing a pink blouse, a navy blue jacket with lapels, a matching knee length skirt and stilettos. In her early thirties, she must have been at least twenty years younger than George and they looked every inch the gangster and his moll from prohibition Chicago.

McCabe smiled as the couple walked towards them. George was also smiling but the blonde was serious and not happy. McCabe had never seen George Lee with the same woman twice and he wondered what the story was with this one.

"Come along, dear boy," commanded George airily as he turned away and waved his right hand. "To The Mermaid Inn," and he and the blonde linked arms and headed off along Church Square with McCabe and Tricia following.

The Mermaid Inn stands near the top of Mermaid Street and is one of the most picturesque hotels in the whole of England, with its half-timbered frontage and leaded light windows surrounded by a covering of ivy. Famous not only for the fact that it has sheltered travellers for 600 years, but also famous in fiction for its association with Russell Thorndike's Doctor Syn novels which describe the adventures of an 18th century criminal who was also the vicar of Dymchurch. Notorious during the middle years of the 18th century, the inn was the secondary headquarters of the Hawkhurst Gang, a ruthless band of murderous smugglers who terrorised Kent and Sussex. Far from being the glamourous folk heroes of myth and a popular Kipling poem they were loathed by the general population until finally, in 1749, over seventy of them were either hanged or transported to the Colonies.

George, the blonde, Tricia and McCabe climbed the flight of three brick built steps and entered through the open front door of the hotel, walked past the reception desk and in the small lobby area George stopped. He whispered something to the blonde and gave her the violin case to carry. Without a backward glance at McCabe and Tricia she started up the narrow flight of carpeted stairs towards the bedrooms on the upper floors. George patted her gently on the backside to help her on her way.

Turning to McCabe and Tricia, George waved them into the lounge where they seated themselves side by side in, rather than on, a long, spacious, leather Chesterfield sofa, one of six similar sofas spaced around the room with their backs to the walls. There were four people at the other end of the lounge but, at this time of day, the hotel was quiet with most guests being in the town or in their rooms. They had a minute to take in the romance of the room with its timbered ceiling, brick and stone fireplace and black oak panelling. Above the panelling to their right was a quotation by Shakespeare beautifully drawn in Gothic script, "And when love speaks the voice of all the gods makes Heaven drowsy with the harmony".

A waiter entered the room and positioned a small oak table in front of them. George ordered champagne without even asking them what they would like to drink and, when the waiter had gone, he said, "I'm so sorry, I should have asked you what you wanted. You both like champagne though, surely?"

He twisted one way and then the other to look at them both in turn with a quizzical expression.

They both nodded, "Who doesn't?" said McCabe while Tricia remained silent.

"How are you both? Especially you, sweetness," asked George turning, smiling and leering at Tricia.

She felt uneasy as George held her eyes for a fraction too long, forcing her to look down at her hands to escape him. "I'm fine," she replied.

McCabe, who was never really sure about George but was obliged to be polite as they played in the Reinhardt's Allstars together, took control of the conversation forcing George to turn to him instead of Tricia.

"We're both well, George. What have you been up to?"

George turned his attention to McCabe and sat back smiling, "Just the usual, Chad. Gigs, racecourses, bars and women."

McCabe had always wondered where the money came from for George's lifestyle and had come to the conclusion that it was provided by his women. There was always a steady stream of them, always glamourous, always well presented, expensive and never seen more than once before George turned up with a different one.

The waiter returned with a bottle in an ice bucket and three champagne flutes. They sat back quietly while he went through his champagne opening ritual, removing the foil and wire, holding the bottle in a white linen napkin in his right hand, gently easing the cork out with a quiet pop with his left, then pouring into the three glasses one after the other with his left hand behind his back, the thumb of his right hand in the punt in the base of the bottle.

"Put that on my bill, will you?" asked George.

"Certainly, Mr Lee," replied the waiter as he placed the bottle back in the ice bucket and draped the napkin over the top of the bucket.

"Will there be anything else, sir?"

"Anybody?" asked George twisting again to look at his two guests.

When they shook their heads George smiled at the waiter, "That will be all, thanks."

With a nod the waiter left the lounge.

"What brings you to Rye?" asked George.

Tricia joined in, "We were sailing past and had some engine trouble, so we came in to Rye this morning."

"Are you staying long?" asked George.

"We've fixed it now," replied McCabe. "We'll be on our way again in the morning."

"Where to?" asked George.

"Up the Thames to London," replied McCabe.

"I don't blame you for getting away after that business at Reinhardt's last week and poor Bronek getting shot," said George.

"It's worse than that. They killed his wife as well," answered McCabe.

"I know they did, dear heart. I read it in the Argus."

"Did you know her?" asked Tricia.

"No, I never met her," replied George looking serious. "They had a daughter too according to the paper."

"They did, and it was me who found her." McCabe picked up his glass and took a sip of champagne. The others followed suit.

"That must have been a bit grim," said George.

"It was. I just went along there to see if she was alright and found her dead in the kitchen. Up until that point I thought that they'd shot Bronek by mistake and they were really after me."

"Why would they be after you?" asked George.

"Do you remember that business with the drugs last year?"

"Ah, yes," replied George. "I do remember that?"

"Well we thought that the people I'd upset might have wanted me killed but they got Bronek by mistake."

"You might be right, of course," said George without much conviction.

"I don't think so now, otherwise why would they have killed Bronek's wife? It's clear that they were after Bronek but we've no idea why."

"Better to be safe than sorry," replied George.

"You're right," said McCabe. "We're going to keep away from Brighton for a bit, anyway."

"Where are you going to go in London," asked George.

"St Katharine Docks," replied McCabe. "We're going to have a holiday."

"Your life is an endless holiday, Chad," laughed George. "Rather like mine. Don't forget we've got a gig at Le QuecumBar in Battersea the week after next."

"No, I won't miss that," McCabe smiled.

George topped up their champagne glasses, filled his empty one and turned the empty bottle upside down in the ice bucket and they chatted about gigs and music while Tricia sat quietly listening. They had almost finished their drinks when, as if on cue, the waiter appeared again and hovered respectfully by their table until McCabe had finished speaking. He enquired whether they would like another bottle of champagne.

"My round, I think," said McCabe.

George patted himself on the stomach and replied with a smile, "No that's enough for me, thanks. I've got to play at the church again at eight o'clock."

McCabe leaned forward and looked enquiringly at Tricia.

"No thanks, Chad. I'd like to go back to the boat and get some sleep."

George answered the waiter, "No thank you," and the waiter withdrew.

They drained their glasses and George stood up buttoning his jacket, "Well, my friend upstairs needs my attention, so I'll say goodbye."

McCabe and Tricia both stood. George grabbed Tricia's shoulders again and kissed her on both cheeks then he picked up his hat and shook hands with McCabe saying, "Goodbye old thing. I'll see you at Le QuecumBar."

"Bye, George," they both said at the same time and he strode out of the room fedora in hand to attend to the blonde upstairs.

McCabe and Tricia left the hotel and, leaning back slightly because of the steepness of the hill, strolled slowly in the hot sunshine, down Mermaid Street towards the river and Honeysuckle Rose.

Tricia spoke, "What do you make of him, Chad?"

"I'm never sure with George, Trish. He doesn't work and sees himself as super cool. He's had two wives and a string of girlfriends who pay his bills until they get wise to him. Not everybody likes him. He talks big and has no visible means of support apart from girlfriends and gigs. He's a good musician though, which is all I'm concerned about."

They walked on in silence for fifty yards and Tricia, who was normally very forgiving of people, suddenly said, "I don't like him. He's a sleazeball."

Chapter Thirteen

Strand Quay, Rye - 0802 BST Monday 23rd July

Half an hour before high water McCabe and Tricia cast off from their mooring, and Honeysuckle Rose, with just her mainsail hoisted, motored and nosed her way towards the Rock Channel again. Theirs was the only boat moving. The visiting yachts from France and Holland had their curtains drawn against the day and their occupants were sleeping. The weather was warm and still with small white cumulus clouds appearing to the west and the sun was already starting to feel hot on their faces. They turned into the Rock Channel and motored slowly ahead retracing their passage of the day before. Turning to starboard they followed the River Rother towards the sea, motoring against the last of the incoming tide which had been rapidly filling the channel and covering the mud on either side. Watching them from the viewing point near the Ypres Tower, as they disappeared into the distance, Quietus considered his next move.

After half an hour they cleared the river entrance and continued to motor in a south easterly direction on a mirror flat sea, making a course that was not the most efficient but which would keep them clear of the military firing ranges on their port side at Lydd. McCabe couldn't see any red flags or red lights which would warn of live firing about to commence but he had a firm belief that, if there might be bullets flying about, it was best to stay at a safe distance. After five miles McCabe turned the boat east and held that course until the headland at Dungeness was directly on their port beam and then slowly brought Honeysuckle Rose around until they were on a north easterly course which would take them up channel, two miles clear of the westbound commercial shipping lane which was on their starboard side. He hoped to be able to hold this course for the next four hours until they reached the South Foreland near Deal where they would turn to the north. They cleared Dungeness at 0940 and the neap tide which they were experiencing would give them about 0.5 knots of easterly lift in their favour over the next couple of hours, after which it would turn against them and slow them down. Not by much though, maybe half a knot in the other direction by the time they reached South Foreland, so the east and west tides would pretty much cancel each other out for that part of the journey. The crucial part of the journey would be at the North Foreland where, in nearly eight hours' time at about 1715, the tide would be in their favour to carry them into the Thames Estuary and on to Queenborough at the mouth of the River Medway. There they would moor up and wait for another favourable tide to carry them up to London. If they missed the tide at North Foreland they would have to put into Ramsgate and wait, or stay at sea and battle against the tide all the way to The Medway.

The weather forecast predicted that the wind would increase from the south west and remain at a steady force 3 or 4 for the rest of the day so, although McCabe had hanked on a genoa to the forestay and lashed it, bundled up, to the guardrail to stop it from going overboard, he didn't expect to use it. Instead he had rigged the boat's cruising chute ready for use but had left it by the mast in its bag until they cleared Dungeness. The wind had increased to the forecast south westerly and was coming from directly behind them. Tricia took over at the wheel while McCabe left the cockpit and, holding on to the shrouds and the handrail which ran the length of the coachroof from the cockpit to the mast he made his way forward. Using a spare halyard he hauled the cruising chute, contained in its nylon snuffer, to the top of the mast and cleated off the halyard at the base of the mast. The tack of the chute was already secured by a line to the bow and he hauled the line tight and cleated it off. The snuffer now looked like a huge orange windsock hanging diagonally from the top of the mast to the bow. McCabe grasped the line attached to the snuffer, hauled it down and the snuffer quickly concertinaed its way to the top of the mast releasing the cruising chute as it went. The chute ballooned out ahead of the boat securely fixed at the bow and masthead but flogging in the wind on the port side of the boat. McCabe secured the snuffer line to a cleat on the mast and quickly returned to the cockpit where he grabbed the thin rope which was the sheet secured to the clew of the cruising chute. He quickly turned it twice around the port side sheet winch. He pulled it tight and then inserted a handle into the winch turning it several full revolutions to take up the slack on the sheet before the flogging of the chute could begin to start tearing its thin MP-70 nylon fabric. As McCabe cleated off the sheet the blue and red cruising chute snapped taut like a horizontal parachute and Rose surged forward as it began to pull her along. Tricia put the engine into neutral and fought with the wheel to keep the boat on course. McCabe hauled on the mainsheet to get control of the mainsail and boom which was threatening to snap across the boat.

"Keep her like that, Trish and I'll put a preventer on the main."

He secured a good rope the thickness of his thumb to an eye on the underside of and about half way along the wooden boom, then made his way forward again and fed the other end of the rope through a block which was fixed to the centre of the foredeck. He fed the rope through another block fixed to the starboard side of the coach roof then he brought the rope back to the cockpit and dropped it. He took the mainsheet in both hands.

"Ready, Trish?"

"OK," she replied.

Tricia turned the boat a fraction to port to get the wind behind the mainsail and McCabe eased out the mainsheet bit by bit until the boom and sail had been eased out to the point where the boom was almost at ninety degrees to the direction of the boat. This was the most dangerous part. If Tricia lost control of the boat and the wind got behind the sail in its new position, the heavy boom would whip across the boat damaging itself and anyone who got in its way. McCabe and Tricia made sure that their heads were below boom height as he cleated off the mainsheet, grabbed the rope that he had secured to the foredeck, pulled it up tight and secured it to a cleat on the starboard side deck. The rope was now acting as a preventer, literally preventing the boom from swinging and causing damage or injuring the crew.

McCabe went back to the cockpit and wound the sheet winch slightly to adjust the set of the cruising chute, he pulled the lanyard in the floor of the cockpit which decompressed and stopped the engine and then stood back in the cockpit and looked up at both sails. With the mainsail boomed out to starboard and the cruising chute flying ahead of the boat and slightly to port they were goose winging their way up the English

Channel at a steady five knots. He looked astern of them. The wind was steady, a straight wake was streaming away from them, the sun was shining, the sea was calm and the horizon was miles away. A perfect morning.

"Would you like me to steer, Trish?"

"Why not?" she replied. "I'll make some coffee and sandwiches."

They continued like that for the next four hours, taking turns to steer for an hour each time. The occasional yacht passed them travelling west, a few fishing boats were visible in the distance and large commercial ships passed them travelling in the opposite direction five miles away out to sea. To port, five miles away, lay the Romney Marsh behind its long sea wall and, as they passed Dymchurch, McCabe thought of Dr Syn and the Mermaid Hotel at Rye. He watched as they began to close with the land which curved out towards them at Folkestone.

They passed Folkestone at midday and an hour later they were two miles out to sea and about to pass Dover Harbour and the famous cliffs, not white but green from the vegetation that covers a large part of them. McCabe glanced up the mast at the old fashioned octahedral type radar reflector hanging from the port crosstree, aware that Honeysuckle Rose was being tracked by all of the shipping in this busy part of the Channel and, more importantly, by the CNIS, the Channel Navigation Information Service which monitors movement in the Dover Straits of over 400 commercial vessels every day and is ready to intervene if there is any danger of collision. The main hazard for McCabe and Tricia would be from cross Channel ferries entering and leaving Dover Harbour, which could run them down, and they kept a more careful than usual watch until they had passed the eastern harbour entrance and the danger was over.

Seven hours after they had left the mooring at Rye and with the wind dying they reached South Foreland where they had to make a turn to the north to sail inside the Goodwin Sands and along the Kent coast to the Thames Estuary. McCabe released the sheet controlling the cruising chute and went forward to the mast and hauled on the snuffer until it was once again a long nylon tube containing the chute from the top of the mast to the bow. He released the halyard and lowered the snuffer to the deck and lashed it in four places to the guard rail to prevent it from escaping over the side. Now they were sailing with just the mainsail up and their speed had slowed considerably. McCabe removed the preventer from the boom as Tricia carefully kept the boat on a steady heading. He returned to the cockpit and quickly hauled on the mainsheet until the mainsail was sheeted in tight fore and aft. He started the engine. Two miles ahead of them to the east lay the beginning of the Goodwin Sands, a treacherous sandbank ten miles long which holds the wrecks of over two thousand ships.

"OK, Tricia. Due north please."

The boat turned onto its new northerly heading keeping the jeopardy of the Goodwins on her starboard side and now there was a knot of tide against them which would get even stronger over the next few hours. Tricia pushed the throttle forward and Honeysuckle Rose was making progress over the ground at a rate of 5 knots still with 17 nautical miles to go before they reached the point past North Foreland where they could turn into the Thames Estuary. That would take at least another 4 hours now that the tide was against them. The wind had disappeared and the sea was calm but they were conscious of the power of the water as it surged against them trying to push them back to where they had come from and McCabe was thankful that they had put into Rye and serviced the engine.

They had now left the English Channel and were in the North Sea. Tricia steered and McCabe spent most of his time below studying a paper chart of the area, reading the local tide tables and carefully plotting their position every half an hour, marking it on the chart in pencil with a triangle and the time written next to it. Every ten minutes or so he would go up into the cockpit to look around. Each time Tricia would be concentrating on the course that she was steering and looking determined.

"Alright, Tricia?"

"Alright, Chad," she replied with a huge grin to show that she was thoroughly enjoying herself.

An hour after South Foreland they were passing the town of Deal on the east Kent coast and McCabe studied the chart carefully taking note of the profusion of red and green channel buoys and black and yellow cardinal buoys all marking various hazards to be avoided. Apart from serving as a warning, the buoys were also useful in helping McCabe keep track of where they were. Tricia would call out to him every time she saw a buoy so that he could come up and check their position against it by confirming that it was the one marked on the chart that he expected to see next. The area that they were sailing through is known as The Downs, a patch of sea used as a sheltered anchorage by navies and merchant ships for hundreds of years when Deal was one of the most important ports in England. Marked on McCabe's chart and repeated many times were the letters Wk each noting the position of a wrecked ship, hundreds of them all over the chart to remind him, as if he needed reminding, how dangerous the waters that they were sailing through are.

They passed Ramsgate, which was their fallback port if they missed their tidal gate and had to return to seek shelter, and then Broadstairs was in sight and, as each hour passed, the tide pushing them south east towards the Goodwins became stronger and their progress slower. McCabe took over the steering from Tricia for an hour to give her a rest and then she took it back again as they drew level with the North Foreland so that McCabe could go below and plot their position. He returned with cups of strong coffee for them both and they sipped at them gratefully.

"OK, Trish. Steer 330 degrees on the compass please and that should take us to a red can marking the edge of Longnose Ledge. Keep well seaward of it and we'll be in Margate Roads. That's where we turn to go up the Thames. Well done."

Feeling pleased with herself and always happy when she received any praise from him, she made the course adjustment and gazed steadily forward looking for the red buoy. McCabe also stared ahead looking for it. They were late and the tide flowing against them was still getting stronger, but if they could get there in the next hour they could make the turn and then have the tide into the Thames Estuary in their favour.

The white cliffs and white lighthouse of North Foreland slowly slid past them a mile away and the Thames Estuary started to open up on their port side. Tricia was the first to spot the red Longnose Buoy and adjusted her course slightly again to keep to seaward of it. Neither of them spoke, both silently willing the boat forward to the point where it could escape the adverse current and turn towards their destination. When they were due north of the red buoy McCabe spoke again.

"Ok, Trish. Great job. We've done it. Turn her due west to 270 degrees please and I'll go down and start plotting our course to the Medway."

He went below and Tricia was filled with a sense of achievement, pride and love for this man who she would go anywhere with. She turned the boat onto the new course and, still with the mainsail up and running on the engine, they headed into the Thames making for the South Channel off of Margate. It was 1810 and they had made the turn almost an hour late but they had escaped from the south going tide which was now pouring down the East Kent coast. Tricia sat back and steered with one hand as the west going tide lifted them into the Thames Estuary and she felt Honeysuckle Rose speed up as they headed towards The Medway with 25 miles still to travel and 5 hours until the tide turned against them again.

Chapter Fourteen

Brighton - 1911 BST Monday 23rd July

Quietus was sitting at the bar in Reinhardt's with a gin and tonic in his hand. It was early, he was the only customer there and he was pumping Jimmy the barman for information. They were talking about the members of the Reinhardt's Bar Allstars.

"Do you know how long he's gone for?"

"A few weeks, I think," answered Jimmy polishing a glass with a cloth. He placed the glass on the shelf above the bar then took another one from the dishwasher basket and carried on polishing. "He's gone in his boat. He told me he's going to leave it at St Katharine Docks and hire another boat and go up the River Thames. Alright for some."

"Have you ever done anything like that?"

"Not in a boat. No chance. I have to work behind this bar. Worked in a bar near St Katharine Docks once. I liked it there. Lots of character. One of the nicer parts of London. What about you? Do you know it?"

"Yes, I've spent a bit of time around there. I know it quite well," answered Quietus. "Did he tell you where he was going on the Thames?"

"No," answered Jimmy, "he's a bit of a dark horse is Chad; doesn't give much away. I know he was going to leave on Saturday. How long does it take to sail to London in a boat? He might be there by now. I know that he's playing at Le QuecumBar in Battersea on the 2nd."

Quietus decided that to ask any more questions about McCabe would look strange so he changed the subject, "How's business after the shooting?"

"Fantastic. Not tonight 'cos it's Monday, but we've been rushed off our feet all weekend. Ghoulish, aren't they? People we've never seen before who just come in to have a look at where it happened. That poor man just sitting over there," Jimmy gestured at the stage, which was really a low dais about a foot high. He screwed up his face and pulled up his shoulders in a camp mock shudder, "and then his wife!"

Quietus glanced at the stage and then decided to leave, "Time I left you to it." He stood up and finished his drink, put the glass on the bar and headed for the door, "Bye, Jimmy."

"Bye," called Jimmy and he went back to polishing the glasses.

Quietus stepped out into the street. As an assassin he was extremely successful, largely because he had never left any clues to his identity at the scene of his crimes and he always planned his hits meticulously. He made sure that he only killed when it was absolutely safe for him to do so. He enjoyed his work and took his time, considering himself to be an artist. He particularly enjoyed the sense of power he felt at the moment of his victim's death. He regarded himself as a cultured individual and had chosen the pseudonym by which he was known to his clients carefully. While watching a production of Shakespeare's Hamlet at the Theatre Royal in Brighton, on his own as he often was, he heard in the famous "to be or not to be" speech the line, "When he himself might his quietus make with a bare Bodkin?" As soon as the play had finished he settled himself with a large glass of brandy in the velvety Victorian plushness of the Colonnade Bar next door to the theatre and researched the speech on the Internet using his phone. When he discovered a definition saying that the word quietus means "a finishing stroke; anything that effectually ends or settles" and then another defining the word as "death or something that causes death" he knew that destiny intended that word to be his professional name.

Now, deep in thought, he walked slowly through the North Laine considering his options. Not all serial killers are psychopaths and Quietus believed that's how it was with him. It was a living not an obsession and he took pride in the fact. He chuckled to himself at the thought that it was his living not his victims'. He always took his time before he actually completed a commission, as he liked to think of it. There would be too many people about for him to successfully stage an accident at St Katharine Docks. The River Thames on the other hand offered all sorts of possibilities: drowning or a boat fire, for example. He hadn't been able to find out from Jimmy where McCabe would be going in the hire boat so he would have to intercept him at St Katharine Docks and follow him. Deciding how to kill him, and possibly the girl as well, could wait until later.

Chapter Fifteen

The journey from North Foreland to the entrance to the River Medway was, by Honeysuckle Rose standards, quick. McCabe and Tricia again took turns to steer for an hour at a time, enjoying the windless evening and feeling the illusion of speed as the tide and engine rushed them past the buoys that marked their westward passage along the coast of North Kent. With the engine pushing them along at 6 knots and the tide adding a knot to that, by 1900 they were in the Gore Channel with the Margate Hook sandbank half a mile the north of them and the Kent coast a mile to the south. Once they had cleared the Hook they made a small course change to take them west north west and headed further out into the Estuary. By 2015 as the sun set ahead of them they had passed the town of Herne Bay and in the clear evening, again with maximum visibility, the estuary slowly became a mass of lights: winking lights from navigation buoys, fixed lights, shipping, small boats and the town of Whitstable three miles to the south. To the north east of them were yellow flashing lights marking the Kentish Flats wind farm and, from the tops of the wind farm's turbine towers, red lights flashing the dot dash dash of the Morse Code letter W.
McCabe made sandwiches and coffee which they ate while keeping a careful lookout at the lights and shipping in the estuary, and by 2100 they were in the Four Fathoms Channel and approaching a green light flashing twice every 5 seconds marking the small Spile Sandbank, which they left on their starboard side. The tide was slackening fast now, but with only 5 miles to

go until they reached The Medway they were confident that they could make it before the tide turned on them. At 2156 they were nearing the buoyed channel which they would follow into the River Medway and the tide was slack, poised to turn east again in an hour's time. McCabe was steering and Tricia had been studying a cluster of four flashing yellow lights on the other side of the channel about a half a mile away from them.

"What's that, Chad?"

"I was waiting for you to ask me that. It's an accident waiting to happen, Trish. The SS Richard Montgomery. Have you heard of it?"

"No, should I have done?"

"Not many people seem to be aware of it, so I'm not surprised," he replied. "It's the wreck of a World War II American Liberty ship which ran aground there in a gale in 1944. It contained thousands of tons of explosives and phosphorous, and later it broke its back and couldn't be refloated. It just sits there a couple of hundred metres from a busy shipping channel with its three masts sticking up above the water. Sometimes phosphorous floats up from it and catches fire when it's exposed to the air."

"Why haven't they removed the explosives?" asked Tricia.

"They removed some of them at the time but then they stopped the work because it was considered too dangerous. If they try to get more out, the whole lot could go up. There are an estimated 1,400 tons of bombs still in it, probably very unstable. Do you see the land lights over to the north west?"

"Yes."

"That's Southend. And the lights over here to the south?"

"Yes."

"That's Sheerness. We're going to turn into the River Medway just past there and tie up at Queenborough on the Isle of Sheppey. The lights further on from Sheerness are on the Isle of Grain, the largest natural gas terminal in Europe. It has huge tanks which store liquified gas. It's reckoned that if the Richard Montgomery exploded it would create a tsunami which would wreck a lot of Southend and Sheerness and send a tidal wave complete with burning phosphorous up the Thames to London, across the gas tanks on the Isle of Grain and along the Medway nearly all the way to Maidstone. The damage and possible loss of life would be huge."

"Could they close the Thames Barrier to keep the tidal wave out?"

"It would depend on how fast the wave was travelling," he replied. "The barrier is about 30 miles from here and the wave from an explosion like that could easily travel at 30 miles an hour. It takes 90 minutes to close the barrier by which time the wave would have gone through and be on its way to central London. If it overflowed the river's banks in London it could even flood the Underground system at Embankment Station which is where the Circle, District, Bakerloo and Northern Lines meet. The Thames Barrier was designed to stop that happening."

She looked at him wide eyed, "Surely they can't just leave it like that?"

"Well they've left it there since World War II. Questions get asked in Parliament sometimes but nothing's done about it. When we leave Queenborough we'll be coming out in daylight, so you'll be able to get a better look at it. Let's start heading in."

McCabe slowed Rose and waited just outside the shipping channel which leads into the River Medway, as a large ship, its decks lit up like daylight, was already in the channel and passing them inward bound. In the dark it looked massive and McCabe kept well away from it. After the ship had passed, and with no other vessels in sight, McCabe crossed to the north side of the channel and then turned to port following the conical starboard buoys marking the channel which, after a mile, brought them safely into Sheerness Harbour.

Although he'd been there before McCabe new better than to take shortcuts across any harbour in the dark and continued to follow the buoys. In the distance ahead of him he could see a green light flashing every 5 seconds. The light was on top of a buoy called Grain Hard and it would be his turning point to make the run into Queenborough Harbour, the entrance to which was on the other side of Sheerness Harbour just over a mile away. When they reached Grain Hard Buoy McCabe turned Honeysuckle Rose onto a course due south and began looking for a white light flashing three times every ten seconds. The flashing light indicated the position of the Queenborough Spit East Cardinal Buoy and, if he passed close to it leaving it on his starboard side, his southerly course would lead him into the channel towards Queenborough. McCabe spotted the light easily and, 12 minutes later, they were passing it and had arrived at Queenborough Harbour which is also the western entrance to The Swale, a tidal channel separating The Isle of Sheppey from mainland Kent.

McCabe slowed the engine and, while Tricia steered, he went on deck and hauled down the mainsail, lashing it to the boom with sail ties to be tidied up later. Then he stood at the bow with a powerful lamp scanning the water ahead until he spotted a yellow visitors buoy. He pointed it out to Tricia who steered slowly towards it. A slight tide had started to run in the direction in which they were travelling as The Swale began to empty back into the Thames Estuary at the eastern end of Sheppey, so Tricia brought Honeysuckle Rose around to face the way they had come and then stemmed the slight current while McCabe tied up to the buoy, passing the rope over the bow roller where the anchor chain would normally go if deployed. He signalled to Tricia and she put the engine into neutral, letting Rose slowly fall back with the current until all of her weight was being taken by the buoy. Satisfied that they were secure, McCabe went back to the cockpit, turned off the engine and sat on a side cushion opposite Tricia. The sudden silence after the many hours of engine noise was palpable and they both listened, not speaking, to the sound of water trickling past the hull. They looked around them at lights from the land reflected from what appeared to be a vast expanse of water, but McCabe knew from a previous visit that it was mostly mudflats with a shallow covering at high tide.

"Glass of wine?" offered Tricia.

"Good idea."

She went below and returned with a chilled bottle of Sauvignon Blanc from the fridge and two glasses. This was their ritual at the end of every passage and she removed the cork, poured the wine into the glasses and handed one to McCabe.

"Cheers, Chad."

He smiled at her and raised his glass, "Cheers, Trish."

Chapter Sixteen

Little Venice, London - 1122 BST Tuesday 24th July

Ulrich Fleischer, arms folded, stood at the floor to ceiling first floor window of his UK headquarters and looked across Warwick Avenue to the postage stamp of a park which is Rembrandt Gardens, at this time of the year in full flower. Through the trees lining the water's edge on the far side of the gardens he could see several colourful canal boats moored in Browning's Pool. Behind him Ernst Kegel his UK enforcer, muscle bound, mean spirited and English born of German parentage, was stumbling over his words as he tried to explain himself.

Fleischer's organisation had many properties in different parts of the world from which he ruled over the hundreds of operatives who carried out his orders, always without question and with ruthless efficiency. He hardly listened to Kegel as he watched a narrowboat emerge from the Regent's Canal and slowly cross the pool until it turned right and disappeared under the low arch of the bridge which marks the beginning of the Paddington Arm of the Grand Union Canal. Of all of his properties, this early Victorian, three storey, six bedroomed and luxuriously furnished house in the heart of London remained his favourite. Externally painted white, like all of the other properties in this select area of the City of Westminster, it was an expensive, anonymous house with wealthy, anonymous neighbours who minded their own business. An oasis of calm whenever he visited England.

Handsome and tanned, with piercing blue eyes, black hair going grey at the sides, Fleischer was in his late fifties. He wore a light grey tailored two piece suit, light blue shirt, dark blue tie, dark blue socks, expensive handmade black leather shoes, and looked every centimetre the successful German businessman that he liked to present himself as. Once a high ranking officer in the infamous, repressive East German security police known as the Stasi, he now controlled one of the world's most successful international criminal organisations, the Schild Schwert und Vergeltung, known to police forces the world over as the SSV.

Fleischer spun around suddenly angry, unfolded his arms and fixed Kegel with a stare that immediately shut him up. He held his underling in that way for a few seconds and then spoke, "Why do you want to kill this man McCabe?"

Kegel, hesitantly trying to find the words that wouldn't anger his master further, "Because he visited the wife and she gave him a letter to deliver. I managed to get that much out of her."

Fleischer glared at him, "You are a brute Kegel, and you lack finesse. Our client wanted Kowalski dead, but he also wants the list of names of the traitors that he was emailing his propaganda to. So what do you do? You kill Kowalski without finding the list. Then you kill the wife without finding the list. Now you want to kill the man who she gave a letter to. Do you not think that it would be better to follow him and see where he takes us and who else might be involved? We have an extremely impatient client who won't tolerate failure and neither will I."

"The wife told us everything that she knew, which wasn't much." Kegel felt that he was on safer ground now that he had an answer for his actions. "We had to kill her to stop her talking to the police. I don't think that she knew much about her husband's activities anyway."

Emboldened now, Kegel continued, "Klaus Stritter has made enquiries in Brighton and discovered that McCabe and a woman are travelling to London by boat. Stritter and Stefan Merk will be waiting for them at St Katharine Docks, which is apparently where they are heading. There are only certain times that a boat can pass through the lock there so they will be easy to see when they arrive."

"And where are they now?"

"At the moment they are somewhere on the South Coast of England and will arrive at St Katharine Docks in the next few days."

"Make sure that you find them, Ernst, and follow them."

Kegel nodded, "I will, sir."

Fleischer looked intently at him without speaking while Kegel inwardly squirmed then, turning to look out of the window again, he said, "And what of the other matter?"

"Everything is being prepared at the Shiplake house, sir. We have planned the operation for three weeks' time on the night of the 13th of August to coincide with the client's wishes and a spring tide when the sea level will be at its highest. Everything will be in place by then."

"Make sure that it is, Ernst. The client is one that I would not wish to offend. You may go."

With a sense of relief Kegel turned and left the room and Fleischer continued to look out at the tranquil scene before him. After several minutes he crossed the room to his antique Chippendale writing desk, sat behind it in a modern swivel office chair and picked up the telephone. His male secretary answered, "Yes sir?"

"I want a woman. Get me one."

Chapter Seventeen

Queenborough - 0530 BST Wednesday 25th July

From Queenborough to Tower Bridge is approximately forty miles and, with careful planning, the journey along the Thames can be made in a single tide. Ten minutes before slack low water, Tricia Knight slipped the rope that had been holding Honeysuckle Rose securely to the mooring buoy for the last 30 hours. McCabe put the boat's old engine into forward gear and they headed along the channel out of Queenborough Harbour towards the Thames Estuary, reversing their journey of two evenings ago. To the east of them the sun had been steadily climbing into a cloudless sky for the last twenty minutes proving that the weather forecast had probably been correct when it promised a windless day with full sunshine, perfect conditions to take the tide up to London but no chance of sailing.

No other boats were moving, which gave Tricia and McCabe that early morning feeling that they had stolen a march on the rest of the world and that Nature had set this morning up just for them to enjoy. Not that this part of their journey was in any way picturesque, as Tricia had learned yesterday morning when she left her bunk early to have a look at their surroundings in daylight. Queenborough was a convenient place for them to break their journey but pretty it was not. Surrounding them were mud flats and expanses of flat water interspersed with marsh, rusting fishing boats and small pleasure craft which sat on the mud at low water and she had wrinkled her nose at the stagnant smell of the place. At high tide the vista changed into an expanse of flat water with, in the distance, electrical pylons, chimneys and cranes randomly placed around the limits of visibility. It was an industrial landscape that made no attempt to appeal to the visitor preferring to mind its own business and get on with its work.

While McCabe steered, Tricia hauled up the mainsail and then returned to the cockpit and sheeted it in tight. It was the only sail that they would need today, not so much to give them any propulsion but to help steady the boat if any sort of breeze did blow up or if wash from passing ships hit them. There would be no time for tacking or changing sails today, the important thing would be to make progress and to get to London with the tide which would be in their favour for the next seven hours. If for any reason they didn't reach their destination at St. Katharine Docks before the tide turned against them, they would either be driven back down the Thames by the current which, in some places, can reach up to four knots or, at best, they would have to motor hard against it for hours until it turned again. The lock at St Katharine's would be available today from about 1120 to 1450 and after that it would be closed again until the following day and there would be nowhere to anchor if they didn't make it. McCabe had already phoned to confirm their mooring at St Katharine's, so they were expected, and he had also checked that the Thames Barrier at Woolwich would be open. Everything was ready. The weather was good, the conditions were right and all they had to do was keep up a reasonable speed and avoid any hazards. For that reason they would rely only on the engine to get them there in time.

They left Queenborough Harbour and crossed the River Medway without incident. When they reached the Grain Hard buoy they turned to the north east and, keeping just outside of it, they followed the shipping channel out of Sheerness Harbour. After a mile they turned to the north making for the red port hand buoy called Nore Swatch and, as they approached it, they had a clear view on their starboard side of the SS Richard Montgomery's three huge black masts sticking twenty feet out of the water covered with green slime. Around the wreck, one at each cardinal point of the compass, were four bright yellow buoys to warn shipping to keep away.

"The central mast of the three, marks the point where the ship's back was broken," said McCabe.

The knowledge that it contained tons of dangerous explosive made Tricia shiver but McCabe had seen the wreck so many times that he appeared not to be bothered by it. When they reached the Nore Swatch buoy McCabe steered to the north west and, an hour after casting off, they reached the Yantlet Channel half a mile east of the Sea Reach No 5 buoy and turned to the west to follow the channel and begin their journey up The Thames proper. McCabe took care to keep close to but out of the channel, leaving it to his north, knowing that it is used by large commercial vessels and that, as long as he kept out of their way, they would avoid being run down by any passing ships. At the same time he was acutely aware that to the south of his position were the Yantlet Flats and then Blyth Sands, mud flats at times only a quarter of a mile away, both of which at this state of the tide were hardly covered and on which they would run aground if he steered onto them. With Southend and its mile long pier and Leigh on Sea clearly visible only two miles to the north of them Honeysuckle Rose began to pick up speed as the incoming tide lifted them. They continued to keep to the south of the channel as they passed Canvey Island which kept them well clear of the London Gateway container port to the north.

"OK Trish. We need to keep a really sharp lookout from here on. There's all sorts of floating junk in the Thames: logs, plastic sheet, dead things, bits of floating rope, if we hit any of it we can damage the hull, or if we go over it we can foul the propellor or even break the propellor shaft. We're doing about 8 knots over the ground at the moment so, if we do hit anything, we're going to do some damage."

Two hours after they had cast off they passed the Mid Blyth North Cardinal buoy and the river began to narrow and then took a bend to the south. As they reached the Lower Hope buoy McCabe, after checking that there was no shipping about to bear down on them, steered Rose across the channel and they would now stay on the starboard side of the river until they reached London.

"I thought the River Thames was supposed to be pretty," said Tricia.

McCabe smiled, "Not here it's not, but I promise it will be when we go to the non-tidal Thames at the weekend."

She looked past a sewage works and out across the mud flats and marshes, "It's all the same. Just flat and empty. Look at this green buoy we're passing," she read the name as they passed, "it's called Mucking No 5. Very appropriate."

McCabe handed over the steering to Tricia and went below to set the VHF radio to channel 68 to listen for warnings of any ship movements out of Tilbury Docks which they were approaching fast.

The river swung to the west and they continued past Gravesend on their port side and the cruise ship terminal on their starboard. There was small boat traffic here but they had not seen any shipping for the entire journey so far. Now there were 2 knots of tide under them and they swung to the north past Tilbury Docks, the river all the time becoming narrower and the current increasing. At Grays the river swung around to the south west and Honeysuckle Rose hurried along Fiddler's Reach, engine pulsing and propellor spinning and pushing her along at 6 knots with the current adding another 3 knots; speed over the ground 9 knots and really making progress. The river bent to the right and they were in Long Reach with the Queen Elizabeth II Bridge at Dartford a mile ahead of them. The sun glinted off of hundreds of cars which the bridge was carrying high above the river on the southbound carriageway of the M25 motorway, all nose to tail and hardly moving. Without warning there was a huge bang and a shock wave coursed through the boat. Her bow reared up into the air and Tricia and McCabe were thrown violently forward as she came to a dead stop. At the same time the engine cut out and there was a sudden silence.

Chapter Eighteen

Klaus Stritter, alcoholic and sly, and Stefan Merk, thuggish and mentally thick, were standing, fifty yards apart, near the lock which links the Thames with St Katharine Docks, even though they knew that it wouldn't be opening for at least another two hours. Merk had just arrived and Stritter was about to leave. They had been told to wait there by Ernst Kegel until McCabe showed up with his boat, and what Kegel told them to do they did without question. Both men were hardened and tough career criminals but they were afraid of Kegel in the same way that Kegel feared Fleischer. Fleischer had found that his organisation functioned at its best when fear was transmitted down the line. He also knew that the only loyalty that he could expect from any of them was based on the considerable sums of money that he paid them; that and the knowledge that nobody had resigned from the SSV and survived. They waited and watched in shifts of about one hour each; more or less an hour to avoid any onlooker noticing a pattern to their movements or that they were working together. Neither man acknowledged the other. Stritter spent his watch seated on a bench by the lock, pretending to read a book which was something that he would normally never do. Merk wandered about the marina looking at boats, or walked along the embankment in front of The Tower Hotel while appearing to study the massive structure of nearby Tower Bridge and boats passing on the river. All the while he kept an eye on the lock.

They had waited there yesterday and the day before, arriving two hours before the first lock opening time and not leaving until the final closing five and a half hours later. They were bored.

Chapter Nineteen

McCabe got to his feet slowly. The cockpit forward bulkhead had prevented them from being thrown too far and, fortunately, neither of them had been launched through the open hatch into the saloon. He went over to Tricia who was sitting on the cockpit sole with her back to the bulkhead checking herself for injuries. Apart from a couple of bruises neither of them was hurt. He looked towards the bow and saw that it was higher than it should be and that Honeysuckle Rose was heeling to starboard. A glance at the river bank a hundred yards away showed him that they were still travelling upriver but more slowly than before, carried along by the current. He looked over the port side and could see immediately a waterlogged tree trunk half the length of the boat and almost completely submerged. They had hit it hard and the cast iron keel of the boat was wedged on the branches which extended out from the trunk.

"We hit a tree, Trish."

She stood up and looked over the side, "What's a tree doing here?"

"Remember what I said earlier? There's all sorts of junk floating up and down the river. We didn't see it because most of it's below the water."

McCabe went below and lifted a floor board in the saloon to make sure that there was no water coming in. The bilge was as dry as it always was. He returned to the cockpit and resisted the temptation to start the engine on the assumption that if there was anything fouling the propellor he might make it worse. Grabbing a boat hook he went up to the bow of the boat and knelt on the deck. He looked around to see that there were no boats in the vicinity and he also noted that Rose and the tree were beginning to perform a slow pirouette as the current played with them. He pushed with the boat hook at the tree trunk with as much force as he could muster but it remained securely attached to the boat. McCabe sat on the deck and thought for a moment. What was holding them together? Branches! Caught around the keel and probably wrapped around the propellor as well. He needed the power of the engine to dislodge it. Returning to the cockpit he looked at the control panel. The ignition was still on and the Morse lever was still in forward gear. He put the lever into neutral.

"Can you keep a lookout please, Trish? We should be OK but watch out for any boats or ships."

Tricia looked anxious, "Should we get on the radio and call for help?"

"I will if we have to but we're alright for the moment."

She looked at the riverbank passing and the slow circling motion of boat and tree and wasn't convinced.

McCabe turned the key to start the engine in neutral and it fired up first time. Instead of pushing the Morse lever forward to select forward gear he pulled it back to send the propellor spinning the opposite way as if to go astern. The engine immediately stalled, the propellor bound up by twigs and branches. He tried this four times, each time stalling the engine. Next he tried a different approach. This time he put the engine into reverse gear before he started it. Turning the key he was rewarded by the awful sound of the starter motor labouring to turn the engine, but it was turning albeit slowly. He had a picture in his mind of the twigs and thin branches wrapped around the propellor and gradually unwinding as the engine turned the propellor shaft. Then he had another mental picture of the starter motor burning out and he switched off the ignition. He would either manage to clear the propellor with the engine or he would have to call for help, be towed in somewhere and either be dry docked or lifted out, or arrange for a diver to go underneath the boat and clear the tree away. If he couldn't clear the obstruction himself they would keep drifting until help arrived or until they hit something. There was also the possibility of being run down by a larger vessel. He decided to try again with the engine.

McCabe started the engine in neutral again and then put the engine into reverse. For a moment it continued to run and then stopped. Progress. Something must have cleared from the propellor. He tried again, this time in forward gear but the engine stalled immediately. Had he made it worse?

"We've got a choice to make, Trish. Either I keep trying to clear it or we call for help."

"What do you think's wrong?" she asked.

"Twigs and branches jamming the propellor."

"I could go over the side and try to clear it?"

Even though the situation was serious McCabe couldn't resist smiling at her. "If we were anchored in the Med I'd let you try that, Trish, but not while we're performing circles in the middle of the River Thames. Brave of you to offer though."

She shrugged, "What are we going to do then?"

"I'll try to clear it with the engine again and, if that doesn't work, I'll radio for help."

McCabe put the Morse lever into neutral and started the engine again. He pushed the lever into reverse and, for a couple of seconds, the propellor turned and then the engine stalled again. He tried three more times with the same result until, on the fourth attempt, the engine continued to run. Instinctively he pushed the lever back into neutral, the engine still running, while alongside the boat bits of twig and leaves which had been stripped from the propellor and shaft floated to the surface.

"Well done!" Tricia jumped to her feet, excited.

"We're not clear yet," said McCabe. "We've still got to get rid of the tree."

Tricia sat down again, "How are we going to do that?"

"The only thing I can think of is to drive the boat hard forward and steer it into the tree. That might break the stern free. The downside of that is that we might foul the propellor again. What do you think?"

"Let's do it."

"OK. Here goes."

McCabe turned the wheel hard to port and then gently put the Morse lever into forward gear. The engine continued to run and he slowly eased the lever forward. The tree and boat, still locked together, began to circle more quickly. He increased the revs to full throttle and they circled even more rapidly until, quite suddenly, water pressure wrenched the tree away from the boat with a tearing noise as branches were ripped off and the keel was wrested away from the tree's clutches. As soon as they were free McCabe put the Morse lever into neutral and then hard astern and they backed away from the tree, which was still pirouetting, as quickly as they could. He put the Morse lever into neutral then forward gear and, with considerable relief, turned Rose's bow upriver as they continued with their journey. They had probably only lost fifteen minutes or so but timing was crucial. He hoped that there would be no further delays.

"Well done. Are there a lot of trees in the river, Chad? Where do they come from?"

"Fallen trees that float down the river for miles. Not many I suppose but it's not the first one that I've seen. We're OK. No damage as far as I can tell. There might be some scratched paintwork but I can live with that."

Tricia took the wheel and watched the surface of the river more intently than before. McCabe went below to confirm that there was still no water coming in under the floor and then he made coffee for them both. Nine minutes after freeing themselves from the tree they were under the QEII Bridge gazing up with a sense of awe at its underside fifty metres above them, still with its burden of almost stationary vehicles, and then they were past it and picking up speed. The high-rise shapes of Canary Wharf and The Shard came into view as if to convince Tricia that they really were travelling into London by boat.

At the end of Long Reach by Crayford Ness the river swung to the west and, a mile later as it bent to the north again into Erith Reach, McCabe went below and switched the VHF radio to channel 14 to listen for any instructions given by the Thames Barrier Control.

The Thames turned north west again and Honeysuckle Rose swept past Rainham and then, at Dagenham, the river turned to the west again into Barking Reach. On their port side they could now see the Thamesmead Development Area, the beginnings of the urban sprawl which is Greater London.

At 1005 they were approaching Tripcock Point and McCabe went below again and called Thames Barrier

Control on Channel 14. He announced their presence and asked for permission to pass through the flood barrier three miles ahead of them. Permission being granted he returned to the cockpit as Tricia, thoroughly enjoying herself, was following the river and steering Rose around to the south west. He pointed at the beacon on their port side.

"That bit of land is called Margaret Ness, Trish. Also known as Tripcock Point. It was right where we are now that the Princess Alice pleasure steamer was run down by a cargo ship called Bywell Castle in 1878. They don't know how many people died because, in those days, that sort of vessel didn't keep a passenger list, but it was between six and seven hundred. The worst inland waterway disaster ever in this country and nobody seems to remember it. They were fishing bodies out of the river for weeks."

Tricia, without realising, looked astern to make sure that there wasn't a ship bearing down on them and stared at the water, picturing it full of struggling people in their heavy Victorian clothes, "That's awful. How did it happen?"

"It was a Tuesday. The Princess Alice was full of trippers from London returning from Sheerness after a day out. They were making the same journey that we're making this morning. They got to where we are now as it was getting dark and the Princess Alice took the wrong line along the river. The Bywell Castle, coming downstream, sailed straight over her and cut her in half so that she sank almost immediately. What made it worse was that there was a sewage outlet here and they'd just released millions of gallons of sewage into the river. Most of the passengers drowned but, of the people that they managed to rescue, which was over a hundred, many died as a result of inhaling or swallowing the polluted river water."

Tricia shuddered, "How horrible."

"It was. It must have been an appalling scene. It shows the importance of keeping a good lookout and following the correct course."

They continued along the river in silence for five minutes both thinking of the people, now forgotten, struggling and dying in the filthy water 140 years earlier until, as they rounded Gallions Point, quite suddenly, straddling the river were the huge, shining steel shells of the Thames Barrier rising out of the water a mile ahead of them.

McCabe took over the steering and slowed to avoid the Woolwich Ferry, which was crossing the river ahead of them, and then he increased speed again as he steered the boat towards the green arrows on the barrier showing which of the six channels through the structure was open to traffic. The channels that were closed were marked with red crosses. They passed through the barrier without incident and now the scenery, which had been desolate or industrial for most of their journey, became interesting and Tricia, who had been hiding her gradually rising excitement, knew that they had arrived in London. Not excitement that they were in London, which she knew well, but that they had actually made the journey by sea and river. She began to tick off mentally the well known landmarks as they passed.

As they rounded the bend into Bugsbys Reach, immediately ahead of them was the massive Millennium Dome, in terms of usable volume the ninth largest building in the world, shining white in the late morning sunshine. At the top of Bugsbys Reach the river performed a hairpin turn to port around the dome which was now on their port side as they passed over the two Blackwall Tunnels buried deep beneath the river bed, each carrying a constant stream of vehicles crossing between the north and south banks.

Honeysuckle Rose continued south along Blackwall Reach and the imposing stonework and domes of the National Maritime Museum began to appear in front of them. As they turned into Greenwich Reach the masts of the Cutty Sark were visible. Tricia went below and looked at the paper chart to check their exact position in relation to the museum. She saw the great uvula shaped Isle of Dogs on the north bank and that they were about to follow the Thames around to starboard and enter Limehouse Reach travelling north. She went back to the cockpit and looked ahead. The river was busier now with fast Clipper passenger boats, Thames Lighters being towed by tugs, and small pleasure boats. It was choppy for the first time since leaving Queenborough and there was more flotsam in the water.

At the top of Limehouse Reach the river swung around to port again as they passed the famous Grapes pub on their starboard side and then they were in the Lower Pool of London and passing The Prospect of Whitby pub on the north bank. At Wapping, McCabe slowed Rose down to nose her gently through a line of scum and floating rubbish which stretched from one side of the river to the other and then they were passing the Metropolitan Police Pier with its moored blue and yellow police launches. Rounding the next bend to starboard, suddenly, half a mile ahead of them was Tower Bridge. Immediately before the bridge, on their starboard side, lay their destination, St. Katharine Docks. The journey had taken them just over six hours and they were in good time to pass through the lock into the dock. Tricia radioed the marina office on channel 80 to announce their arrival and, with superb efficiency, as they reached the lock the outer gate began to fold down. Their arrival had already been noted by Klaus Stritter and he was phoning the information to Ernst Kegel.

From the window of his room overlooking the docks, on the sixth floor of the Tower Hotel, Quietus had also observed their arrival and was considering what to do next.

Chapter Twenty

St Katharine Docks - 0840 BST Thursday 26th July

The day started well and McCabe and Tricia breakfasted together in Honeysuckle Rose's cockpit, enjoying the sunshine and discussing their forthcoming cruise along the non-tidal Thames, the picturesque section of river which, for anything but small boats, begins at Lechlade in the Cotswolds and meanders for 122 miles to Teddington Lock in the London suburbs. After Teddington it becomes tidal and is known as the Tideway. They wouldn't have time to navigate the entire river, so the plan was to leave Rose at St Katharine Docks and travel by train to Reading which was 73 miles up river from their current position. McCabe had arranged to rent a boat from an old friend who owned a boatyard a short taxi ride from Reading Station.

Peacefully enjoying their al fresco breakfast, they were unaware that they were being watched by Quietus from a nearby coffee shop. Quietus, in his turn, was unaware of Ernst Kegel who was watching him from across the marina while keeping an eye on Honeysuckle Rose at the same time. Kegel had not yet discovered who Quietus was or what he was up to and was content, for the moment, to wait and see what developed.

After breakfast, Tricia left to catch the tube from Tower Hill to Paddington Station, travelling ahead of McCabe to Reading where she was going to stay with friends. As soon as she left he locked up the boat and walked to Whitechapel to deliver the letter to Shapiev.

With the aid of Google Maps on his iPhone, McCabe easily found the address written on the envelope which Tushka had given to him, about a mile from St Katharine Docks and close to The Royal London Hospital. He was standing in a quiet, narrow street. In front of him, on the other side of the road, was a terrace of five slate roofed, brick built, two-up, two-down Victorian houses each with a front door, a single sash window on the ground floor and two sash windows on the first. As he crossed the road to the house that he was looking for, he saw an elderly man walking slowly towards him. The man stopped at the front door of the house that McCabe wanted, fumbling to insert a key into the lock and, by the time that McCabe reached him, he had succeeded in opening the door and was entering the house. He turned with painful effort as McCabe spoke.

"Excuse me. Does someone called Shapiev live here?"

The man looked furtively up and down the street then directly at McCabe. He spoke with an Eastern European accent, "What do you want with Shapiev?"

"I have a letter for someone called Shapiev at this address."

"Why would you have a letter for Shapiev? You don't look like a postman."

The man eyed him suspiciously.

"It's a letter from Bronek Kowalski."

"Bronek is dead."

"I was asked to deliver it by his wife."

"His wife is dead too."

"I know that but she asked me to deliver it before she died," replied McCabe with a hint of irritation. "Are you Mr Shapiev?"

The man studied him intently for a moment and then he said, "Yes. You had better come in. Close the door behind you."

Shapiev shuffled off along the dingy hallway which had a staircase starting a third of the way along it on the left, and two doors set into the wall on the right. McCabe followed, closing the front door as instructed. Shapiev stopped at the first door and struggled again to insert a key into the lock until, finally succeeding, he opened it and went in. McCabe followed him into a bed-sitting room and closed the door behind him. He studied the room and the man who occupied it.

Shapiev was probably in his late seventies, maybe early eighties. He was thin and short and his weak voice suggested asthma. His white hair was thinning and his clothes were shabby but they must once have made him look very dapper. He gave the impression that he didn't eat properly, probably because he couldn't afford to. The room was shabby with old dark furniture. It contained a sink and draining board, a single bed, two well worn armchairs facing each other with a small wooden coffee table between them, a wooden kitchen table with two chairs, an ancient Baby Belling electric cooker and, in front of the window, an old gateleg table that served as a writing desk which was strewn with papers. The single sliding sash window covered by a net curtain looked out onto the street and heavy, faded red velveteen curtains hung on either side of it. Equally faded flock paper covered the walls probably dating from the time when the building had been a single house. On one wall was a small flat screen television. The floor was covered with a threadbare brown carpet and McCabe guessed that there was a shared bathroom along the corridor or upstairs somewhere. It reminded him of his bed sitter in Brighton over thirty years ago, when he was 17 years old and fending for himself for the first time in his life.

"Please, sit," said Shapiev and gestured to the armchairs.

One chair had a deep impression in the seat cushion which indicated that it was the most used and probably Shapiev's favourite. McCabe sat in the other one which had no impression in the seat and less wear, which suggested that Shapiev didn't get many visitors.

"Can I offer you some tea Mr …?"

"McCabe."

Shapiev wrote the name in ink on a piece of scrap paper which was lying amongst the other papers on the writing table. "I have difficulty remembering names Mr McCabe, so I find it better to write them down. Could you spell that for me?"

McCabe spelled his name out loud as the old man wrote and Shapiev put the pen down, satisfied.

"Tea, Mr McCabe?"

"Yes please." McCabe had intended to deliver the letter and leave but he was intrigued.

Shapiev filled an old electric kettle and switched it on, then pottered about draping an old fashioned linen cloth with floral embroidery over an even older looking two handled tea tray. On it he laid out two cups and saucers, tea spoons, a tea strainer, a small silver milk jug and an antique porcelain bowl containing cubes of white sugar and a pair of silver sugar tongs. He placed the tray on the table between the armchairs then returned to the kettle which had boiled. He warmed an old china teapot with water from the kettle, swilled it around the teapot and then emptied it into the sink. He took a beaten up, tin tea caddy with a picture of two geishas on it from a shelf, opened the lid and put three heaped scoops of leaf tea into the teapot, switched on the kettle again and, when it boiled, he poured the steaming water onto the leaves in the teapot. Finally he put the lid onto the teapot, carefully carried it to the tray and put a stained, embroidered tea cosy over it. McCabe, who hadn't seen tea made in that way since he was a boy sat quietly and waited, understanding the importance of such a ceremony to his host.

Shapiev sat in his armchair and looked at him, "So, you said that you have a letter for me."

McCabe took the letter from the inside pocket of his jacket and passed it to him.

Shapiev studied the handwriting on the front of the envelope and then stood up and crossed to the writing table. He picked up an ivory handled letter opener and prised the point under the edge of the envelope flap then slit it open. He gently removed the single sheet of paper from the envelope. It was handwritten on one side of the paper and Shapiev read it carefully before placing it face down on the table with the letter opener on top of it. Then he returned to his chair and looked at McCabe.

"Thank you for delivering that, Mr McCabe, it is important."

"Well I'm glad to be of help."

"Did you know Bronek well?" asked Shapiev.

"Not really. We played in a band together."

"Ah yes, his Jazz Manouche. He often talked about it. Was he a good player?"

"Like me," replied McCabe with a smile, "competent but not the genius of Django Reinhardt."

"I met Django several times when I was 16, so that must have been …" Shapiev paused, "… let me see … 1952, in a cafe in Samois-sur-Seine in France."

McCabe was interested. He had never met anyone who had actually met Django before.

"My father knew him but I never thought to ask him how."

"Did you hear him play?" asked McCabe.

"No, I never did. According to my father he had virtually stopped playing guitar by then. He seemed to spend all of his time fishing and talking to friends in the cafe."

"He would have been 42 then and he died the following year," answered McCabe.

"That's right. It was a great shock to everyone when he died."

"You don't sound French," suggested McCabe.

"I'm not," answered Shapiev. "My family wandered through Europe a great deal."

"Bronek was Polish, I think."

"Not Polish, Mr McCabe, but not far from there."

"His wife told me that he was involved in trying to overthrow his country's government."

Shapiev poured the tea through the strainer into the two cups.

"Did she?" he replied thoughtfully. "That was very indiscreet of her. What else did she tell you?"

"Nothing else, but she was frightened of something."

"As well she might be," said Shapiev. "Milk and sugar, Mr McCabe?"

"Yes please, two sugars. Do you know who killed her?"

"Not exactly, but I can tell you that they were probably working for the government of my home country, which was also Bronek's country. We are patriots, Mr McCabe, but our government doesn't see it that way which is why we are in England and not at home." He handed the cup of tea to McCabe.

"I found her body," said McCabe. "It's been haunting me ever since."

"I was told what they did to her," said Shapiev. "It gives you an indication of the type of people that we have working against us."

"Do you know why they tortured her like that?"

"I can guess. We have a small anti-government publication which is produced by me and sent free of charge to all of our subscribers by email. I know nothing of computers so, once I have completed the newsletter, it is - or I should say was - delivered to Bronek in Brighton who would turn it into something that he called an E-zine. It was sent electronically to thousands of our sympathisers across the world, even in our home country. I have no idea who these people are, just that they share our ideals. Bronek was responsible for adding new people to the list of names and email addresses and he is the only one who had the list. That is what they were after, I think."

McCabe thought of Tushka, her hands nailed to the cheap pine table, burns and bruises to her body, and he thought again of how much she must have suffered before they killed her.

"When you arrived here today with the letter," continued Shapiev, "I thought it was the list of names. It was important but it was not the list. If the police in my country now have the names then thousands of people are in danger."

McCabe now knew why Arthur Barnard had been at the scene of Tushka's murder. Clearly, the British security people were taking an interest and it wasn't just a police matter.

"Did Bronek confide in you at all and talk about the list, Mr McCabe?"

"No. As I told you, I didn't know him well. He wouldn't have confided in me."

"Then all we can do is start building a new list of subscribers to our newsletter," replied Shapiev.

They finished drinking their tea in silence until McCabe, unwilling to pry further, said, "Well thank you for your hospitality, Mr Shapiev. I must go."

They both stood and walked out of the room to the front door of the building which Shapiev opened to let McCabe out. On the pavement they shook hands and Shapiev said, "Thank you for delivering my letter, Mr McCabe. It was dangerous for you to do that but you weren't to know."

"I hope that no more harm comes to any of your people," said McCabe, "and I wish your cause well for the future."

McCabe turned away and Shapiev went back into the house.

Quietus, who had tailed McCabe from St Katharine Docks, watched from a distance and then discreetly followed him as he walked away.

Through the tinted windows of a Volkswagen Touran with German plates, parked fifty yards away from the house, Ernst Kegel, the murderer of Bronek and his wife, looked on with Gunter Meise thuggish and a born follower. He waited until McCabe and Quietus had walked past the van then, leaving Meise to continue the watch on Shapiev's house, Kegel got out of the vehicle and followed.

Unaware that he was being tailed, McCabe walked back to Honeysuckle Rose and, after he had unlocked, he sat in Rose's cockpit gazing out at the moored boats and the tourists in St Katharine's while he tried to decide what to do. Should he tell Barnard about his visit to Shapiev or just let it go? Why? Shapiev didn't appear to be doing anything illegal? He decided to forget about it. It was innocent enough. He had delivered a letter, that's all, and he didn't want to create any trouble for the old man who had treated him so civilly. He seemed to have trouble enough.

Glad to have some time on his own, McCabe decided that he would put in some practice for the gig at Le QuecumBar in Battersea in a week's time. Not that he needed much practice but it was always good to keep his fingers supple and make his muscles remember the chord shapes and solos that they had repeated so many times over the years. He never got bored with playing the same numbers over and over, year after year. His repertoire was considerable and it was what the audiences wanted to hear, but he often thought that it would be good to learn something new. That thought reminded him that Bronek's Licks and Tricks flash drive was still in the guitar case in the forward cabin. He went below and walked through the saloon to the forepeak. Opening the case, he removed Bronek's guitar and took out the flash drive, then he replaced the guitar and closed and secured the case. Returning to the saloon he sat at the table where his old Acer laptop was ready for use, switched it on, and after it had booted up he took the flash drive out of its protective holder and inserted it into one of the three USB ports on the back of the computer. Using the mouse and Windows Explorer, McCabe found the flash drive Local Disk (H:) on screen and clicked the mouse to open it. There was only one folder on the drive. It was named Licksandtricks. He double clicked the mouse on the folder and it opened to reveal a subfolder named db and five files. He double clicked on the subfolder and revealed a file with a name that was just a jumble of numbers and letters. Double clicking on the file produced a query asking him to specify a programme that could be used to open it. He chose the Notepad programme and a box appeared displaying a quarter page of what looked like hieroglyphics. McCabe closed Notepad and looked again at the five files. Three of them were data files and opening them with Notepad produced the same mess of symbols that the file in the subfolder had done. The fourth file was named vault.ico and double clicking on that produced a picture of a strongroom door in the centre of the screen so cleverly detailed that McCabe double clicked the image in the hope that it would open, which it did not. He closed the image down and looked at the only file which he hadn't attempted to open yet which was named desktop.ini. He double clicked the file and was rewarded with the text: "[.ShellClassInfo]IconFile=vault.icoIconIndex=0InfoTip=Encrypted Vault".

It didn't take a computer genius to know that the files on the flash drive were encrypted, and there was no way that he was going to see what they were about. But why would Bronek have bothered to hide his licks and tricks?

    He closed the laptop's lid, put it in its bag and put the flash drive into the pocket of his cargo pants. Picking up his Harmsworth and Willis practice guitar he began to play slowly and with feeling through the chord sequence of the tune J'attendrai adding grace notes and embellishments as he did so. Hardly aware of the guitar and chords that he was playing, his mind pondered the puzzle of Bronek and Tushka and then he thought again of their little girl, orphaned, being absorbed into the local authority social care system and no longer part of a family.

Chapter Twenty One

Whitechapel, London - 1104 BST Friday 27th July

Shapiev's cleaner turned into his street for her weekly visit and walked the short distance to the old man's front door. She was pushing a stolen, wobbly wheeled supermarket trolley full of cleaning materials and thinking of her husband, who treated her badly, and her two small boys who she could afford to feed but not clothe or indulge as she would like. She was in her late twenties, dark haired, attractive but weary, worn out by the constant fight to provide for her family for the two years since they had arrived in the UK. She was from Shapiev's own country and his bedsitter was the second property that she would visit today. Before she finished, late this evening, she would have dragged and pushed the trolley to, and cleaned, five more.

The cleaner took a bunch of keys from the trolley, all labelled with her own code in case they were lost or stolen, found the two Shapiev keys, opened the front door, dragged the trolley into the hallway and closed the door behind her. She moved along the hall, knocked on the door to Shapiev's room and, knowing that the old man would be expecting her, using the second key she unlocked it pushing it open with her back as she dragged the heavy trolley into the room at the same time calling out to him.

"Only English today, Mr Shapiev. If I speak only the language of the old country, I will never learn. How are you today?"

Shapiev didn't reply and, when she turned to see him, seated at the table which served as a writing desk, she began to scream. She continued to scream uncontrollably as she fought her way past the shopping trolley and ran into the street. Curtains twitched, doors opened and people came out of their houses. After a few minutes a police car arrived and one of the officers dealt with the sobbing cleaner. The other policeman, young and new to the job, entered the property. He found Shapiev stripped to the waist with his hands nailed palms down to the table and his severed thumbs placed side by side between them. There was a gash in his neck. His bare arms and torso were covered in burns and his face, visible through the layers of cling film which were wrapped around his head, was bloodied and bruised his mouth wide open in a terrified rictus as if still fighting for breath.

Chapter Twenty Two

St Katharine Docks - 1004 BST Friday 27th July

Quietus had not found the opportunity to kill McCabe yet. He watched from his hotel window as Zac Battersby arrived at Honeysuckle Rose, having travelled by train from Brighton. He was sorry that he had missed Tricia but was pleased when McCabe hugged him as if Zac was his long lost father. The two friends sat in Rose's cockpit and drank coffee for twenty minutes, exchanging news and information. Zac would stay on Rose while McCabe and Tricia were away and take advantage of the opportunity to revisit some of his old Merchant Navy contacts in London. McCabe knew that his friend would also apply some varnish to the boat if he got the chance. Between them they had restored Honeysuckle Rose 16 years before and Zac, quite correctly as far as McCabe was concerned, treated her as if she was his own. Zac, now in his 73rd year, felt himself blessed that he had a friend as good as McCabe and that he could still maintain his contact with the sea and enjoy his love of boats through the old Hillyard that they both treasured.

By 11.00am, McCabe was at Tower Hill tube station where, after standing back while the Circle Line underground train emptied its cargo of excited tourists visiting The Tower of London, he boarded it to travel to Paddington. Over his left shoulder he carried a rucksack containing his laptop in its bag and all the things that he required for a few days on the Thames. Slung over his other shoulder was his Harmsworth and Willis guitar in its soft Ritter bag. When he boarded the train, which had previously been packed, he had the carriage almost to himself, apart from a teenage boy and girl a few seats away who were totally engrossed in each other. Quietus had got into the next carriage without McCabe noticing him, and Gunter Meise was at the far end of Quietus's carriage. The modern through-train made up of carriages joined but completely open, each to the next, allowed the two men to watch McCabe from the adjoining carriage without being obvious. Quietus, focused on McCabe who was sitting with his back to him, took no notice of anyone else on the train and stood by the sliding doors ready to get out when McCabe did. Both Meise and Quietus, not knowing their final destination, had used prepaid Oyster cards to get past the ticket barrier.

Twenty four minutes and ten stations later, the train reached Paddington Underground Station and the three men got out. McCabe followed the signs reading National Rail with Quietus behind him, then Meise. If McCabe had turned to look behind him he would have easily seen the men following him, but nobody turns around on underground stations for fear of holding up the relentless progress of the crowds of people behind them. They stepped off at the top of the escalator and walked along the wide passageway which would lead them out of the station. Then the three men took the short escalator up to the vast concourse of Paddington mainline railway station and spread out in different directions. McCabe walked to the ticket office, Quietus crossed to a coffee stand from where he could observe the ticket office main doors, and Meise took up position by a burger stand from where he could see the ticket office and Quietus.

Six minutes later, after queueing for and buying a ticket, McCabe reappeared then stopped to look up at the digital boards displaying the platform, destinations and times of departing trains. After studying the boards for a few moments he turned and walked to the automatic ticket barrier at Platform 8, inserted his ticket into the reader on one of the gates, retrieved it as the barrier opened for him and passed through onto the platform. The digital board above the barrier showed that the train waiting at the platform was scheduled to leave in four minutes and would be travelling to Oxford, stopping at Slough and Reading en route. Quietus and Meise followed in turn, both again using Oyster cards to pass through the barrier. The Oyster cards, issued by Transport for London, would legitimately cover the cost of the journey as far as West Drayton on the outer edge of London Fare Zone 6. After that they would be travelling without a ticket.

As the train began to pull out of the station all three were seated in the same carriage, only McCabe knowing what their destination was. The open plan carriage was half full of passengers and Quietus, making sure that he wouldn't be seen by his target, had no difficulty watching him, having made sure that he was seated where McCabe again had his back to him. Meise sat separately and carefully watched McCabe and Quietus at the same time. Sixteen minutes later the train stopped at Slough and more passengers got on, so that now all of the seats were filled and some had to stand. As the train pulled away an inspector moved purposefully through the carriage checking tickets. He discreetly challenged Meise and, shortly after, Quietus, insisting that they pay an excess fare charge to their destination from West Drayton, which they had already passed. Both men, not knowing where they were going, were obliged to pay for a ticket to Oxford where the train would make its final stop. They paid with cash trying not to draw attention to themselves and, twenty nine minutes after leaving Paddington, the train began to slow and nearly half of the people in the carriage, including McCabe, rose as one as the train stopped at Reading Station. McCabe had arranged to meet Tricia outside the station and he stepped onto the platform with Quietus and Meise following.

Quietus lost sight of his target as McCabe got onto the escalator which carried him and over a hundred other people up to the wide enclosed bridge which spans eight platforms of Reading Station, but he assumed correctly that his target was leaving the station. When he reached the top of the escalator Quietus looked to the left and then right and saw shops, people, takeaway outlets but no sign of McCabe. He had a choice: turn left to the old southern station frontage which leads to Reading town centre or right which would lead to an exit on the north side of the station with access to the River Thames and Caversham. For no particular reason, other than that he had to make a decision, Quietus turned left and hurried towards the Reading town exit. As he reached the top of the escalator which would take him down to the exit he saw McCabe, far below him, pass through the ticket barrier and disappear from view as he left the station. Quietus hurried down the narrow escalator brushing past people in his attempt to catch up with his quarry. Meise followed Quietus, on the assumption that he knew where he was going, and they exited the station in time to see Tricia Knight greeting McCabe with a beaming smile and a kiss on the cheek as she hugged him. McCabe and Tricia crossed the wide expanse of paving between the station and the road, and climbed into the back seat of the first in a line of several black cabs which were waiting at the kerbside. They settled back as the taxi pulled away, and talked animatedly to each other as if they hadn't met for years.

Quietus, overweight, ran forward, jumped into the next cab on the rank and fell back onto the seat breathing heavily from the exertion and calling out loudly to the driver, "Follow that cab!"

The driver turned around to look at him and asked, "Which cab?"

Quietus pointed down Forbury Road at the disappearing taxi, "That one!"

The driver, who by his appearance could have been from any number of Arabic countries or perhaps Afghanistan, proved that he was British born and bred by replying, "We're not in a bleedin' movie, mate," but he put the cab into gear and moved off. Meise had already got into the next cab on the rank and was following Quietus.

The dense nose to tail traffic and seemingly endless succession of traffic lights soon impeded the three taxis and they made slow progress as they edged their way out of the busy town centre. They speeded up as they reached the Oxford road and made steady progress for a few miles, the rear two taxis keeping a discreet distance from each other. The occupants of the two leading cabs were so intent on looking ahead that they weren't aware that they were being followed. The leading cab turned away from the main road and continued along a lane followed by the other two then pulled into a boatyard by the Thames. Quietus's taxi continued past the boatyard. Meise's taxi stopped to drop him off, then turned around and went back to Reading. Meise walked back to the boatyard and reached it as McCabe's cab, empty, pulled back into the lane and headed towards Reading. He stepped into a clump of trees inside the gate from where he could see, unobserved, the boatyard office which McCabe and Tricia Knight had just entered. Quietus's taxi returned and dropped him off outside the gate from where he could also see the office.

In the office, McCabe was already drinking tea and catching up with his old friend Phil Maypiece, from whom they would be hiring the boat for a few days. Tricia watched them both with amusement suddenly realising that they knew each other from way back, confirmed when Phil insisted that he wouldn't accept any payment for the hire.

McCabe, in turn, insisted that he would pay but, eventually, Maypiece won with the words, "I won't hear of it, Chad. Just pay for any fuel and enjoy yourselves. She's insured, fuelled up and the water tank is full. Are you ready to go?"

They gathered up the bags and guitar and the three of them left the office and walked along the old wooden pontoons to a brand new widebeam cruiser, 57 feet long, waiting quietly for them in the afternoon sunshine.

"We built her for a customer who didn't have the money to pay for it," said Maypiece. We're going to rent her out as a hire boat but she's free at the moment and you're welcome to use her."

They loaded the bags and guitar on board and Maypiece showed them around the boat. She was built of blue painted steel with a beam of 10 feet and had two double cabins with heads and shower, a well-appointed galley and saloon, and the whole boat was lined internally with expensive hardwood panelling. Looking rather like an oversized narrowboat the steering was done from the stern which was protected by a black canvas wheelhouse that could be folded down if required. On the bow was painted the name Summer Breeze in white lettering. Compared to Honeysuckle Rose she was huge and McCabe and Tricia thought that she would do very nicely and said so.

"Are you ready for the off?" asked Maypiece.

"We certainly are," replied Tricia.

McCabe turned the key to start the 55 horsepower diesel engine and Phil Maypiece stepped off and cast off the bow and stern lines, waving them away with a cheery, "See you in a few days."

They both waved at him as McCabe increased the engine revs and reversed away from the pontoon then put her into forward gear, turned the wheel hard over to the left to turn downstream and they headed back towards Reading obeying the speed limit at a sedate five knots.

Gunter Meise, hidden in the clump of trees, waited and watched Quietus who had now pulled a mobile phone out of his pocket and was Googling taxi companies. When Quietus found the nearest one, he telephoned for a cab and waited for twenty five minutes until it arrived to pick him up with instructions to take him to the nearest car rental company. As Quietus left, Meise phoned his immediate boss, Ernst Kegel, to report in and arrange for a car to meet him so that they could begin their search down river for McCabe and Tricia's boat.

Chapter Twenty Three

Sonning, Berkshire - 1922 BST Sunday 29th July

McCabe finished his pint of London Pride and glanced up again at the ancient wisteria covered facade of The Bull Inn. Situated in the centre of the usually quiet village of Sonning-on-Thames, the 16th century pub had, as always, attracted a large crowd on this sunny day, but as the Sunday afternoon drinkers had started to drift away he had been lucky enough to find a table free in the courtyard at the front of the pub. He glanced at his watch and realised that he was late, having told Tricia that he would be back at the boat by seven. He stood and walked across the courtyard to the gate leading to St Andrew's Church and entered the ancient churchyard, which was free of living people and sleepy in the evening sunshine. Leaving the sounds of the pub behind him, he strolled along the crushed stone path past the well-kept graves of long dead people and mused on how short life really is. He was reminded of the lines from Gray's Elegy which he had been forced to learn at school, "Each in his narrow cell for ever laid, the rude forefathers of the hamlet sleep... The paths of glory lead but to the grave," and thought how important it is to enjoy the days as if each one is the last. It was that poem which had profoundly affected his attitude towards life and helped lead him to his off-grid lifestyle. He went through another gate and walked down a gently sloping earthen path towards the river, surrounded by the evening chorus of birdsong. Whenever he came to Sonning he was reminded of the description by Jerome K Jerome in his famous book Three Men in a Boat, that

Sonning, "... is the most fairy-like little nook on the whole river".

At the end of the path he turned right and followed the riverside Thames Path through trees and bushes the short distance to Sonning Bridge. There he stopped to stare at the river, which was flowing gently through the eighteenth century red brick arches mirrored in the smooth water so exactly as to make perfect circles. He descended the bank to go under the nearest arch which, at this time of the year, was dried out sufficiently to allow anyone who knew that it could be done to walk through on the well beaten earth without getting their feet wet. The alternative was to wait for the traffic travelling over the bridge to stop, and cross the busy road. McCabe stooped as he walked under the bridge, ascended the grass bank on the other side, re-joined the riverside path and walked past the Great House Hotel its lawn full of deckchairs and still busy with customers talking, drinking and enjoying the remains of the evening.

He walked on and could see Summer Breeze moored to the bank where she had been for the last 24 hours. When he reached her he called out, "Sorry I'm late Trish."

He stepped onto the stern deck into the wheelhouse and went down the steps into the saloon, but Tricia wasn't there.

"Trish?" he called, thinking that she might be in her cabin. There was no reply.

McCabe looked into both the sleeping cabins and then came back into the saloon. She had left. On the drainer in the galley was a salad, part prepared, and a half empty glass of white wine. He went back to

Tricia's cabin and noted that her leather shoulder bag was not there; a sure sign that she had gone out.

He went up the steps to the wheelhouse and looked up and down the river bank but couldn't see her. He thought that she might have gone to find him, but why would she leave the boat open to anyone who cared to walk in? He sat on the helmsman's seat and wondered whether to go and look for her. Then his phone began to ring.

He pulled the iPhone from his pocket and looked at the screen which displayed the words Tricia mobile. Stabbing the green Accept with his finger he spoke into the phone, "Where are you? I was beginning to worry."

A slow, deep, slightly German accented male voice replied, "You would do well to worry, Mr McCabe. Miss Knight is with me and she is in considerable danger."

McCabe was stunned into silence and the voice continued, "My men went to your boat to find you but they found Miss Knight instead. If you want to see her again unharmed then listen very carefully to what I am about to say to you. Do I have your attention?"

McCabe bristled, "I don't know who you think you are, but you can't scare me with …"

"I said, do I have your attention?"

"Who am I speaking to? If you think you can just kidnap people and get away with …"

"I will only ask once more, Mr McCabe. Do I have your attention?"

"Yes."

"Very good. The first thing I must tell you is that if you contact the police about this, Miss Knight will disappear without trace. Do you understand?"

"Yes."

"Good. You have something that I want. Something that was given to you by your friend Bronek Kowalski. Where is it?"

"Bronek wasn't my friend. I hardly knew him."

"Really? Then why were you visiting his wife after he died?"

"To see whether she needed any help."

"And why, after that, did you visit the man Shapiev?"

"She asked me to deliver an envelope to him."

"And what was in the envelope?"

"I don't know."

"You know more than you are telling me, Mr McCabe," and then to someone else, "Bring the girl over here and hurt her."

McCabe heard a scuffle and then Tricia's unmistakable voice crying out in pain. He shouted, "Stop, stop. I'll try to help you."

There was silence for a moment and then the German replied, "Good. We are not animals, Mr McCabe, and no more harm will come to her if you are helpful. You know what I want. I will give you 36 hours to produce it. Do you know where Beale Park is?"

"Yes."

"You will meet my men on the river bank there, with the information, at ten o'clock on Tuesday morning. You will come alone."

The line went dead and McCabe sat there with the phone still held to his ear wondering what to do next.

Chapter Twenty Four

Lower Shiplake - 1957 BST Sunday 29th July

Ulrich Fleischer switched off Tricia's phone and removed the sim card. He placed the card and the phone in the top right hand drawer of his desk, closed the drawer then leaned back into his high backed, black leather swivel chair. On the other side of the desk and bent forward over it was Tricia Knight. Her head was being forced back by Fleischer's man, Ernst Kegel, who was standing behind her pressing her against the desk with his groin and gripping a handful of her hair. Holding her left arm behind her back stood Gunter Meise impassive while he waited for instructions. Forcing her right arm behind her back and up, excited by the pain that he was inflicting, stood Klaus Stritter. Tricia, looking tiny between the three men, her clothes dishevelled, a bruise on her left cheek and her teeth clenched, stared defiantly across the desk at Fleischer.

"Take her back to her room and try not to damage her unless it's really necessary," ordered Fleischer.

Kegel released her hair and the two men holding her arms turned without a word and dragged her, struggling, backwards from the room.

Tricia kicked and shouted, "You bastards, get off of me …" but gave up when Stritter applied more pressure to her right arm.

Kegel closed the door behind them and turned to Fleischer, "I can make her talk," he offered.

"That's what you said about Kowalski's wife and Shapiev, Ernst. But you didn't make them talk, did you? All you did was leave behind a mess for the police to investigate."

Kegel looked sheepish, "I did my best to …"

"But, yet again, your best wasn't good enough. You let your base instincts run away with you and you failed to get any information from them, so we are reduced to trying to discover whether this man McCabe knows anything. I don't believe that the girl does but at least we can use her to influence him. Keep away from the girl, Ernst. I don't want any more corpses here at the moment."

Ernst grunted in reply and thought of the words that his father had drummed into him, *Was du nicht weißt, kann dir nicht schaden - what you don't know can't hurt you* - the motto which he had lived his life by. Fleischer would be leaving the country in three days' time and then Ernst would decide for himself whether he would keep away from the girl or not.

Chapter Twenty Five

Sonning - 2001 BST Sunday 29th July

McCabe, having poured himself a large shot of Laphroaig whisky, was sitting in the wheelhouse of the hire boat and staring upriver towards Sonning Bridge as he wondered what to do. The river traffic had all but ceased with only the occasional late arrival looking for somewhere to moor. At this time on a Sunday evening there was plenty of space left by the weekenders who had gone back to their various marinas. He took a sip of the whisky and looked across the river at a plantation of trees through which he could see the sun nearly at the horizon, turning the sky pink in the distance.

The German had told him that, if he called the police, Tricia would disappear and McCabe believed him; the man was obviously responsible for Bronek and Tushka's deaths and would be capable of anything. What could he do to help her? Nothing that he could think of except to follow instructions and be at Beale Park on Tuesday morning.

Who else might the German have grabbed? Zac? Was Zac alright? McCabe pulled out his phone, found Zac in his contacts and pressed his mobile number.

Zac answered almost immediately, "Hello Chad. Good to hear from you."

"Hi Zac. Everything OK there?"

"Fine. Most of the tourists have gone now so St Katharine's is a lot quieter than it was earlier. I'm just about to cook myself a fry up."

"Good, well look after yourself ..." McCabe ran out of things to say.

"Are you alright, Chad?"

"Fine thanks. Just making sure that you are. Give me a call if you need anything."

"I will, don't worry, have a good holiday."

Zac put the phone down, puzzled.

McCabe felt relieved that Zac was OK and then he thought of Tricia's sister, Caz. Should he tell her that Tricia had been kidnapped? Probably not, she might call the police. What if she was in danger as well as Tricia? He had better call her to make sure that she was alright.

He dialled the number she had given him and waited as it rang.

She answered, "Hello?"

McCabe could hear George Ezra singing Shotgun loud in the background.

"Hi, it's Chad McCabe."

"Who?"

"Chad McCabe."

"Hang on. I'll turn the music off."

McCabe waited, a fantasy image in his mind of her naked, as she was when he had first met her, and probably dancing around her flat come film studio in Brighton with a glass of wine in her hand. The music was suddenly switched off.

"Who?"

"Chad McCabe."

"Chad. How lovely to hear from you." Then lowering her voice to a seductive, sultry tone, "What can I do for you?"

She had immediately reduced him to flustered adolescent status. How did she do that?

"I… I was just making sure that you're OK."

That wasn't what he'd wanted to say at all.

"Of course I'm OK. Why wouldn't I be? Has something happened?"

"Everything's fine, I was just ..."

"Something's wrong," she said.

"No. Nothing's ..."

"Let me talk to Tricia," she interrupted.

He began to regain his composure, "Can't do that at the moment."

She raised her voice, "What's going on McCabe? Let me talk to Tricia."

How was he going to explain anything to her without triggering a phone call to the police? He thought quickly and then decided to abandon caution.

"Caz, Tricia's not here. There's been a problem and she can't come to the phone. She's alright, she's not ill or injured or anything like that ..." he hoped that was the case, "but she can't talk to you right now."

There was silence and then McCabe heard anger in her voice as she said, "What have you done to her, McCabe?"

"Nothing, I promise you. I haven't done anything to her."

"Then why are you ringing me?"

"I was ringing to make sure that you were alright."

"We're going round in circles here, McCabe. Where are you?"

"I'm at a place called Sonning. It's near Reading."

"And where is Tricia?"

"I'm not sure. She's disappeared."

He heard Caz sigh as she replied, "What's she up to now?"

"It's complicated ..."

She interrupted him, "Alright McCabe, something's not right. I'm going to come and see you. What's the best way to get there?"

A good outcome thought McCabe. No more questions on the phone and he could explain to her what was going on face to face,

"Are you in Brighton?" he asked.

"Yes."

"Your best way would be by train Brighton to Victoria, then to Reading from Paddington and I'll meet you at Reading Station."

"OK. It's Monday tomorrow," she replied. "I've got nothing going on. I'll catch a train in the morning. Should we call the police or do you think that she'll turn up?"

"No. No need to call the police. I'll explain everything when I meet you tomorrow. Text me when you leave Brighton and I'll wait for you at Reading."

"OK, McCabe. You'd better not be fooling with me," and she cancelled the call.

McCabe knocked back the whisky, stood up, went down the steps to the saloon then returned to the wheelhouse with the bottle and poured himself another large one.

Chapter Twenty Six

Reading, Berkshire - 1214 BST Monday 30th July

Caz Knight's green eyes were blazing with anger as she pushed her way through the barrier at Reading Station and, swinging her overnight bag in her right hand as if she was about to use it as a weapon, she charged towards McCabe who was waiting for her.

"What's she been up to this time? What's going on, McCabe? Why all the mystery? What can you tell me that you couldn't tell me on the phone?"

She stared up at him seething with a fury that had been pent up since his phone call the previous evening. The steady flow of people walking past took them to be lovers having a tiff and avoided them.

McCabe took a step back and held both hands up palms toward her, "Let's go somewhere and talk. I need you to be calm."

"You tell me now!" she shouted. "You phone me and say that there's a problem with my sister but you won't tell me what, so I travel half way across the country to meet you. What's the big secret?"

"Calm down …"

"Shut up McCabe and stop trying to fob me off …"

"OK, OK," he lowered his hands, "I'll tell you but not here."

"Where then?"

McCabe glanced around and looked up at the imposing facade of the station pub, The Three Guineas, and pointed to it, "In there."

She turned without a word and hurried towards the pub with McCabe trailing after her.

When they were inside she asked, "Where do you want to sit?"

McCabe who had often waited for trains here pointed to some steps which led to an area behind the bar. At this time of day, they could talk there without being overheard.

"Can I get you a drink?" he asked.

"Sure, I'll have a gin and tonic."

"Any particular gin?"

She looked at him with impatience, "Any gin, McCabe."

"Any particular tonic?"

She flashed her eyes at him again, "Just a gin and tonic, McCabe. Can you do that?"

Determined to ignore her rudeness he turned to the bar and ordered two gins and tonic.

"Any particular gin?" asked the barman, who had been listening to the altercation.

McCabe, forgetting for a moment the seriousness of the situation, smiled at him, "Gordon's please," and the barman smiled back.

He waited while the drinks were prepared, paid for them and then carried the two glasses and part full tonic bottles to where Caz was seated under a ceramic tiled sign set into the wall which read God's Wonderful Railway. It was a play on the initials GWR, an acronym for Great Western Railway, the company which built the line from London to the west of England, Wales and parts of the Midlands in the nineteenth century. A glance around the pub would show that the bar was designed with a railway theme, but McCabe had seen it many times before and Caz was too keyed up to notice. He placed the drinks carefully on the marble topped table, sat down and looked at the beautiful, fuming woman sitting opposite him as he wondered where to start.

She picked up her drink, took a sip of it and looked directly into his eyes, still angry and smouldering, ready to explode. Through clenched teeth she ordered, "Just get on with it McCabe."

He had already decided that there was only one way to break this news to her so he just said, "Your sister's been kidnapped."

She stared at him in silence for a few moments and then quietly but with venom replied, "You were supposed to be looking after her, McCabe."

"I don't think it was my fault," and for the next few minutes he explained what had happened from the time that Bronek was shot to Tricia's disappearance, then to his phone conversation with the German.

Caz sat quietly and listened carefully and seriously to everything that he was telling her and, when he had finished, the anger gone and only determination left, she just asked, quietly, "What do we have to do?"

"Well we can't go to the police because the German said that she'll just disappear and I believe him. We'll keep that as an option if we have to but at the moment all we can do is meet him at Beale Park tomorrow."

"The police could wait for them at Beale Park and grab them," offered Caz.

"But what if Tricia isn't with them? They could just deny everything and then we'd never see her again. That won't work."

They both sipped their drinks while Caz thought about that and then she said, "I know people who can act as muscle for us. Is it worth getting them along?"

McCabe had half expected her to say something like that and replied, "Beale Park is a huge empty space on the river. There are trees and bushes that you could hide an army in but not close enough to the river that they could help us. That's probably why they've chosen it as a meeting place. We could hide people on the boat that I've borrowed but, if the kidnappers decided to check, it could just escalate."

"Then we'll just have to meet them on our own," replied Caz.

"No! I can't take you with me, Caz. There's no telling what they might do."

"Well you're not going without me McCabe and that's the end of it."

He wondered for a moment whether it was worth arguing with her and then decided that it would be pointless.

"Come on then," he said. "Drink up and we'll get back to the boat."

They finished their drinks in silence and then left the pub. Crossing the station concourse to the taxi rank McCabe thought back to his meeting here with Tricia three days ago and hoped that she was being treated properly and wasn't suffering.

Once free of the nose to tail traffic in Reading town centre, the black cab, identical to a London taxi, gathered some speed and the four mile journey from the station took nineteen minutes. Caz stepped out of the cab by Sonning Bridge and studied their surroundings while McCabe paid off the taxi driver. It was hot and sunny. The noise was overpowering and completely contrary to what a rural beauty spot should sound like. There was engine noise from a long line of cars crossing the bridge, a loud buzz of conversation on the other side of the hedge from where she was standing which came from the diners eating al fresco at The Coppa Club, part of The Great House Hotel. Added to that were the rattling of the taxi's diesel engine and the screams and shouts of a crowd of teenagers beginning their school holidays and choosing on this sweltering summer day to meet by the river, lounge on the grass in swimwear or jump from the bridge into the water.

McCabe joined her, carrying her bag, and they walked together through the gate and along the river bank the two hundred yards to where Summer Breeze was moored. As they walked, the noise from behind them slowly receded until, by the time they reached the boat, the scene was the tranquil Thames idyll that it was supposed to be.

For the first time since meeting Caz at Reading Station, McCabe took note of what she was wearing: deck shoes, jeans, white blouse and dark blue jacket all very expensive. He suddenly felt shabby in his every day boating wear of blue cargo pants, blue polo shirt and beaten up brown deck shoes. He was impressed that she had come wearing practical clothes.

"Here she is," he said. "Summer Breeze."

Caz stood back and appraised the boat in front of her. "OK," was all she said and she climbed on board and waited in the wheelhouse for McCabe to follow.

He placed Caz's bag on the deck and hoisted himself onto the boat, at the same time feeling for the boat keys in his pocket. After unlocking the double doors, he picked up Caz's bag and then stepped to one side, "After you."

She stepped through the entrance, went down the steps into the saloon and looked around as McCabe followed, bringing her bag with him.

"Right," she said. "What's the plan?"

"The plan is to go up river to Beale Park this afternoon and moor there ready to meet them tomorrow morning."

"How long will that take?"

"Eleven miles and four locks. Four to five hours I should think."

"OK," she replied. "Can I freshen up before we leave?"

"Of course. You can have Tricia's cabin. Along here."

He showed her to the cabin and, taking her bag with her, she closed the door behind her.

McCabe called after her, "Have you eaten?"

Her muffled voice came back through the bulkhead, "Not since breakfast."

"I'll make some sandwiches."

He busied himself in the galley but couldn't get out of his mind the sound of Tricia crying out in pain on the phone. Were they doing the right thing?

Chapter Twenty Seven

At Sonning, Quietus turned and walked back past the line of boats where, less than an hour before, McCabe and Caz had cast off and started their journey up river to Beale Park. He cursed quietly to himself, bored with the tedium of searching all of the many locations on both sides of the river where they might be moored. Not a man much given to aesthetic appreciation, for him the riverbank was a location where his quarry might be hiding and its beauty and charm were lost on him. Ahead of him a man of about twenty years, tall, dark, trendily dressed and good looking, was idly leaning against the low, thin iron railed fencing which encloses the garden of the Great House Hotel. He had a glass of beer in one hand, a cigarette in the other, and he gazed out across the river while exhaling a cloud of smoke. Perhaps, thought Quietus, this man might have seen them. He stopped to engage him in conversation.

"Lovely day."

The man looked back at him with suspicion and didn't answer.

"A lovely day," Quietus repeated.

"S'alright," the man replied and took a long drag of his cigarette, holding the smoke in for a couple of seconds and then exhaling loudly. As far as he was concerned, a man that you didn't know who spoke to you for no reason was either mentally ill or queer. He took a swig of his beer and, pointedly ignoring Quietus, continued to stare across the river.

"I'm looking for a man," continued Quietus. "Perhaps you've seen him. Tall, dark hair, quite good looking ..."

The man turned on him, gritting his teeth and snarling, "Look! I'm not interested, see? Bugger off," and he took another quick, nervous drag of his cigarette and looked away across the river again.

Quietus understood and, hiding his impatience and the temptation to punch the man in the face, he took a non-threatening step backwards.

"Ah, no, you misunderstand. I'm looking for a friend who is travelling with a woman in a boat called Summer Breeze. I thought that they might be moored here. Sorry to bother you."

As Quietus began to walk away the idler visibly relaxed and called after him, "Sorry mate. I'm with you now. You've just missed them."

Quietus stopped and turned, "They were here?"

"An hour ago."

"Definitely Summer Breeze?"

"Yeah, definitely. They got here a couple of days ago. I'm interested in boats so I check 'em all out. One day I'm gonna get one. It was definitely called Summer Breeze."

"Do know where they went?"

"No. They were here earlier when I arrived but when I came out for a fag just now they'd gone. The river's like that. Boats come and go all the time."

"Any idea which way they went?"

"No, sorry."

"OK. Thanks," said Quietus and turned to walk away again.

"Funny thing," the man called after him. "The woman who was with him when he arrived was a brunette, but the woman with him today was a redhead. Cracking bit of stuff too."

Quietus was thinking and didn't respond but carried on walking towards the hotel car park. Had the man got the wrong boat? Redhead, brunette? What was that about? He definitely recognised the boat name so, presumably, it was the correct one. Which way did they go? On the basis that they were not likely to go back the way they had come, they must be continuing their journey down river. He reached the inconspicuous dark blue Ford Focus which he had hired, sat in the driving seat and opened his copy of The River Thames Book which he had purchased at the marina in Caversham earlier. He quickly flicked through the pages until he found the map with Sonning shown on it. Following the river downstream on the map he could see that the next major town where they might stop was Henley-on-Thames but, before reaching Henley, there were at least half a dozen moorings in the countryside where they could have stopped. To check those he would have to park the car and walk across fields to reach them. It was going to be a long, tiring process. Quietus started the engine and drove out of the car park heading for the first possible moorings shown on the map, near an isolated island called Hallsmead Ait close to Shiplake. He was convinced that if he could find them in a place like that it would be the perfect spot to kill McCabe and whoever was with him.

Chapter Twenty Eight

McCabe and Caz on Summer Breeze arrived at Beale Park just before sunset and moored in an isolated spot away from other boats. They were both tired and, after eating in near silence a salad which Caz had prepared while underway, they went to their separate cabins. Neither of them could sleep, both anxiously anticipating what would happen at the meeting with Tricia's kidnappers the next morning. McCabe dozed and woke, read a book and dozed, and was wide awake as daylight started to push through the curtains on his cabin windows. He looked at his watch, saw that it was just past 5.30, and got up. Dressing quickly in the same clothes that he had worn the day before, he went up to the wheelhouse. Caz was sitting in the helmsman's chair with a duvet wrapped around her and was staring out at their surroundings which were slowly appearing in the grey dawn light.

"Can't you sleep either?" he asked.

"No, I've been awake all night."

"Me too, pretty much. Coffee?"

"Yes please," she said and smiled at him.

Five minutes later, McCabe appeared with two steaming mugs of instant coffee and passed one to her.

"Black two sugars, right?"

"Yes, how did you know?"

"Because it's the way I have it," he replied, "and Tricia once told me that you do as well."

"Does she talk about me much?" asked Caz.

"Non-stop. She looks up to you, I think."

"Yes, because I'm older. She always did. Has she told you what I do for a living?"

"No."

"She probably doesn't like to tell people," said Caz.

McCabe remembered what Caz had said to him the first time that they met in her flat, "I make movies here, of the adult type but with a storyline," and he decided to change the subject.

"A shame we won't see the sunrise here." He pointed across the river to the heavily wooded hillside climbing up from the opposite bank, "It rises behind that hill, so it won't appear for a while."

"What is this place?" she asked, looking out at the river bank to which they were moored. "It just looks like a huge field with trees and bushes around the edge of it."

"Yes, perfect place for a meeting, isn't it? Nowhere to hide ambushers close to the boat. Where we are it's quiet, but behind the trees over there is a zoo, gardens, children's play area, It's a local attraction, ideal for a family day out, started up about sixty years ago."

"In different circumstances I'd be enjoying this trip, McCabe. Might even go to the zoo."

"Do you like boats?" he asked.

"I do. I've done a lot of shoots on private yachts in some very exotic places."

He looked at her and saw that she was smiling at him.

"I'd better get dressed," she said. "I can't sit around naked all day. I'll take the coffee with me."

As she stood up and reached out for the coffee cup it was obvious that she was wearing nothing except the duvet. McCabe watched as, barefoot, she padded across the wheelhouse and went down the steps to her cabin and he wanted her more than any woman that he had ever met.

Chapter Twenty Nine

Shiplake - 0922 BST Tuesday 31st July

Quietus had parked the hire car near Shiplake College and was walking the Thames Path in a futile hunt for McCabe who had travelled up river to Beale Park in the opposite direction to the area that he, Quietus, was searching. He had followed the map to two small islands, The Lynch and Hallsmead Ait, both heavily wooded and their west sides visible from the towpath. Boats were moored to the islands and also to the river bank where he was standing but not McCabe's hire boat. He was feeling the heat as the sun beat down on him and that, coupled with his normal lack of exercise and the exertion of his search, was making him irritable. Quietus was heading back to the car when his phone rang. He pressed the answer icon, put the phone to his ear and waited without speaking.

"Hello?" Ricky Bishop's voice, "Hello?"

"Yes?"

"What's happening?"

"I'm working on it," replied Quietus.

"You've been working on it for nearly two weeks. Why haven't you done it yet?"

Quietus remained calm. "You know how I work. I take my time, do it right and it looks like an accident."

Bishop raised his voice, "Never mind all that bollocks. Just get it done. I've already paid you half the money up front and nothing's happened. I'm not sitting around all day with a little phone up my arse just to call people like you who tell me that they haven't been able to do something. Get on with it."

Quietus sounded calm but inwardly he was seething, "I've told you that it will be done at the right time. Don't push me."

"If I wasn't stuck in this prison all day I'd do it myself instead of hiring prats like you. I'll give you another week to finish it. If you haven't done it by then I want my money back and I'll get someone else to do the job."

Bishop ended the call and Quietus put the phone back in his pocket. He continued to walk along the riverbank towards his car and imagined what he might do to Bishop if he had the chance. He wanted the money for this hit because life was expensive, but he didn't need it that badly and he wasn't going to be insulted by the morons who employed him. He would do this job but maybe he would have Bishop done as well, just for the fun of it. Being locked away in prison wouldn't protect him. Quietus could reach him anywhere.

Chapter Thirty

McCabe had been carefully watching the river for the past hour. A narrowboat came towards them and two large, white, fibreglass cruisers but none of the boats moored up and they continued on their way up river towards Goring-on-Thames. A strong breeze had sprung up and it blew steadily through the trees on the opposite bank, sighing and rustling as McCabe and Caz waited.

She called up to him from the saloon, "I want to come up, Chad."

"No. Stay there. They told me to come on my own. If they see you, who knows what they'll do?"

He looked astern and, in the distance, coming towards him on the long reach from Pangbourne, he could see a large motor cruiser travelling fast.

"This might be them. They're ignoring the speed limit and they'll be here in a couple of minutes."

The vessel grew larger as it got closer and, as it drew alongside, McCabe could see that it was a sleek, steel, sea going cruiser, dark blue in colour, probably sixty feet long and flying the horizontal red white and blue of a Dutch ensign. The name Wilhelmina was painted on the bow in Gothic script. She pulled into the bank in front of Summer Breeze and two powerful looking crewmen jumped off onto the grass and stood, one at the bow and the other at the stern, holding her in position with ropes. Another crew member lowered a gangway from the waist of the vessel and Ernst Kegel appeared holding Tricia's arm. They came down the gangway then stopped and were followed by Kegel's backup, Gunter Meise and Klaus Stritter who stood behind and to either side of Kegel. They stared threateningly at McCabe who had left Summer Breeze and was walking towards them. He was ten feet away from them when Kegel shouted at him, "Stop!"

He stopped. For a few moments they confronted each other. Nobody spoke and the only sound was the wind moving the long grass then, at exactly 10am, McCabe's phone rang.

"Answer it," ordered Kegel.

McCabe pulled the phone from the pocket of his fleece jacket, and looked at the screen - Tricia's phone. He accepted the call and putting the phone to his ear he heard the German's voice.

"My men are standing in front of you and you can see that they have the woman. Now, where is it?"

"Where is what?" replied McCabe.

"If you play games with me, Mr McCabe, Miss Knight will be killed."

"I don't know what you want. If you tell me what you want I'll try to help, but I can't if I don't know what it is you want."

The line was silent for a few moments and then Fleischer spoke again, "I know that you visited Kowalski's wife and then you visited the man Shapiev. Why did you do that?"

McCabe glanced at Tricia and could see that she was watching him with an imploring expression on her face.

"I told you before, I visited his wife to see if she needed any help and I delivered an envelope to Mr Shapiev for her. I didn't know her and I didn't know Shapiev."

"What was in the envelope?"

"I don't know. Just a single sheet of paper I think."

"What did you and Shapiev talk about?"

McCabe thought quickly. The less he told this man the less he would have to be suspicious about, "Nothing really. I just gave him the envelope."

"Don't lie to me, Mr McCabe. You were in the house for nearly half an hour."

McCabe decided that the best way forward was to tell the truth, "We had tea."

"And you talked?"

Not all the truth, "Not about anything in particular."

The line was silent while Fleischer considered this. He replied, "I believe you, Mr McCabe, but there is something more. I know that you wanted to give Kowalski's wife his guitar so you must have it in your possession. Is it in a case?"

"Yes, but I don't have it with me."

"I have other things to attend to, Mr McCabe, and this is a small matter. While you find what I want, Miss Knight will remain as my guest. That will keep your attention focussed, I think. You have three days to find it."

"But I don't know …"

"That is all Mr McCabe. Pass the phone to the man who is holding your friend. I wish to speak to him."

McCabe held the phone out and offered it to Kegel, "He wants to speak to you."

"Throw it over here," said Kegel.

McCabe tossed the phone into a clump of grass near Tricia's feet and Klaus Stritter stepped forward, picked it up and passed it to Kegel who was still holding on to her.

Kegel spoke into the phone, waited, then answered, "Yes." He dropped the phone onto the clump of grass again and started to move backwards pulling Tricia with him. His two bodyguards moved back with him. Suddenly they froze.

Caz appeared by McCabe's left shoulder. With her right hand she was pointing a small, black pistol directly at Kegel, and she was angry.

She shouted, "Stand still, you bastards." Five feet two inches of auburn haired spitfire, she waved the pistol at Kegel and snarled, "You bring my sister over here."

Kegel thought for a moment then slowly and carefully he edged forward towards the unexpected, petite redhead who was threatening to shoot him. At the same time he computed distance and angles until, using Tricia as a shield, he stopped directly in front of her. Behind him, Meise and Stritter produced handguns and trained them on McCabe who looked on, horrified at the sudden turn in events, unable to intervene. Silently he willed her to stop. What was she doing? You can't wave pretend guns at these people. They'll shoot you.

"Now let her go," ordered Caz.

Carefully, Kegel removed his left arm which had been across Tricia's chest, his hand gripping her right shoulder. Tricia, shrugged away from him and stepped to her left. Kegel swivelled his right forearm upwards and, with his fist clenched, knocked the gun away. The force of the blow caused Caz's finger to tighten on the double action trigger firing the gun and two 9mm bullets sped harmlessly away across the field. Kegel grabbed the front of Caz's shirt with his left hand and slapped her hard with his open right hand across the side of her head. McCabe leapt at him as Kegel released Caz and she fell to the ground. Kegel stepped back and stopped McCabe with a straight left arm and open hand to his chest and then punched him hard in his stomach with his right. McCabe fell to the ground winded as Meise and Stritter ran forward grabbing Tricia and dragging her backwards, kicking and screaming, forcing her onto the Wilhelmina and out of sight below deck.

Kegel sneered at Caz and McCabe, both still lying on the grass, "Stay here for two hours. I have a man with a high powered sniper rifle hidden in the trees on the other side of the river. If you try to leave before that time he will shoot you."

He kicked McCabe in the chest then walked backwards to the Wilhelmina, not taking his eyes from them for a second. Kegel climbed aboard and the two crewmen holding the ropes followed him. The Wilhelmina immediately pulled away from the bank, turned and made its way down river at speed in the direction that it had come from.

McCabe sat up winded and struggling to breathe from the punch to his stomach and the boot in his chest. Trying to ignore the nausea that was threatening to overwhelm him he dragged himself to where Caz was still lying motionless on the grass. He got to his knees beside her and gently stroked to one side the mass of auburn hair that was covering her face. Her eyes were open but she stared vacantly ahead. He feared the worst.

"Caz, are you with me?" he asked, shaking her shoulder gently.

She blinked.

"Wake up, they've gone."

She suddenly frowned and sat up, then put her hand to her left ear and winced, "That hurt. My head is ringing. That bastard slapped me so hard."

"Are you surprised? You were pointing a starting pistol at him. He wasn't to know it's one of your studio props."

Caz turned and on her hands and knees searched the tufts of grass, almost immediately finding the weapon which had been knocked from her hand. "Here it is! It's not a studio prop, it's real."

McCabe took it from her and examined it, small and black with twin barrels, "You're joking. What are you doing with a real gun?"

"Someone gave it to me ages ago for protection. It's called a Double Tap Derringer. It fires two shots and there are two spare bullets in the grip."

"You know it's illegal to carry one of these around, don't you?" McCabe said.

"Sure it is but sometimes I have to do business with some really unpleasant people. Give it back to me."

"I'm tempted to throw it in the river, Caz"

Suddenly her eyes narrowed and he saw the flash of anger that he had seen the first time that he had met her; the same anger that had made her pull a gun on Ernst Kegel.

"Give it back to me."

He handed it back to her without speaking and her manner changed as if nothing had happened.

"Did you see which way they went?" she asked, scrambling to her feet.

McCabe slowly pulled himself up and picked up his phone, "They went downstream towards Pangbourne."

Caz turned in the direction of Pangbourne and saw the Wilhelmina a mile away, fast disappearing around a left hand bend in the river, and she shouted excitedly, "I can still see them. Let's follow them," and she started to run towards Summer Breeze.

McCabe went after her, "Wait!"

He caught up with her as she stopped by the boat.

"Wait," he lowered his voice as if their conversation could be overheard. "That thug said that they'd left a sniper here who will shoot us if we leave without waiting for two hours. Didn't you hear him?"

"No, I was stunned for a bit after he whacked me. Do you believe him?"

McCabe glanced around and his eyes searched the trees opposite, "I'm not sure. It's possible. It's not worth risking anyway."

Caz suddenly remembered, "You had a phone call."

"It was their boss. The man who called me before. He's given us another three days to get him whatever Bronek had that he wants."

"What is that?"

"I haven't the faintest idea."

"Well we can't just let them take my sister away and not do anything."

McCabe looked at her and smiled, "Come on. We're going to rescue her but we have to wait for two hours. Let's get on board. I'll make some coffee and we'll talk through what we're going to do."

Chapter Thirty One

The journey from Beale Park had taken the Wilhelmina nearly five hours and Tricia had counted five occasions when the boat had stopped briefly and she heard male and female voices. She guessed that they were holiday makers whose boats were sharing a lock with them. If she'd had a chart or pilot book which she could refer to she would have been able to work out, by counting the five locks, roughly where she was. She had felt the Wilhelmina turn sharply after she was bundled below at Beale Park, so she knew that they had travelled downstream. She was locked in one of Wilhelmina's cabins, wood lined with a single bunk and a small porthole with opaque glass that she couldn't see through and which she couldn't open. There was a doorway to an adjoining heads containing a shower, washbasin and toilet. Tricia had spent most of the journey lying on the bunk, wondering what was going to happen to her.

The boat was slowing down and came to a stop and again she heard voices, but this time she knew that it was the crew only who were talking. The cabin door was suddenly thrown open and Ernst Kegel filled the opening as he stooped to enter. Tricia sat up and quickly swung her legs over the side of the bunk and stood up as he reached out and grabbed her right arm. He dragged rather than led her out of the cabin and along the passageway which led to a companionway leading up to the wheelhouse. Kegel pushed her up the steps and at the top led her through the wheelhouse, out onto the side deck and down a gangway, pulling her with him. As she reached the bottom of the gangplank she stumbled, still squinting as her eyes became accustomed to the sudden daylight. She was in a huge well-kept garden. Behind her was the river and in front of her a large house. She smelled new mown grass as Kegel pulled her to her feet and then hurried her across the lawn, up steps onto a stone paved terrace and through French Windows into the house. Without pausing in the expensively and tastefully furnished sitting room Kegel forced her through another door, along a corridor and then down some steps and into a small room, high ceilinged with a single bed, a wash basin and a small window high up in the outside wall. The window was below ground level and looked out onto a lightwell with an iron grid across it. Kegel slammed the door behind her and she heard him lock it. She was familiar with this room which had been her cell for the two days since they had first brought her here. The only times that she had been allowed to leave it was to go to the lavatory in a small room along the corridor while one of the men stood guard outside, and when she was taken out in the early hours of this morning for the journey to Beale Park. On the bed was a change of underwear, a clean summer dress, a fresh towel and a clean bath robe which replaced the one that had been in the room when she had left that morning.

Tricia sat on the bed for a few minutes fearful and anxious and then decided to do something positive. She stripped off all of her clothes and folded them neatly on the chair by the bed and then put the towelling bathrobe on. It was white and fluffy and the feel of it lifted her spirits briefly. She went to the washbasin, ran some hot water and took off the bath robe. She took a flannel and soap and began to wash herself. The feel of the water and the roughness of the flannel felt good against her skin and she smiled to herself as she soaped her face, her arms, her armpits, the front of her body, as much of her back as she could reach, between her thighs, her buttocks, then her legs and feet. Finally, she rinsed the soap away with the flannel and fresh warm water. She took the large blue bath towel which had been placed on the bed and dried her body then put the bathrobe on again. A strip wash was not a bath but it was better than nothing. She suddenly heard the sound of the key in the lock and quickly wrapped the robe tighter around herself, tying it as the door flew open. Tricia gasped as she saw Ernst Kegel standing in the doorway glaring at her with lust in his cruel, malevolent eyes.

Chapter Thirty Two

"They can't hide a boat the size of Wilhelmina, Caz, unless they travel down to Teddington, then onto the tidal Thames and take her out to sea."

"Perhaps they've done that," she replied and cast a sceptical glance in McCabe's direction.

He didn't reply and continued to stare fixedly ahead, carefully keeping control of Summer Breeze, unaware of how much Caz had lost confidence in him.

They had waited at Beale Park for two hours, as instructed, and then had set off in pursuit of the Wilhelmina, although what they would do if they found her they had no idea. So far they had passed through five locks. The first four: Whitchurch, Mapledurham, Caversham and Sonning were all manned and the lock keepers at each one confirmed that Wilhelmina had passed through a couple of hours previously. By the time they had reached the fifth, Shiplake Lock, the keeper had finished for the day and Caz operated the gates after McCabe explained to her what to do. The Thames locks are electrically operated with push buttons and she had no difficulty opening the gates and sluices while he drove the boat in, held it steady with ropes as the lock emptied and drove it out after Caz opened the bottom gates. He waited on the lock landing while Caz closed the gates behind him and, as soon as she was aboard, they set off again in pursuit of Tricia and the Wilhelmina.

They motored under the railway bridge which carries the local line from Henley to Twyford, passed the picturesque St George and Dragon pub at Wargrave on their right and rounded a long left hand bend. As they exited the bend they saw open countryside on their left and, in the distance, they could see dinghies pulled up on the right bank at Henley Sailing Club. As they drew level with the club, ahead of them on the left bank was a line of houses, upmarket and expensive. McCabe saw, in front of one of the houses, a flash of red, white and blue, the horizontal bars of a Dutch ensign. It was the Wilhelmina moored to a floating pontoon which ran almost the entire width of the property, an imposing house set back from the river with lawns and a solidly built boathouse on the upstream boundary.

He slowed the boat, "There she is Caz."

Caz leapt up from her seat, excited, "Let's call the police."

"No!" McCabe turned the boat across the river and they started to head back the way they had come. "The German said that, if we do that, Tricia will disappear."

"Well we've got to do something, McCabe," she replied, her anger flaring up again.

"We are going to do something. We're going to wait until it's dark and then we'll go and investigate. What we can't do is let them see us."

In silence they motored back to Shiplake Lock and moored on the lock landing. Caz angry and frustrated, McCabe calm now and forming a plan in his mind.

Part of Summer Breeze's inventory was an inflatable dinghy and an outboard motor which hung on the guardrail. McCabe, with Caz's help, pulled the heavy dinghy from its locker and hoisted it over the rail and onto the wooden boards of the lock landing, then he stepped off and unpacked it from its bag. It was an old Suzumar dinghy suitable for three people and seemed to be in good condition. He removed the foot pump from the bag, connected it to one of the dinghy's three air chambers and began to inflate it. He repeated the process with the other chambers and then pumped up the floor and keel as well. Standing back, he waited for signs of any leaks and, when he was satisfied that there were none, he took the oars from the bag and fitted them to the rowlocks on the inflatable's side tubes. It was ready. McCabe searched until he found two long ropes in one of Summer Breeze's lockers and he attached them to the D rings on either side of the dinghy's bow. He pushed the dinghy into the water and then attached both ropes to Summer Breeze's stern cleats, one port and the other starboard, as a towing bridle. That done he went back to the wheelhouse where Caz was waiting with coffee and sandwiches.

"What's the plan, McCabe?"

"As soon as it's dark we'll go back without being seen and moor just up river from the house where the Wilhelmina is, but on the opposite bank. There's a line of riverbank moorings there which I've used before at a place called Lashbrook. We'll row across the river in the dinghy and check out the situation and then decide what to do. I say we because I'm pretty sure that you won't let me go without you."

"You're right, I won't."

"OK, but you leave the gun behind."

She frowned at him for a moment then answered, "OK."

"Good. That's agreed then."

"What if we can't find her?" asked Caz.

"She'll either be on the Wilhelmina or in the house, I hope. If we find her we'll try to release her."

"And if we don't find her or we can't release her?"

"We'll have to think of something else."

"No!" Caz's temper flashed again. "We'll call the police. If we can't help her we'll have to get people who can."

McCabe thought for a moment, "You're right. If we have to, we'll get help. The German has given me three days to find something for him and I don't even know what I'm looking for but he says she'll be safe until then."

"Well you might believe him but I don't," Caz replied. "If we don't rescue her tonight I'm calling the police myself."

Chapter Thirty Three

Tricia was incapable of movement, fixed to the spot like a mouse in front of a cobra. Too late she realised that there must have been a hidden camera watching her wash. Kegel continued to stare at her as he stood in the doorway, then he stepped into the room and slowly and quietly closed the door behind him. He crossed the room and seized the front of her bathrobe tearing it open. He threw her onto the bed and fell on her feeling for her mouth with his lips and grasping at her breasts with both hands. His weight was crushing her and, as he found her mouth, she smelled stale beer on his breath. She emitted a loud and primitive growling sound from the back of her throat as she bit hard on his bottom lip piercing it with her incisors and clamping his face to hers. Kegel screamed into her face as he tried to rise from the bed struggling to get away from her while she continued to bite into him. As he rose he lifted her, and her full weight was held by his lip until it tore through and she fell back spitting a piece of his flesh out. He stood above her panting, his injured lip ripped open in a jagged tear and he stared down at her, hatred on his face and blood pouring down the front of his shirt. Ignoring the blood and not noticing the pain, he fixed his eyes on hers and slowly began to unbuckle his belt as Tricia cowered helplessly in front of him. He released his belt and unbuttoned the top of his trousers then, as he unzipped, a loud hammering began on the door.

"What?" shouted Kegel spitting blood across the room.

Stefan Merk, who knew better than to interrupt Kegel when he was with the woman, shouted from the hallway, "The boss wants you on the phone, now."

A command from Fleischer was the only thing that could have dissuaded Kegel from what he was about to do and it stopped him in his tracks. "Tell him I'll be there in a minute," he shouted, spraying more blood over Tricia.

Kegel zipped up his trousers and refastened his belt, all the time staring at the terrified woman as she lay on the bed in front of him. "I'll be back for you when I've dealt with this phone call."

He suddenly became aware of the blood running from his mouth and, without saying anything else, he pulled a grubby white handkerchief from his pocket and put it to his lips where it instantly began to turn crimson. Backing across the room and still fixing her with his eyes he reached the door, opened it, went out and locked it again.

Tricia slowly sat up, pulling the robe around herself again, and swivelled her body until she was sitting on the edge of the bed in shock, her bare feet cold on the vinyl tiles of the floor, the taste of him, beer and blood, still in her mouth. She wrapped both arms around herself, hugging herself, taking comfort in the warmth of the blood spattered bath robe as she waited anxiously for Kegel to return.

Chapter Thirty Four

Sunset, officially, was at 2053 and they waited for another hour until it was truly dark. Summer Breeze, not showing any lights, slipped into a vacant space at Lashbrook Moorings on the Berkshire side of the river and McCabe jumped off and tied her fore and aft to the short but sturdy wooden posts spaced at intervals along the bank. In front of them was a moored narrowboat, seemingly unoccupied, and behind them was a large, white fibreglass hire boat with light streaming from its windows and its occupants below deck. On the landward side of the mooring were high hedges and trees separated from the boats by a narrow grassy path. Caz and McCabe could see, slightly downstream of them on the other side of the river on the Oxfordshire bank, the outline and cabin lights of the Wilhelmina still moored where she had been earlier. They watched for twenty minutes during which time there was no sign of activity either from the house or from the Wilhelmina.

"OK Caz. Let's go across there. Can you see, on the right where the garden meets the river, an area in deep shadow? We'll row across in the dinghy and tie up there. We can't use the outboard motor because it would be too noisy so we'll leave it here."

Caz, who had changed into black cargo pants, a dark blue sweater and deck shoes, held the dinghy steady with a boathook while McCabe climbed down into it. He, in turn, held the dinghy firmly against Summer Breeze as Caz stepped down to join him, then he cast off the towing bridle. Caz sat in the stern of the inflatable while McCabe, dressed in his usual navy blue cargo pants and fleece, rowed them steadily and quietly across the river aided by the slight current which was carrying them slowly downstream.

The night was cloudless and the sky bright with stars which made them feel visible and exposed against the light grey colour of the dinghy but McCabe knew that, as long as they remained in the middle of the river, they were virtually undetectable from the bank. Before leaving Summer Breeze he had checked the moonrise time and noted that it would be at 2239, which gave them only half an hour to find and release Tricia. After that, the moon, waning but still nearly full, would begin to bathe the river in light; something he would normally have welcomed, especially sitting on deck with a glass of wine and the beautiful Caz for company. They drifted with the current until they drew level with Wilhelmina and, as they passed, McCabe taking care not to splash, pulled on the oars and propelled them silently and efficiently into the shadowed area of bank which they had spotted from the other side of the river. He shipped the oars and tied the dinghy's painter to a mooring ring and they waited for any shouts to indicate that they had been seen. Nothing. Wilhelmina and the house were still spilling light onto the river and lawn but there didn't appear to be any form of lookout or guard. McCabe, keeping low, climbed out of the dinghy and then, crouching, held the little boat, keeping it stable while Caz climbed out of it and joined him on the lawn. With Caz following him, he crept forward and they both took cover behind a patch of rhododendron bushes twenty feet from the water's edge. Looking back, McCabe was satisfied that the dinghy was hidden in shadow and would only be noticed if someone took the trouble to walk to that part of the garden. They both studied the house and could see the brightly lit terrace and French

Windows. The curtains were drawn in all of the windows facing the river and there didn't seem to be much point investigating the terrace and the rooms facing onto it. They saw that the lawn and a gravel path continued around the side of the house nearest to them and rose gently away towards gardens at the front, which were also bathed in light. The side of the house was in shadow with only a dim light from two small windows at first floor level, and there was a faint glow from a window at basement level which cast light onto the brickwork above it. Expecting to be challenged at any moment, McCabe and Caz crept forward, staying on the lawn to avoid making any noise on the gravel. When they reached the glow from the basement they stopped and were looking down into a small light well covered by a metal grille which, in daylight, would allow some meagre light into the room. The window was curtainless and light streamed out from the room casting the upward glow which they had seen from the bushes. Caz, on her hands and knees, crawled forward to peer down into the room and tried to lift the steel grille which covered the lightwell.

Lying on her side on the bed, curled up and hugging her knees, Tricia had been waiting for Ernst to return for more than five hours. Five long hours during which she had lain waiting for and dreading the sound of a key in the lock, which would signal the man's return and her punishment for tearing at his face. She was thirsty. The bottle of water that had been left for her was empty and she was resisting the urge to drink tap water from the wash basin.

She had put on the clean underwear and dress, then dozed intermittently and now she was suddenly wide awake, sure that a noise had woken her but unsure what it was or where it had come from. She stood up from the bed and crossed to the door and listened. Then she heard the noise again, a scratching sound outside the window. She crossed the room and stood below the window and, as she looked up, she saw through the grille fixed to the top of the lightwell a vaguely lit face which disappeared instantly as the person pulled back surprised at being seen. Tricia stepped back into the room and shook her head. It was her sister's face but how could that be? Had they found her or was she still half asleep? She stepped forward again and looked up and Caz was there looking down at her and gesturing frantically, pointing at her and silently mouthing the words, "Are you OK?"

Tricia nodded, almost crying with excitement, and was about to call up to Caz when she heard the key turn in the lock and the door flew open. She spun around and waited for the attack to start, determined that he wasn't going to win, but it wasn't Ernst. It was his two men Meise and Stritter who had dragged her back to the Wilhelmina at Beale Park earlier on in the day. She had seen them before individually when one or the other of them had brought her food and water. Neither of them had answered her questions or even spoken to her but, unlike Kegel, they had always treated her with respect.

"You come with us," ordered Meise, his English heavily accented revealing his German origins.

Tricia stayed where she was. Whatever happened now she wanted Caz to see it.

"Now," ordered Meise.

Tricia didn't move and both Meise and Stritter crossed the room, violently grabbed her arms and marched her to the door.

Caz quickly pulled back from the lightwell again and excitedly turned to McCabe, "I saw her. She was in there."

As she spoke, the light in the room was turned off and they were in complete darkness.

"Keep your voice down, Caz. They'll hear you. What was she doing?"

"She looked up and saw me and then she was grabbed by two men and dragged away."

"Did they see you?"

"No, they didn't look up."

"Well at least we know she's here," replied McCabe. He crawled forward and looked down into the lightwell but, without the light from the room, he couldn't see anything. He tested the metal grille but it was firmly bedded into its concrete surround and he couldn't lift it.

"We've got to get into the house Caz. We can't get in this way and the back of the house facing the river is too well lit. The only way is through the front."

Caz was already moving and he quickly went after her, both of them staying in the shadows as they followed the path until they reached the corner of the house. From there they could see more lawns and flowerbeds, a large turning space and a long drive stretching away into the distance with more rhododendron bushes lining either side. The front of the house was completely floodlit by powerful lights which were sunk into the flowerbeds and it was obvious to McCabe that they weren't going to be able to get into the house from this side either. It wasn't obvious to Caz though and he had to reach out and grab her as she stepped out into the light eager to find her sister. He pulled her back into the shadows, struggling.

"Let go of me," she hissed. "What do you think you're doing?"

"You can't go out there. They'll see you."

"Well I'm not staying here," she argued in a loud whisper. "You didn't see what they were doing to her. They had her by the arms and they …"

McCabe had grabbed her by the shoulders and was shaking her, "Stop it! Be quiet."

Caz stopped arguing and he repeated, "You can't go out there. If they see you they'll grab you and they'll have two hostages. Just stop and we'll think."

As McCabe finished speaking they heard voices and he peered around the corner of the house, hidden by the rose bushes which were planted as a feature along the frontage. Meise and Stritter had appeared, leading Tricia between them, and were walking her to a group of cars parked side by side at the far edge of the turning space. They stopped by a top of the range BMW and together they pushed Tricia into the back seat. Stritter got in with her and Meise got into the driving seat and started the engine. He backed the car out then turned towards the drive and pulled away.

"We've got to stop them," shouted Caz and sprang forward into the full glare of the floodlights with the derringer in her hand, as if to chase the rapidly disappearing car along the drive.

Chapter Thirty Five

Quietus had parked the hire car in Willow Lane and walked along a narrow footpath which led to the river. Trees and bushes hemmed him in on either side of the path and blotted out any light, so ahead of him was complete blackness. He stopped and pulled his phone from his pocket and switched on the torch function. The light from the phone showed that the path stretched away from him for a hundred yards, dead straight and narrowing as the untended bushes tried to spread their foliage to cover it completely. He pushed forward and emerged onto the old towpath as the moon began to rise above the trees and paint the riverscape with a pale eerie light. He switched off the phone and put it back into his pocket and waited while his eyes adjusted themselves to the moonlight.

Across the river he could see large, opulent houses each in their own grounds leading down to the water. Some had light shining from their windows, others appeared to be unoccupied. To his left, the hedge which defined that side of the footpath continued to the water's edge blocking any access in that direction. To his right a narrow, rough path continued along the riverbank and he knew from a study of the map earlier that it would lead him to Lashbrook Moorings. He began to walk slowly along the path taking care to avoid tree roots and uneven ridges which were waiting to trip him up. Almost immediately he could see in front of him a line of moored boats. A narrowboat, a white hire boat with light from its saloon spilling out onto the path, and Summer Breeze. He had found her.

Quietus crept forward quietly and stood by Summer Breeze and listened. No lights were on and there was no sound from inside. If McCabe was there and asleep this would be an ideal opportunity to wake him up and arrange a quick drowning accident but the smoker at Sonning had said that there was a woman with him and that would make an "accident" more complicated. Quietus turned and retraced his steps back to the car. He would return early in the morning and see whether McCabe was alone. If not, then there would have to be two accidents and tomorrow night would see the contract completed.

Chapter Thirty Six

McCabe leapt forward and caught up with Caz after twenty yards. He grabbed her by the waist, put his left hand over her mouth and carried her kicking and protesting back into the shadows. The car with Tricia in it had already disappeared from view and probably, by now, had reached a road and was on its way.

"What do you think you're trying to do?" he hissed in Caz's ear. "Shut up!" then again, "Shut up!"

She slowly stopped struggling and he grabbed her right hand and forced her to give up the derringer which he slipped into the pocket of his fleece jacket. Then he released her and she turned on him.

"Get off of me. We've got to help my sister."

"Keep your voice down," he ordered. "You're not going to help her by getting us both killed."

"Well I'm not going to just ..."

"Be quiet," he ordered, "and listen."

They listened for a full half minute. Complete silence. Perhaps the house was empty now but McCabe wasn't prepared to wait around to find out.

"Nobody saw us," he said with relief. "Let's get back to the boat. It's time we got some help."

They retraced their steps back past the window where they had seen Tricia, then across the lawn to the shadows of the first rhododendron bush. From here they could see that the back of the house, still with lights on, was quiet and nobody was on the terrace. Wilhelmina was exactly as they had seen her before, and they were about to leave their hiding place when McCabe saw the glow of a cigarette being dragged on next to the boat's wheelhouse. Much to her annoyance he grabbed Caz's arm to stop her from walking out onto the lawn.

"Stop. There's someone on the boat."

She shrugged her arm away, "Where?"

"On the other side of the wheelhouse."

She stared hard at the Wilhelmina, "I see him."

They waited for the man to finish his cigarette. He walked along the deck towards the bow and flicked the stub into the river with a shower of sparks and went back into the wheelhouse. They still waited. Had the man gone below decks or was he still in the wheelhouse somewhere. It was impossible to tell as the glare from the floodlights which fringed the river and pointed back at the house left the Wilhelmina in shadow.

"We've got to take a chance and go, Caz," whispered McCabe.

"OK. Say when."

"Now!"

They ran towards the dinghy, keeping low as they crossed the floodlit grass. Someone shouted from the direction of the Wilhelmina and as they reached the dinghy McCabe stopped to help Caz in. He jumped in himself as Caz leaned out of the boat to release the painter from the mooring ring. McCabe sat on the thwart and grabbed the two short aluminium oars. He dug them into the water and pulled away from the bank as rapidly as he could. As he rowed away he could see that the crewman from the Wilhelmina had reached the spot where the dinghy had been moored and was shouting angrily at them in German. McCabe continued to pull steadily away and, instead of taking the shortest route across the river back to Summer Breeze, he rowed hard downstream towards Henley, remaining on the same side of the river as the Wilhelmina which now fired up a searchlight swinging and probing across the water for them. Within seconds it had them pinned in its beam lit up as if it was daylight.

They could hear shouts and commands in German as the Wilhelmina launched a tender which had been hanging in davits on her stern. It took time and when they finally had it in the water and had started its outboard motor, McCabe and Caz had escaped the beam of the searchlight and he was still rowing hard downstream. Spaced along the bank were houses, all individual and detached but built close together, some with boathouses roofed and enclosed on three sides and open to the river at the front. Several of the houses had small boats moored along the bank. They presented a number of hiding places and McCabe hoped that he had given their pursuers the impression that they had been heading for one of the boathouses. Opposite the houses, in the middle of the river, is an unoccupied and completely overgrown island called Handbuck Eyot and McCabe suddenly pulled hard on his right oar and swung the dinghy towards it. He rowed furiously with rapid strokes as hard as he ever had in his life and, as they crossed the fifty yards or so of water between the riverbank and the island, he was sure that they would be caught. Coming towards them was the Wilhelmina's tender shining a spotlight ahead. The light from the spotlight was so bright that Caz thought that they must have been seen and she crouched down in the bottom of the dinghy, but they were outside of the main beam and it was not as powerful as Wilhelmina's searchlight which had been switched off. They reached the island within twenty seconds and McCabe drove the dinghy hard under an overhanging tree, its foliage reaching to within a few inches of the water. As the branches clawed at their faces and closed around them, they crashed into bushes that seemed to be growing out of the river, hung onto them completely hidden from view and waited in the darkness.

Neither of them spoke and they stayed low and watched through the foliage as their pursuers drew level with the first boathouse and shone the spotlight into it. Then they proceeded to do the same with the next one, carefully examining the interior and moving on to the next, probing with the light and examining the banks and gardens as they slowly moved downstream. McCabe and Caz watched anxiously as the boat with two men in it drifted past them twenty yards away. The slow current, with an occasional short burst of the engine to straighten their boat up, carried them down for a good five minutes as they examined the row of boathouses and gardens, searching for Summer Breeze's inflatable. When they reached the end of the row of houses they put out the spotlight and switched off the boats engine. Caz was not sure what was worse, seeing the two men hunting for them or not being able to see them at all.

"They want us to think that they've gone downstream. They know I was rowing and that we won't have got far without an engine, so it's only a matter of time before they come back and check the island. We've got to get the dinghy out of the water and hide it in the undergrowth."

"OK. What do you want me to do?" whispered Caz.

"Change places with me and I'll see if I can pull us into the bank."

As quietly as she could, Caz crawled to the centre of the dinghy and McCabe moved up to the bow. His eyes had become accustomed to the darkness and he could see the vague shapes of bushes with the occasional break between them. Grasping a handful of the nearest bush he pulled the dinghy hand over hand until it reached a gap. Grabbing the dinghy's painter in his left hand and a tree root on the bank with his right, he crawled over the side of the boat and onto the island managing to dip both of his legs into the water up to his knees with a splash. He lay still, face down on the earth smelling the damp soil and feeling the coldness of it against his cheek. He waited for a shout or for the spotlight to be turned on to show that they had been discovered. Nothing. No sound, no light.

"Are you alright?" hissed Caz.

"Yep," he answered, struggling to sit upright, "Come on, I'll give you a hand."

Caz crept forward and climbed out of the dinghy falling onto him in the process, something that he found not unpleasant as he let go of the painter and wrapped his arms around her to stop her rolling back into the river.

"Alright McCabe. That's enough." She shrugged him off and got to her feet.

He stood and they both listened for a moment for the sound of a boat engine, but they could hear nothing except the river's night noises and a breeze rustling through the trees above them.

"We've got to get the dinghy up onto the bank and out of sight before they come back," he whispered as he hauled on the rope and pulled the bow up towards him.

Inflatable dinghies are heavy - the Suzumar that he was hauling up weighed 40 kilograms - and they are awkward to handle out of the water, but if you can slide them, rather than lift, one person can manage them. McCabe was grateful that he hadn't attached the outboard engine to the boat which would have made it even harder to handle. Caz helped. They lifted the bow onto the thin line of low bushes at the water's edge and pulled until the centre of the dinghy was on top of them, then pulled downwards to pivot the boat over the bushes and dragged it until it dropped off of the bushes with a loud rubbery bang onto a small patch of open ground. The spotlight snapped on a couple of hundred yards downstream and they heard the boat's engine start.

McCabe, Caz and the dinghy were hidden from the river now by the overhanging trees and the dense bushes which lined the edge of the island and they waited as they heard the boat approaching. Light flickered through the foliage like sunlight on a summer afternoon as the Germans swung the spotlight to and fro, ignoring the houses now and searching and probing along the island. They drew level with Caz and McCabe and the flicker of light grew brighter until they could see each other dimly, but the boat carried on slowly past them as the two men looked for any sign of the dinghy. The search carried on to the upstream end of the small island then returned past McCabe and Caz's hiding place continuing downriver for a few minutes. They heard the engine revs increase and suddenly the search boat was roaring past them, still with its light probing the banks as it returned to the Wilhelmina having given up the search.

"They've gone," said Caz.

"Right, but we've still got to get back to Summer Breeze without being seen."

"Do you think that they'll still be looking out for us?"

"They will if they've got any sense," answered McCabe. "We were creeping around in their garden, after all."

"How will we get back?"

"The hard way, but let's wait and make sure that they've gone."

After five long minutes McCabe broke the silence, "OK. Let's go."

He stood and pulled the dinghy around so that the bow was pointing at the river and, together, they repeated the process of pushing and hauling it over the bushes. From there it was an easy matter to slide it into the water and, once it was floating, Caz climbed in. As she did so, McCabe took her derringer pistol from his pocket and quietly slipped it into the river, then got into the dinghy himself. They waited for a few minutes to make sure that the German's hadn't floated back to trick them, then McCabe pulled the bow of the boat to the overhanging tree branches and carefully leaned through to look up and down the river. In the distance he could see the Wilhelmina, deck lights blazing and crew on her deck with the tender tied alongside.

"OK, Caz. They've gone. Mind your eyes. I'm going to pull us through these branches."

The moon had disappeared behind clouds and, in complete darkness, McCabe began to row quietly downstream away from the Wilhelmina and immediate danger. As he rowed he thought of Tricia and how best they could help her.

Chapter Thirty Seven

Zac Battersby, sleeping soundly in Honeysuckle Rose's bow cabin, was startled by the crunch of the saloon door splintering as it was kicked in by Stefan Merk. Not one to wait for information in the face of danger, Zac swung out of his bunk and lunged for the cabin door, throwing it open and stopping in his tracks as a powerful torch was shone into his eyes by Ernst Kegel. Zac backed towards his cabin and the torch came after him.

From the darkness behind the torch a voice, distorted and muffled, ordered, "Stand still old man."

"What do you want? Get out," shouted Zac as the torch came towards him. An unseen hand in the middle of his chest gave him a violent shove and he fell back onto the bunk hitting his head on the hull lining.

The cabin light was switched on suddenly and now Zac could make out his attacker standing above him and threatening him with the torch which he held over Zac's head like a club in his huge fist.

"Be quiet, do what I tell you and nothing will happen to you," snarled Kegel. "Be difficult and you won't like what we'll do to you."

Kegel, mindful of Fleischer's jibe about leaving bodies everywhere was going to be careful this time.

"Where are Bronek Kowalski's things?"

"I don't know Bronek Kowalski. You've got the wrong boat."

Kegel grabbed Zac by the front of his pyjama jacket, pulled him up from the bunk and dragged him into the saloon where Merk stood impassively with his arms folded, having found the saloon's overhead lights and switched them all on. Kegel forced Zac to sit at the dining table and stood back. Zac saw that his assailant's chin and part of his mouth was covered by cotton wadding held on by tape, which explained why his voice sounded strange.

"Your friend McCabe told us that you have a guitar case belonging to Bronek Kowalski. That's all we want, so where is it?"

"I don't know, mate. I'm just the help. Chad isn't here and I'm looking after the boat while he's away." Zac knew that there were two guitars in the stern cabin and they would find them so there was nothing to be gained by stalling. "It's not in my cabin and it's not in here so, if it's anywhere, it must be in the stern cabin. Help yourself."

Honeysuckle Rose had a centre cockpit which allowed access to the stern and forward cabins by any intruder who came on board, so the doors were locked at night. Stefan Merk had already gone up the steps into the cockpit and Zac winced as he heard the mahogany splinter when the stern cabin door was smashed in.

Merk returned almost immediately with Bronek's guitar case, "Here it is. It has his name on it."

"Good. Go!" ordered Kegel.

As Merk left, taking the guitar in its case with him, Ernst Kegel turned to Zac and threatened him, "You stay here and wait for at least half an hour before you go outside. Do you understand?"

Zac nodded, "Yes."

Kegel turned, mounted the steps to the cockpit and clambered over the side. Zac remained where he was and listened to his attackers' footsteps disappearing along the wooden pontoon. When they had gone he stood up and put the kettle on, then he inspected the damaged doors already working out in his mind how he was going to repair them.

Chapter Thirty Eight

As McCabe quietly rowed them away from danger neither of them spoke until they had rounded the downstream end of Handbuck Eyot, putting the island between themselves and the Wilhelmina.

"What are we going to do, McCabe?" asked Caz, her voice a loud whisper.

He pulled steadily across the river and then turned the dinghy upstream before he answered, "We're going to row back to our boat and get away from here. Then we're going to work out how to get Tricia back."

"We're not going to get her back without help, are we?" She sounded frightened.

"No, we're not. We have to get the police involved."

"We should have done that from the beginning, McCabe."

"It wouldn't have worked, Caz. If you'd heard the man who phoned me you wouldn't have risked calling the police. I told you what he said. If I called the police, Tricia would disappear. And she would have done. She's OK at the moment but we've got to find out where they've taken her."

"How are we going to do that?"

"We'll talk about it later. Let's get back to the boat without being seen first."

As he spoke the moon reappeared from behind the cloud and bathed the river in a pale light. At the same time they reached the upstream end of the island and the Wilhelmina, on the other side of the river, came into view again her deck lights still blazing. McCabe rowed slowly keeping as close to the bank as possible, putting the tall trees which grew along it between him and the moon in the hope that in their shadow the dinghy wouldn't be seen. Nobody was visible on the deck of the Wilhelmina, but the wheelhouse, which was unlit, might still have somebody on watch in it.

They made slow but steady progress, feeling exposed and all the time expecting a shout and the searchlight to be switched on, but it didn't happen. In ten minutes they had passed the Wilhelmina and could see the line of moored boats and Summer Breeze in the middle of it. McCabe pulled the dinghy into the bank and they climbed out, relieved that they hadn't been seen. With Caz's help he secured the dinghy to Summer Breeze. They boarded and went down into the warmth of the saloon and collapsed onto the settee berths facing each other across the dining table.

Caz was the first to speak, "What now?"

"We go. We've got to get away from here before it's daylight and they see us. Dawn will be in another three hours."

"And then what? Police? We don't have to wait until daylight. We can call them now."

"Not the normal police. I have a contact, Caz. I'll call him in the morning and tell him what's going on. I promise you he's the right person to deal with it. I know what I'm doing."

For the first time since they had met at Reading Station she smiled at him, "I'm starting to believe you, Chad."

They took the time to make and drink coffee and then, working as a team, they cast off and without showing any lights pulled away from the bank heading downstream with the engine quietly ticking over. As soon as they had Handbuck Eyot between themselves and Wilhelmina, McCabe switched on Summer

Breeze's navigation lights and opened up the engine to a normal cruising speed, heading for Marsh Lock thirty minutes down river at Henley. They passed more islands: Poplar Eyot, Ferry Eyot and then, where the Hennerton Backwater joins the Thames, turned to port. Ahead of them, flooded with moonlight, was a long wide straight with dense woodland on their right, open countryside on their left, Marsh Lock in the distance and no other boats in sight.

As they reached Marsh Lock, Caz took a torch, stepped off onto the lock landing and walked forward to operate the electric gates. The lock was full and in their favour and she shone the torch onto the control panel, pressed a button and the gates slowly opened. McCabe drove the boat straight in and then climbed onto the boat's roof. Caz closed the gates and took the long bow and stern lines from him, passed each one around a bollard and gave them back to him. She walked to the gates at the downstream end and pressed the button on the polished steel panel, opening the sluices to let the water out. He felt the boat surge forward slightly and began to feed the bow and stern ropes out as the water went down until, after what seemed an age, the water in the lock had fallen 1.33 metres and was at the same level as the water outside the downstream gates. Caz pressed another button and the gates opened. He slipped the ropes and made them tidy then drove Summer Breeze slowly out of the lock and moored up to the lock landing on the starboard side to wait for her. She closed the lock gates and pressed another button which closed the sluices, then walked down the steps to the lock landing, boarded Summer Breeze and they pulled away and continued down river.

After half a mile they passed Rod Eyot another small island, this time with houses on it. As they reached the downstream end of the island McCabe steered the boat to port. Ahead of them were boats moored to the bank and, as they continued to turn to port to go around the island they could see more boats in a long line almost all the way back to Marsh Lock. It was the summer holiday season and, at this time of the year, Henley-on-Thames was one of the busiest towns on the river. They motored slowly along the narrow channel between Rod Eyot and the riverbank and saw a space just large enough for Summer Breeze. They pulled into it both jumping off when the boat had stopped and tying her fore and aft to conveniently placed mooring rings. They boarded again and McCabe switched off the engine and the navigation lights. They listened to the silence.

"Peaceful, isn't it?" he said.

"It certainly is."

"It won't be later. All of these boats are visitors so they're full of sleeping people, but it'll get busy when they wake up."

"And that's what we should do," she replied as she went down the steps to the saloon. "Goodnight Chad."

"Goodnight, what's left of it. Sleep well."

He went down the steps and switched off the saloon lights, then went through to his cabin and closed the door. He stripped off his clothes, washed quickly, fell exhausted into the double bed and switched off the bedside light.

McCabe was dozing off and half asleep when he heard his cabin door open and then quietly close again. As he woke he felt movement and then warm skin against his as Caz got into the bed and nestled against his chest. He put his arms around her and, without speaking, they fell asleep together.

Chapter Thirty Nine

The sound of McCabe's phone woke him at exactly 6am and, for a moment, he was confused as to why he was lying on his side spooning with a naked, sleeping woman, his right arm over her and his hand on her left breast. Then he remembered. The phone was insistent and he reluctantly turned over and picked it up from the bedside locker. He swung his feet out of the bed and sat there as he looked at the screen. Zac was calling him. He switched it on and put it to his ear.

"Zac."

"Hi Chad. I'm sorry to ring you so early mate but there's been a bit of bother here."

"Go on."

"Well I had a break in last night. A couple of hooligans busted in and stole one of your guitars."

McCabe heard a noise behind him and turned to watch, in the dim light filtering through the curtains, Caz, still naked, as she gestured that she would make a drink for them both. His eyes followed her as she left the cabin and then he mentally shook himself. Concentrate.

"Zac, are you OK?"

"Yeah, I'm alright. They pushed me about but that was all. They've damaged the boat though."

"Go on."

"Saloon and stern cabin doors. Smashed where they kicked them in, but don't worry, I can fix that."

"OK. As long as you're alright. Any idea who they were?" asked McCabe, although he already knew the answer.

"Don't know. They said that you'd told them that you had a guitar belonging to Kow… Kowel…"

"Kowalski."

"That's the one. They found it in the stern cabin and took it. I'm sorry, Chad. I couldn't stop them."

"It's alright, Zac. Not your fault. Don't worry about it. I know who they are and they're welcome to the guitar. I didn't know what to do with it anyway."

"I haven't called the police yet. Should I have done?"

"No need. I'm meeting them today about something else. I'll report it."

"OK. I need to make the boat secure. I'll find a timber merchant and get the bits. It'll be good as new by the time you get back, mate. Don't you worry about that."

"I'm not worried, Zac. Just so long as you're alright. I know you'll take care of everything."

"Bye then."

"Bye."

Chad cancelled the call and sat for a moment thinking of Zac. Dependable, practical, unflappable and a good friend. Between them they had restored Honeysuckle Rose and Zac, even though he didn't own the boat, had spent more unpaid hours and energy on her than either of them.

"Are you off the phone?" Caz called.

Chad stood up, put a towelling robe on and walked into the saloon. Caz had her back to him and was laying up two places at the dining table. She was wearing a thin white robe, similar to the one that he had seen her put on at her flat in Brighton when he had first met her the previous year. She turned and smiled at him and he saw again how beautiful she was.

"Are you hungry, Chad?"

"Not really." He glanced at the clock on the bulkhead," It's a bit early for me. I'd like coffee though."

"Already on its way."

Caz busied herself making a cafetiere of coffee and Chad watched her. Neither of them was going to talk about her visit to his cabin in the night, although all they did was sleep. He knew that he wanted more.

She brought the coffee to the dining table, poured two cups both black, and then sat opposite him with the table between them.

Now she had a serious expression and asked, "What's the plan then?"

"I have this contact," he answered. "Arthur Barnard."

"Police?"

"He says he's a sergeant in Sussex Police but I think he probably works for MI5 or similar. A bit of a mystery man. Tricia and I met him last year when we got caught up in a people smuggling racket which he called The Normandy Run."

"And nearly got yourselves killed. Tricia told me about that."

"Well I saw him again recently. You know that a guy called Bronek Kowalski was shot when we were about to do a gig?"

Caz nodded.

"I spoke to Arthur Barnard at Bronek's house after his wife was murdered a few days later. He said to phone any time day or night if I wanted him."

"OK."

"That phone call just now was Zac Battersby - he's a friend looking after my boat at St Katharine Docks.

He was calling to tell me that the boat was broken into this morning and they took Bronek's guitar."

"Is he alright?"

"He's fine. He's a tough old bird. Nothing much bothers him. I think that the two heavies who busted in on Zac last night were in that group we met at Beale Park yesterday."

"Why did you have Bronek's guitar?

"I tried to return it to his wife but she didn't want it." He thought for a moment, "Why did they want Bronek's guitar case?"

"There must be something in it that's important to them."

"Must be. I looked through it but I couldn't see anything out of the ordinary, unless …"

"Unless what?"

"Hang on a minute," McCabe stood, went into his cabin and returned with his laptop bag. He sat at the table again and rummaged in one of the bag's pockets until he found Bronek's flash drive.

"There," he said, putting it on the table between them. "Licks and tricks."

"What is it?" asked Caz.

"A memory stick."

"I know that," she answered, "but what is it?"

"It was in Bronek's guitar case. I had a look at it but the files on it are encrypted, so I've no idea what they're about, but I'll bet that's what they were after."

"Well done. That's it. We give them the memory stick and we'll get Tricia back."

He looked at her, his face serious, "It's not as simple as that. If it is what they're after they've already killed two people, that we know about, to get it. Do you think that they'll just give Tricia back to us once they have it? And, if it's so important, who else is going to suffer because of it?"

Her expression changed and her anger flared up, "I want my sister back McCabe. Give it to them."

"You forget that I don't know how to contact them."

"You can call Tricia's phone and speak to them."

"The phone will be switched off. They know that it can be traced if it gives out a signal."

Caz's anger increased, "So what do you want to do?"

"Yesterday they gave us three days to get the information. Today is Wednesday, and we've got until Friday before they get nasty with us. We're not even sure that this flash drive is what they're after. Let's talk to Barnard and get his advice."

Her anger subsided, "OK. Do it."

McCabe picked up his phone, looked in the contacts section, found Barnard's details and pressed the number. He held the phone to his ear and listened to the ringing tone.

A male voice, not Barnard's, answered, "Hello?"

"Can I speak to Detective Sergeant Barnard please?"

"There's nobody here of that name."

"I saw Sergeant Barnard recently and he gave me this number."

"I'm sorry. There's nobody here of that name."

The line went dead and McCabe switched off the phone.

"Well?" demanded Caz.

"They say that there's nobody there called Barnard."

Her anger was returning, "So what now?"

Chapter Forty

Tricia Knight slowly became aware that she was in the back seat of a powerful BMW car which was travelling at speed along a motorway. It was dark outside and through the windscreen she could see a large, illuminated, blue overhead sign appearing in the distance. As the car got closer she saw that it read Chamonix-Mt Blanc in white lettering and the number A40 in white on a red background. She kept still, as much as anything to stop her head throbbing and to keep at bay the feeling of nausea which threatened to overwhelm her. The driver and the man in the back seat with her were the two men, Klaus Stritter and Gunter Meise, who had taken her from the house in Shiplake, for which she was grateful because it had got her away from Ernst Kegel. She remembered the journey through Henley, then across country until they had joined the motorway system and had driven for an hour or so until they saw signs for Luton Airport. She had been thirsty and Klaus Stritter the man in the back with her had offered her a small bottle of water which she gratefully drank. Ten minutes after that she began to feel lethargic, then dizzy, and the last thing that she could remember was the car being driven into the airport. Now she was in another car being driven across France.

The water that Klaus Stritter had given to Tricia as they approached Luton Airport was laced with Rohypnol; enough to make her compliant but not enough to make her pass out. At the airport they had been met by another of Fleischer's men who drove the car away after they had removed their hand luggage and Tricia's shoulder bag from the boot. Stritter and Meise with Tricia walking dutifully between them had entered a private lounge where they were greeted by an attractive female receptionist. Not stopping to take advantage of the free champagne and sumptuous seating that was available, they had followed the greeter who stayed with them as they passed through security and passport control. The formalities were made simpler by the fact that Stritter had Tricia's own passport, which she had constantly kept with her in her shoulder bag since she had started to travel with Chad McCabe. Stritter had handed all three passports to the immigration officer who found them in order, handed them back and nodded them through. The receptionist guided them to a chauffeur driven Mercedes which took them the short distance to a waiting six seater private jet. The airstair door was raised and securely closed by the co-pilot as soon as they entered and they crouched their way under the five foot headroom to the front four seats; two facing aft and two facing forward. Waiting for them in one of the forward facing seats, impassive and immaculately dressed in a dark blue business suit, was Ulrich Fleischer. None of them spoke. Stritter had strapped Tricia into the rear facing seat opposite Fleischer and he and Meise took their seats on the other side of the narrow aisle. Without waiting for instructions the two pilots went through their final pre-flight checks and then started the Pratt & Whitney turbofan engines of the Brazilian built Embraer Phenom 300 and radioed for permission to taxi. Twelve minutes later they were on the runway and rolling, thrust levers forward, then nose up and after 700 metres they were being driven westwards into the sky by the twin jet engines at a seemingly impossible angle until they reached their cruising height. One hour forty minutes and 496 miles later they were descending onto the runway at Geneva airport.

None of the passengers had spoken throughout the flight; Ulrich Fleischer because he had contempt for all of them, Stritter and Meise because they knew better, and Tricia Knight because she was in a daze, dozing and waking intermittently. When the aircraft reached its stand, the co-pilot left the flight deck and opened the airstair, and Fleischer stood and exited, still without speaking. Stritter unbuckled Tricia and roused her from her seat and led her to the doorway followed by Meise. Fleischer had already been driven away and the two men helped Tricia down the steps of the airstair and the three of them got into another chauffeur driven Mercedes. Tricia noticed that the car had a Swiss number plate with its distinctive white cross on a red shield but her drugged brain made no sense of it. Their car had crossed the tarmac and left them at the doorway to a VIP Lounge where they were met by yet another attractive receptionist and led through passport control and customs without incident. When they left the lounge they were met by one of Fleischer's men who opened the doors of the BMW which was waiting at the kerb with its engine running. Tricia and Stritter had got into the back seat and Meise drove the car out of the airport. Switzerland has acceded to the Schengen Agreement and from there they were able to enter any other Schengen Area country, in this instance France, without any border control to register their presence. Now, having seen the Chamonix-Mt Blanc sign, Tricia closed her eyes again and listened to the steady, rhythmic, hypnotic hiss of the tyres on the road surface and slept as the car drove on through the night, not knowing or even caring where they were taking her.

In the early hours of the morning the BMW passed Chamonix and crossed the border into Italy and Tricia had woken up and was watching the road signs again, trying to keep track of where they were. She could see from the signs that they were on the E25 driving towards Turin, and lights high up in the distance suggested that they were driving through mountains. Three hours after leaving Geneva and before reaching Turin, they were in flat, open country and the car left the motorway. For ten minutes or so, they followed a smaller road until the car slowed and turned into a driveway. In front of them was a large house. The BMW stopped in front of the house and the driver got out of the car, opened the door next to Tricia, grabbed her arm and dragged her out of the car. She had just enough time to notice how crisp and cold the air was and that the tops of mountains in the distance were slowly appearing as the sun rose, then she was bundled towards the house by her two captors. The front door was opened from the inside, as if someone had been waiting for them, and she was led down a corridor, pushed into a room and the door was slammed shut behind her. For the entire journey from Geneva Airport to wherever she was now, nobody had spoken.

The room that she was in was similar to her room at the Shiplake house: a single bed, a wash basin, a small window with bars but, unlike the house at Shiplake, there was a door leading to a small bathroom. On the bedside table was a tray laid up with cold meats, cheese, bread, butter, a vacuum flask of coffee and a civilised china cup, saucer, sugar bowl and spoon. She sat on the bed and began to eat, even though she wasn't feeling hungry and she was hungover from the Rohypnol. In her mind, Tricia was beginning to think of ways that she might escape and, for that, she would need to keep her strength up.

Chapter Forty One

Arthur Barnard had returned McCabe's call within minutes and he apologised for the subterfuge.

"So sorry. It's a bit sensitive what we do here so we never admit to anything, even peoples' names, until we know who we're talking to. The switchboard records the incoming caller number and, if they check out, we call back. What can I do for you?"

McCabe, who didn't believe that Barnard was using his real name anyway, ignored that and explained briefly what had been happening until the policeman, or whatever he was, interrupted him.

"I think we'd better meet, Chad. Today. Will you be free for lunch?"

"Yes."

"Good. And bring Miss Knight with you."

They arranged to meet at a small Italian close to the river in Henley and at exactly 12.30 pm McCabe pushed the front door of the restaurant open and stood aside for Caz to enter. The room was opulent with mirrored walls, thick carpet, comfortably upholstered chairs and well-spaced tables covered with crisp white linen and silverware. Only half of the tables were occupied and it promised to be an ideal place for a discreet meeting.

McCabe had brought Caz with him, as instructed, but he was still wondering how Barnard knew that she even existed. Barnard was already waiting for them and he stood as the head waiter showed them to the table.

He shook hands with McCabe and then turned to Caz, hand extended, "Miss Knight, a pleasure to meet you. Please …" he gestured at the chairs and the three of them sat down.

"May I call you Casablanca?" asked Barnard.

"No. Nobody calls me Casablanca. Call me Caz but how do you know my name?"

"In my line of work, Caz, I have to know a great many things." He turned to McCabe, "And may I continue to call you Chad now? I think we know each other well enough."

"Of course and what shall we call you?"

Smiling, he replied, "Barnard will do." He continued, "I thought it better that we meet and compare notes. Tell me in detail what's been going on, but not until you've chosen your meal."

McCabe and Caz studied the menu for a minute while Barnard, who had already decided what he would have, waited patiently.

When they folded the menus the waiter approached the table again and they ordered: for Caz, parma ham and melon followed by fillets of sea bass with prawns, ginger and white wine sauce; for McCabe, sautéd tiger prawns with sea salt, black pepper and spring onions to begin and, for a main course, seared sirloin of beef slices served with mixed herbs dressing. Barnard ordered Prosciutto E Melone followed by smoked haddock with garlic, tomatoes, capers and olives. For Caz and McCabe a bottle of Chablis and, for himself, Barnard ordered an expensive bottle of Chianti of which he would only drink half.

The waiter returned to the kitchen and McCabe began to explain the sequence of events since he had last met Barnard outside Bronek's house in Brighton: Tricia's kidnap, the phone calls from the man with the German accent, the meeting at Beale Park, the failed rescue attempt at the house at Shiplake and the intruders on Honeysuckle Rose who took Bronek's guitar. The delivery of Bronek's letter to Shapiev's house in Whitechapel was not important he thought and he left it out.

A different waiter came to the table and poured the wines for tasting, then half filled their glasses and left.

Barnard had been sitting quietly, listening intently and, when McCabe had finished, he was silent for a few moments more until he said, "And is that everything?"

"Yes."

They paused as the waiter served the first course and departed with the words, "Buon appetito" as they began to eat.

"OK," said Barnard carefully inspecting a piece of ham on the end of his fork. "Why didn't you contact the police when Patricia Knight was kidnapped?"

"Because they said that she would disappear if I did," replied McCabe, "and I wasn't going to risk it."

Barnard looked thoughtful and said, "I can see that but let me tell you who you've been dealing with." He picked up his wineglass, first held it to his nose and then took a sip. "The man with the German accent is Ulrich Fleischer and he is one of the most dangerous and ruthless criminals on the planet. He was born in East Germany in 1961, the same year that the Berlin Wall was erected. As a child he informed on neighbours, his classmates' parents, his own parents and other relatives, to the Staatssicherheitsdienst - the State Security Service more usually known as the Stasi. At the age of 16, he left his polytechnic secondary school, and began a career working for the Stasi, quickly rising through the ranks. Fleischer was active in kidnapping, execution, and psychological attacks against anyone who was perceived to be an enemy of the State and he enjoyed his work. In fact, he enjoyed his work so much that when, in 1990, East and West Germany were reunited and the Stasi was disbanded he formed the SSV. The SSV is a criminal organisation which freelances for governments, corporations and anyone else who can use its services. The name SSV is shortened from Schild Schwert und Vergeltung, in English Shield Sword and Retribution, a nod of respect to the motto of the Stasi which was Schild und Schwert der Partei meaning Shield and Sword of the Party.

Fleischer has become hugely successful and wealthy from his activities. The SSV will work for anyone who will pay them, and acts as an enforcer and enabler in acts of terrorism, drug trafficking, kidnapping, arms dealing, the trading of human organs and anything else illegal that might turn a profit. Do you still think that you shouldn't have called the police?"

Caz's anger was rising as she answered, "I told you, McCabe." Looking directly at Barnard she asked, "What do we have to do to get my sister back?"

The waiter cleared their plates away.

"We've been aware of Fleischer's activities for years and we've been watching him," continued Barnard. "To the world in general he appears to be an everyday international businessman and he's never been prosecuted for any of his crimes because he remains at arm's length from them."

"Yes," answered Caz, her voice rising. She repeated, "But how do we get my sister back?"

"I don't think we do at the moment," said Barnard. "That's why I wanted to meet you."

McCabe chipped in, "Well we can't just leave her. You've got to do something. They've given me until Friday, in two days' time, to produce whatever it is that they want and I've no idea what it is."

Barnard looked fixedly at McCabe and held his gaze, "What does the name Shapiev mean to you?"

McCabe looked away, embarrassed at being caught out.

Chapter Forty Two

Quietus was standing on the towpath at Lashbrook Moorings and staring at the gap between the narrowboat and the white cruiser where Summer Breeze had been. Annoyed did not really describe it. Furious, fuming, now he blamed himself. He should have left the hotel in Reading, where he had stayed the previous night, earlier. Instead, having arrived at the hotel late, he had slept soundly and taken a late breakfast, secure in the knowledge that he had tracked McCabe down. Now he had lost him again and he wasn't going to continue the search. He had spent four days catching trains, driving from place to place, tramping across fields and along towpaths in the midsummer heat and it was time to quit. Enough!

He looked at the house on the opposite bank, still with the Wilhelmina moored outside, and imagined what it would be like to live there without all the stress that infected his life. He could certainly afford to buy a house like that with the accumulated fees of years of contract killing. Perhaps it was too large for him by himself, but slightly smaller would do. A plan was beginning to take shape in his mind - something that had been there unrecognised for a long time - and he made a decision. McCabe was going to be the last one and then he would retire from killing and live a normal life.

Quietus walked back along the towpath and turned left under the cool shade of the trees overhanging the footpath leading to the lane where he had parked his car. He felt pleased with his decision; one last job and then take it easy for the rest of his life. McCabe? As Jimmy the barman in Brighton had said, McCabe would be playing at Le QuecumBar in Battersea on the 2nd, which was the following evening. Quietus would have preferred to kill him in this isolated place by the river but he would find him in Battersea and finish the job.

Chapter Forty Three

"How can I help you if you're not straight with me?" asked Barnard.

There was an uneasy silence until McCabe answered, "I didn't think that it was important".

Barnard waited.

McCabe stalled, playing for time, and picked up his glass of Chablis and took a mouthful.

"Shapiev was murdered five days ago," said Barnard. "We found your name written on a piece of paper in his room."

"Murdered?"

"Yes, horribly. Just like Tushka Kowalski."

McCabe felt a chill pass through him at the thought of the old man and Tushka, both murdered in the same violent way and remembered that Shapiev had written his name down so that he could remember it.

"I was there delivering a letter from Bronek that his wife had asked me to take to Mr Shapiev."

"Do you know what was in the letter?"

"No, I didn't read it."

"Do you know what an Ezine is?" asked Barnard.

"I know," said Caz. "It's an emailed magazine or newsletter. I use one in my business to email information to a list of subscribers. It keeps customers up to date with new products."

"Exactly," said Barnard, "and that's what Bronek Kowalski and Alexei Shapiev were doing. Producing a monthly anti-Government Ezine which was emailed to thousands of their countrymen. They were revolutionaries with the aim of overthrowing their country's leadership. Not with guns but using the power of propaganda and the Internet.

"Which country are we talking about?" asked McCabe.

"Better you don't know, but it was previously behind the iron curtain," replied Barnard. "Fleischer has been employed by that government to eliminate the Ezine by killing those that were producing it and also to obtain the list of names that it was being emailed to. Shapiev produced the text every month and your friend Bronek was responsible for transmitting it to the people on the list. So Fleischer has succeeded in the first part of that, because he's closed down the Ezine, but we think that he is still looking for the list. He obviously thinks that you've got it Chad, or that you can get it for him. Could it have been in the letter that you delivered to Shapiev?"

"No, I don't think so. He only took a single sheet of paper out of the envelope so it can't have been a list of thousands of names."

They stopped speaking as the waiter served their main courses and they began to eat.

"We know that Fleischer's people searched both addresses thoroughly," said Barnard. "So if the list was there they would have it now. The fact that they are still holding Miss Knight and are pressuring you suggests that they haven't found it yet."

"Last night," said McCabe, "when they broke into my boat at St. Katharine Docks, they took Bronek's guitar in its case."

"Could the list have been in the case?" asked Barnard.

"If it was hidden in the lining perhaps, but I went through the case and I didn't find anything like that."

"What was in it?"

"The usual stuff: spare strings, tuner, things like that. A flash drive with licks and tricks on it."

"Licks and tricks?"

"Guitarist stuff. Short musical phrases that add colour to your playing."

Barnard looked thoughtful. "Did you look at the flash drive to see what was on it?"

"I tried to but the files were encrypted."

"Are licks and tricks so secret that they have to be encrypted?" asked Barnard.

"Not at all."

"So they've taken an encrypted memory stick with the guitar case," mused Barnard.

"No they haven't. I've got it in my pocket."

McCabe fished around in his hip pocket, produced the flash drive and placed it on the table. Barnard picked it up, examined it for a moment, took his wallet from an inside pocket of his jacket and carefully placed the memory stick inside it.

"I'll have my technicians look at that and see if they can decipher what's on it," he said.

Caz had been quietly listening but now she spoke with irritation in her voice, "That's all very nice but what about my sister?"

"Your sister is no longer in the country," replied Barnard. "Her passport was used at Luton Airport last night and she flew to Geneva on a private jet with Ulrich Fleischer and two of his men."

Caz raised her voice angrily and other diners turned around to look at them, "Well, if you know that, why haven't you stopped them?"

McCabe put his hand across the table and put it on top of hers as she realised that people were staring.

She snatched her hand away and, lowering her voice, she hissed, "Do something, Barnard. Get her back. Are you a policeman or not?"

Barnard ignored the question and looked at her for a moment without speaking, as if wondering what to do. Then, having made a decision, he spoke, "What I'm going to tell you must remain between ourselves."

"OK," said McCabe.

Caz just nodded and looked at Barnard with suspicion.

"Apart from closing down the Ezine," started Barnard, "we believe that Fleischer is planning a much larger operation. The Ezine is unconnected to it, a different job. We don't know what he's up to exactly but our intelligence sources are expecting a major terrorist attack in the UK. It's quite likely that Fleischer's organisation will be carrying it out on behalf of a terrorist group and we want to know what it is. For that reason we don't want to alert him to the fact that we are taking any more interest in him than we normally would.

"But what about my sister?" demanded Caz. "Somebody's got to go to Switzerland and get her back."

"She's not in Switzerland any more. They drove into France and then Italy. You see? We're keeping track of her and I'm sure that she'll be safe as long as they are still waiting for you to find the list for them. You said that they've given you until Friday. Is that right?"

"Yes," replied McCabe.

"Good. Then we've got two days to sort something out."

"How do you know that she's in Italy?" asked Caz.

"Switzerland and the countries that surround it are in the Schengen Area; no borders so free movement," replied Barnard. "Anyone arriving in Switzerland can go off, in any direction to other countries, without any more passport controls, which makes it easy to disappear with the whole of Europe to play in. Fleischer is on a watch list so they took an interest in him at Geneva. He stayed in Switzerland but his two men and Miss Knight were picked up on security cameras. They left the airport in a hired car. We know the make and number of the car and they are being tracked by cameras and our colleagues in Italy as they drive south. We don't know where they're heading for yet but, as soon as we do, I'll let you know. If we stop them now they'll say that your sister is travelling voluntarily with them. The reason that I think she's safe is because if anything happens to her they've already established an official link with her at passport control and we can trace that back to them."

"You'd better be right," Caz said.

"I just want you to leave it to us and not interfere for a few days in the interest of national security," said Barnard. "My Italian counterparts are watching them and also eavesdropping on their conversations; their car was bugged at Geneva before it was delivered to them and it also has a tracker fitted to it. If they believe that your sister is in danger they will intervene immediately. I certainly don't think that they'll harm her before you give them what they want or until they believe that you can't get it. What do you think that she would want you to do?"

Caz and McCabe looked at each other across the table. "She'd want us to help," said Caz.

"There you are then," replied Barnard. "We'll keep an eye on her and do everything we can to make sure that she stays safe."

In his heart McCabe knew that what Barnard had just promised was impossible.

Chapter Forty Four

The lunch ended with Barnard insisting that he should pay for it and standing to shake hands with them both as they left. The head waiter opened the front door of the restaurant and McCabe looked back to see Barnard seated at the table again tapping at the screen on his phone.

McCabe and Caz walked back to their boat along the wide tarmacked towpath, passing the empty bandstand around which hundreds of holiday makers were enjoying the summer sunshine on the lawns of Mill Meadows. Adults seated on rugs laid on the grass were enjoying picnics while their children chased each other squealing and shrieking, all oblivious to the dangers posed by Ulrich Fleischer and his like, all completely in holiday mode. On the river a constant stream of boats went by: small hire boats, large passenger boats running trips along the river, white cruisers and narrowboats. The atmosphere was festive and the noise was a cacophony.

"What do you want to do, McCabe?"

"I've been wondering about that."

They reached Summer Breeze and climbed aboard.

"I've got to play at a gig tomorrow night at Le QuecumBar in Battersea," he said. "Do you want to come to that?"

"I don't think so," replied Caz. "I might as well go back to Brighton until we hear something."

"In that case we can leave the hire boat here and I'll go back to my boat at St. Katharine Docks. I'll ring Phil Maypiece at the boatyard and he'll get one of his people to pick this boat up and take it back to the yard. I'm sure he'll understand."

Between them they tidied the boat up and then packed their bags. Together, they locked up and left, walking across the meadow between the army of trippers, through the car park and along the narrow alley that leads to Henley Station. McCabe bought two single tickets to Paddington and they waited on the platform for only a few minutes until the three carriage train came rumbling slowly along the single track into the end of the line station. They boarded for the twelve minute journey through the countryside to Twyford and, as they stopped at Shiplake Station, McCabe hoped that none of Fleischer's men would be taking the same train. Nobody was waiting on the platform and the little train pulled away again almost immediately. At Twyford they waited for twenty minutes until a slow, stopping train arrived and, nearly an hour later, they were at Paddington Station in London. It felt like an escape, a relief to be away from Fleischer and his men.

"Are you sure that you don't want to come to St. Katharine Docks with me? There's plenty of room on my boat and you're welcome to stay."

"Thanks, McCabe, I'd like the company but I've got some things to attend to in Brighton. Promise that you'll keep me in touch if you hear anything from Barnard, will you?"

"Of course I will. I'll call you immediately I know anything."

Caz gazed up at him and he was aware of an invisible energy passing between them. "Last night…" she hesitated for a moment, "it was nice to be held. It felt safe." She smiled at him and then leaned up as she had at Brighton Marina and kissed him on the cheek. "You're a good man Chad McCabe and I'm looking forward to seeing you again."

She turned and he watched as, oblivious to the heads surreptitiously turning to look at her, Caz weaved her way through the crowd of home going commuters. She reached the escalator and slowly descended out of view to catch an underground train to Oxford Circus, from there to Victoria Station and then a fast train to Brighton.

McCabe remained still, watching the top of the escalator where she had been. The delicious memory of her naked in his arms had come back to him. Finally he turned away and, lugging his rucksack and guitar, he walked to the station shopping complex and took the escalator up to The Mad Bishop and Bear, the nearest pub that he could find. He was in love with a porn actress and he needed a drink.

Chapter Forty Five

Battersea - 1951 BST Thursday 2nd August

"It's bad, Chad. We've all been interviewed by the police but they don't seem any nearer to finding out who killed him. When we play there we keep thinking that someone's going to walk in and start shooting. It hasn't kept the audiences away though."

Andy Mason, solo guitarist for the Reinhardt's Bar Allstars was standing by the low stage at Le QuecumBar and trying to find out whether McCabe knew any more about it than he did. McCabe was doing his best not to let slip that he knew anything.

"I don't know Andy. I was interviewed as well but they don't give much away, do they?"

"You can say that again. Can you make it to Brighton on Sunday, Chad?"

"Not this weekend. I have to stay in London."

"Bugger! I thought you'd say that. Without you and Bronek I'm stuck for a rhythm player and we've got a Sunday lunchtime gig at Reinhardt's. No way I can persuade you, I suppose?"

"Sorry, I just can't make it. Have you asked Roy Mechen?"

Roy normally played rhythm with a trio at Reinhardt's on Tuesday evenings.

"Not yet. I wanted to ask you first. I'm sure he'll do it. No problem."

Quietus, standing at the bar and drinking a tomato juice with trimmings, watched the two musicians talking and wondered whether he could engineer an accident here. He was beginning to tire of this job. If the target was like most people, who stayed in one vicinity

and had regular habits, Quietus could have studied him, trapped him and already killed him. He looked around the room and decided that McCabe was probably in the safest place to be right now, a restaurant full of witnesses. Every table was taken by people keen to see The Reinhardt's Bar Allstars, a lot of fans of course, but others who, although lovers of Jazz Manouche, had never seen them play but were drawn there by the band's recent publicity. There is nothing like a genuine, unsolved, violent crime to sell tickets and bring people in. Maybe after the performance, he thought, he could get McCabe on his own. The Allstars were taking their places on the stage, the room was settling down and Quietus knocked back his drink and put the glass on the bar, then he crossed the room and took his seat.
The audience chatter slowly subsided as, exactly at 8.00pm, Andy played Django Reinhardt's familiar, slow, fifteen chord tease of an intro to I'll See You in My Dreams. The Allstars joined him swinging into the number in 4/4 time at 190 beats per minute, McCabe playing the rhythm a la pompe, and the audience beginning to tap their feet. The Allstars playing for the first time without Bronek.

    Quietus watched McCabe intently. He had realised how he would kill him later in the evening.

Chapter Forty Six

It was starting to get dark outside and Tricia Knight was still coming to terms with her surroundings. She had spent yesterday at the house near Turin. Klaus Stritter had brought her food and drink at midday and again in the evening but refused to speak when she asked him where she was. She had slept well and this morning, after she had eaten another meal brought to her by Stritter, they had bundled her into the BMW again and, with Gunter Meise driving and Stritter seated in the back with her, they had driven past Turin on the motorway and continued through Italy. She saw a sign to Fossano where they turned off of the motorway and began to follow local roads to Cuneo, as they drove deeper into the Italian countryside and climbed higher into the hills. She had given up trying to make conversation with them and gazed at the passing landscape which, if she had been on holiday, would have thrilled her. As it was, she tried to ignore the fear which had been gnawing away at her since they had taken her from the boat at Sonning. The one comfort that she had was that she knew that Chad would be looking for her and would find her if he could. The fear still nagged though. How could he find her when they'd taken her to another country? She put that thought out of her mind and concentrated on where she was. The knowledge might be useful later.

After they had passed Cuneo, Stritter produced a black blindfold and tied it tightly over her eyes. Now all that she could do was guess what was happening. They continued to rise and weave on the twisting mountain road and eventually the BMW stopped. She was taken out of the car, frog marched into yet another house and pushed into a room. Her blindfold was removed and she was locked in. As far as she could tell, Gunter Meise and Klaus Stritter were the only other occupants of the house, but there could be more. Stritter had delivered a meal earlier and Meise had come in an hour later and taken the tray away. The room itself was almost identical to the one in Turin except that the window high up in the outside wall had a steel mesh over it and a small ventilator in the centre of the glass. Occasionally people would walk past the window and she could hear their voices, muffled and speaking French which, after their drive through Italy, puzzled her.

Tricia sat on the edge of the single bed and started to plan her escape.

Chapter Forty Seven

Le QuecumBar had nearly emptied and The Allstars were packing up their instruments and preparing to leave after another successful gig.

Quietus called across the room from the bar, "Anyone want to share a taxi to Victoria?"

McCabe answered immediately, "Sure, I'll do that." From Victoria he could catch a Circle or District Line tube train to Tower Hill and walk the short distance to Honeysuckle Rose at St. Katharine Docks.

"Are you ready to go?" called Quietus.

"I will be in a minute."

"I'll order one," replied Quietus and opened the taxi app on his phone and tapped in instructions.

Within minutes the taxi had arrived and McCabe said goodnight to the other band members. He and Quietus stepped out of the front door and acknowledged the driver who had got out of the taxi to open the boot while McCabe placed his guitar case in it. They settled in the back of the cab and travelled through the almost empty streets of Battersea towards Victoria Station on the other side of the river.

"Good gig," said Quietus.

"Did you enjoy it?" answered McCabe, "It's a nice venue."

"It certainly is."

The taxi crossed the Albert Bridge with its 4,000 white lights illuminating itself and the River Thames below and they sat back, not speaking further, for the short journey along The Chelsea Embankment then through Chelsea and into Victoria. At Victoria Railway Station McCabe insisted on paying the taxi driver after Quietus' mild protest that they should go halves, and

Quietus was inwardly amused that the condemned man was paying for his own tumbril.

The driver opened the boot and handed McCabe his guitar case, then got back into the car and it pulled away from the kerb, leaving them standing on the pavement.

"Which way are you going?" asked McCabe.

"Brighton."

"OK. I'll say goodbye then. I'm getting the tube to Tower Hill. See you at the next Allstars gig?"

"Of course."

They shook hands and McCabe went down the wide flight of steps leading to the Underground and the fifteen minute trip to Tower Hill.

Quietus waited for ten seconds and then went after him. When he reached the bottom of the steps he could see McCabe walking away in the distance. He followed discreetly. There were not many people around at this time of night and an underground station is the perfect place for an "accident"; one quick push as a train comes charging into the station and it's done. McCabe used his Oyster card to go through the barrier and Quietus did the same ten seconds later, tailing him down the escalator to Platform 2 which serves the eastbound Circle and District Lines. As Quietus followed the passage leading to the platform McCabe was out of sight and he could hear the slowly increasing rumble and rush of an incoming train about to emerge from the tunnel. Quietus reached the end of the passage and, through the arch leading onto the platform, he saw McCabe, guitar on his shoulder, facing away from him looking at the tunnel mouth. He walked out onto the deserted platform, looked both ways to make sure that they were alone, and waited. At last he was going to be finished with this job. Quietus felt the rush of air being pushed along by the oncoming train and, as it burst from the tunnel, he walked forward to stand immediately behind McCabe who was too close to the platform edge for safety. The train rushed towards them, rattling and deafening and, when it was thirty yards from them, Quietus reached forward to push McCabe onto the rails. As he did so he looked up and saw two long, white, box shaped cameras back to back twenty feet away and above him. One was pointing along the platform to the tunnel where the train had appeared but the nearest one was staring straight at him. Quietus stopped himself and stepped back as the train rushed past and slowed to a stop, then he turned and quickly walked back into the passage. As the train doors opened McCabe stepped aboard and took a seat in the empty carriage, unaware that he had nearly died under its wheels.

Chapter Forty Eight

St Katharine Docks - 0710 BST Friday 3rd August

McCabe was suddenly woken by the ringtone on his iPhone belting out the first ten bars of Sweet Georgia Brown; the Quintette du Hot Club de France version recorded in London in January 1938. Much as he loved to hear Jazz Manouche, it was too early for it. He glanced at his watch, swung out of his bunk and looked at the phone. A number that he didn't recognise. He pressed the green accept icon on the phone's screen anyway.

"Hello?"

Barnard's voice, "I do hope I didn't wake you, Chad, but we've got a lot to do today."

He had McCabe's full attention, "OK. What's happening?"

"I want you and Miss Knight to fly to Nice this morning."

"You've found Tricia?"

"We never lost her, Chad. She's stopped travelling and I want you both to go to France and be ready to meet her when we get her released. They went to France after Italy so we were waiting to see where they would lead us."

"And Tricia is alright?"

"We've no reason to think she's not, Chad. We've tracked them to a house in a village called Tende, in the mountains behind Nice, and the French police are keeping the place under observation. They'll get her out when it's safe to do so and you and Caz can be the friendly faces when they do."

"You know that today is Fleischer's deadline for me to give him the list, don't you?"

"I'm aware of that. Another reason for you to be out of the country," replied Barnard. "If he contacts you, tell him that you left Bronek's memory stick in Brighton and you think that must be what he's looking for. Tell him that you'll have it for him in a couple of days as long as Tricia is alive and unharmed. We'll have released her by then."

"Are you sure that she'll be safe until then?"

"As long as you have something that Fleischer wants, she'll be safe. Now, you haven't got much time. Your flight leaves at 1140 and you have to check in. If you wait by the South Terminal railway station entrance at Gatwick Airport, someone will meet you with the tickets and I'll arrange for a car to meet you at Nice Airport to take you to an apartment that's been booked for you. All you have to do is relax for a day or two in the South of France and I'll be in touch to tell you what's happening. Is all that clear?"

"Yep. I've got it."

"Good. Well try not to worry and have a good trip," Barnard disconnected the call.

McCabe sat there for a moment and then dialled Caz who answered almost immediately, "Hello?"

"Caz, it's me. I've just had a call from Barnard. He says that Tricia is OK and she's in a village in France called Tende. He wants us to fly to Nice and meet her there when she's released."

"OK. When do we go?"

"Now. Our flight's at 1140 from Gatwick. If I leave in the next half hour I can be there by 1000. Can you meet me then?"

"Yes."

"Will you travel by train?"

"Yes."

"Right," replied McCabe, "I'll meet you where the station exits to the South Terminal."

"OK, I'll be there. Bye."

"Bye," and he pressed the red cancel icon on his phone.

McCabe could hear Zac moving about in the galley and opened his cabin door, "Morning Zac."

"Morning, Chad. Coffee?"

"Thanks. I've got to go away for a few days. Are you still OK to look after the boat?"

"Sure thing, don't worry about her. We'll look after each other."

McCabe quickly washed and shaved, by which time Zac had coffee on the saloon table. They chatted briefly while drinking the coffee, but he thought it wise not to tell Zac that he was going to France in case Fleischer's men bothered him again.

Twenty minutes later he had found his passport, packed a rucksack and was heading for Tower Hill tube station. Twenty five minutes after that and he was back at Victoria Station, unaware that he had nearly been killed there the previous night. He queued for a ticket, then boarded the Gatwick Express and by 0930 he was at the airport where he waited for Caz to arrive.

Quietus had followed him all the way and was watching him from a distance while being hidden by excited holidaymakers milling about and searching for their check-in desks. What was McCabe doing? Where was he going? His phone rang and he answered it, not taking his eyes away from McCabe for a moment.

"Yes?"

"Have you done it?" It was Ricky Bishop.

"Not yet."

"What am I paying you for?"

"I'm busy. In fact I'm watching the target now."

"Well why don't you just get on with it and kill him and stop faffing about?"

"I'm working on it."

"You've been working on it for two sodding weeks. What's wrong? You not up to it?"

"I do things properly. The right time, the right place and…"

Bishop interrupted him his voice rising in anger, "While I sit in this poxy cell waiting for you to sort it out. Have you any idea what it's like in prison, trying to get things done by people who are too useless to do simple things? Sitting here with a stupid little phone up my arse which I have to fish out to call prats like you? I've paid you good money to do this job."

Quietus pictured him sitting on a bed in his cell, red faced and apoplectic, with his little phone held to his ear. He didn't bother to answer Bishop's question with the correct information, that he had no idea what it was like in prison because he hadn't ever been stupid enough to be caught.

"Are you still there?" shouted Bishop his voice rising even further.

"Yes, I'm still here and I'm busy."

"Don't you talk to me like that you freak!" shouted Bishop. "Psychopaths are ten a penny, mate. I can get a dozen people to do that job. I tell you what! I gave you a week, so you've got four days left. If McCabe's not dead by then I'll get someone else to do the job and, while they're at it, I'll get them to do you as well." His voice finally reached a crescendo that must have been heard by everyone in the prison wing as he yelled, "Now get on with it!" and switched his phone off.

Quietus put the phone back in his pocket and made a mental note that he would have to kill Bishop at some point in the future. It is a bad mistake to threaten to kill someone who kills people for a living. Sometimes Quietus killed people for fun and he didn't particularly need Bishop's work. At the very least, he would make arrangements to have Bishop dealt with if he was stupid enough to carry out his threat in the future. He turned his full attention back to McCabe.

Chapter Forty Nine

In her flat near Brighton Railway Station, as soon as the call from McCabe had finished, Caz Knight quickly dressed in designer jeans, deck shoes, and a white silk blouse. She packed a small, wheeled suitcase with clothes suitable for the South of France, located her passport and ate a hurried breakfast of two pieces of buttered wholemeal toast and black coffee. Carefully checking that everything that should be was switched off, she left a light on in the main first floor room that faced onto Queens Road, hoping that it would give the impression at night that the flat was occupied and would deter burglars. She smiled at the memory of the time she had first met Chad McCabe, the previous year, when he was doing just that - burgling her flat at the behest of her sister Tricia.

Caz glanced around one more time and then descended the narrow stairs to street level. At the bottom of the stairs she let herself out onto the pavement and double locked the front door behind her. With a lightweight navy jacket draped over her arm and pulling her flight bag behind her, she crossed Queens Road and quickly walked the one hundred yards to the station. There she bought a ticket to Gatwick Airport and caught the 0912 train which departed on time. As she watched from her window seat, the green fields of the Sussex countryside slid by and she daydreamed as she thought about McCabe, suddenly realising that she was excited to be seeing him again. The train stopped at Gatwick Airport thirty three minutes after leaving Brighton and Caz left the train and exited the station into the vast hall which is Gatwick's South Terminal. She immediately saw McCabe waiting for her.

"Hi McCabe."

She stepped forward and briefly hugged him and he felt his blood pressure surge as she stepped back and looked up at him, smiling.

"This is unexpected."

He was about to reply when an attractive blonde woman in a dark blue business suit, who he had vaguely been aware of for the last few minutes, approached them and spoke.

"Are you Chad McCabe?"

"Yes."

"I'm a police officer. Can I see your passport please?"

He noticed the red, go anywhere, airport security pass hanging from a lanyard around her neck as he took his passport from an inside jacket pocket and handed it to her, "Of course."

She studied it briefly, looking at the photograph before she passed it back to him and then turned to Caz, "You must be Miss Knight."

"Yes. Is there something wrong?"

The police officer smiled, "No, nothing wrong. I've got your travel documents. I was instructed to look out for a tall dark haired man and a stunning redhead and you two match the description. I was told to give them to you, Mr McCabe, but I couldn't be sure it was you until Miss Knight arrived. Together, you're unmistakable." She passed an envelope to McCabe with a smile, "Enjoy your trip, both of you. You check in at the North Terminal and someone will meet you at Nice Airport."

As the police officer turned away they both thanked her and watched her move through the crowd.

"Well," said Caz. "First class service with a smile. You obviously have influence."

McCabe was opening the envelope which contained two easyJet tickets for flight EZY8353 London Gatwick to Nice departing at 1140. He passed Caz's ticket to her.

"There you are. You don't often get an expenses paid trip to the South of France."

"I do actually, Chad. In my line of work I travel to all sorts of places on expenses. Did Tricia tell you that I'm giving it up?"

"No, she wouldn't discuss you with me."

"Because she knows that you're the kind of man I fall for and she wants to keep you to herself."

McCabe smiled at her, his confidence with her growing, "We should discuss that further, I think, but we've got to get a flight. Come on, we need to go to the other terminal."

They took the short walk to the driverless inter-terminal shuttle train, which transferred them to the North Terminal in two minutes, and found the check in desks for EZY8353 where they joined the shortest of the two queues. Quietus followed them at a discreet distance and had his phone in his hand as he tried to book a ticket for the same flight using the easyJet app. The flight was full. There were no seats available and McCabe was getting away.

Kill McCabe here? Not in front of all these people. All he could do was watch and make sure that they actually were going to catch the flight. He waited until they had checked in and then followed them until they disappeared into the wide entrance to the Departures Hall and the pre-flight security checks.

Quietus looked again at his phone and the easyJet app and booked a one way ticket to Nice on the next flight, EZY8357 departing at 1655. Then he made a phone call to a contact in Nice, arranging for McCabe to be followed from the airport to wherever he was staying and be kept under surveillance. He also made an appointment to visit the contact early the next morning. Satisfied that he could do no more, he headed in search of an early lunch and mentally prepared himself to settle down for the long wait until his flight was ready.

Chapter Fifty

The Airbus A319, which was flight EZY8353, flew in over the blue Mediterranean and landed at Nice Côte d'Azur Airport in brilliant sunshine. Five minutes later it had taxied to its stand at Terminal 2 and the twin jet engines were silenced two hours and eighteen minutes after taking off from Gatwick. McCabe and Caz negotiated baggage collection and passport control without any delays and, as they walked through the arrivals hall they saw a short, morose, thuggish man with cropped grey hair, wearing a crumpled brown suit. The man was holding up a makeshift cardboard sign on which the words Honeysuckle Rose had been scrawled. Clever of Barnard to use the boat name instead of drawing attention to their real identities, thought McCabe.

They introduced themselves to the man and, without speaking, he walked them through the airport and out to a dark grey Peugeot which was parked in a No Waiting zone. He took their bags and put them into the boot of the car with the cardboard sign then opened the back door for them to get in, Caz first. She slid across the seat to allow McCabe to climb in and the man closed the door and got into the driving seat. Beside him in the front passenger seat was an impeccably dressed man in his mid-forties who turned and spoke to them in near perfect English as the car pulled away from the kerb.

"Good afternoon. I hope you had a pleasant flight. My name is Jean-Louis Gravier and the gentleman driving is Monsieur Henri Girard. Mr Barnard asked us to meet you and we are taking you to an apartment in

Nice which you are welcome to use as our guests for the few days that you will be here."

Girard neatly manoeuvred his way through the traffic as Gravier was speaking and the car joined the Promenade Edouard Corniglion Molinier and then the Promenade des Anglais, following the airport perimeter and heading for their destination six kilometres away.

"Have you found my sister?" asked Caz.

"Ah yes, Miss Knight. We have," replied Gravier. "I understand that you have discussed this with Monsieur Barnard. He will have told you that she is in Tende and we need to leave her in place for a little longer."

"What are you waiting for?"

"Did Mr Barnard mention a man called Fleischer?"

"Yes," replied Caz.

"We are expecting him to arrive in Tende. When he does, we will have him and can charge him with kidnap. We have to arrest this man for a variety of reasons and this is our opportunity to do so. We will be able to hold him while more charges are brought against him."

The car had left the airport perimeter and was now heading into the outskirts of Nice along a wide dual carriageway with palm trees along its central reservation, white painted apartment blocks and hotels on their left, and a wide promenade and the Mediterranean sparkling in bright sunlight on their right.

"What do you want us to do in the meantime?" asked McCabe.

"We want you to relax for a couple of days and enjoy Nice. On no account try to contact Miss Knight's sister. I cannot emphasise that too much. We have the house where she is being held under observation and are sure that she is quite safe. If we decide otherwise we will go in and get her."

They sat back and watched the wide sweep of the bay open up, the beach, the sunshine, and a few minutes later the car turned left into Boulevard Gambetta and pulled up in front of a large apartment building.

Girard got out of the car and opened the door for them and then opened the boot to take their luggage out which he placed on the pavement still without speaking. They picked up their bags and Jean-Louis Gravier escorted them into the building as far as the reception desk.

As soon as the receptionist saw Gravier enter he turned and took a key card from under the desk, electronic and credit card sized. With a nod of his head and the word, "Monsieur," he handed the key to Gravier and went back to his paperwork.

Gravier walked with them to the lift and pressed the call button. He turned to McCabe and gave him the key card with a slight bow and then a smile to Caz. "There is no need for any paperwork. Please enjoy your stay and I will be in touch with you in the next day or two to let you know what is happening."

Caz and McCabe together said, "Thank you," and Gravier turned and walked away stopping at the desk to speak quietly to the receptionist.

The single lift door opened and McCabe followed Caz into the confined lift car thinking that it was small for the size of the building. She turned with difficulty, "Which floor?"

He looked at the key card, "Five. 521."

She pressed the button for the fifth floor and they stood in awkward silence, slightly too close together for comfort, as the lift clawed its way slowly upwards. When they reached their floor the door opened and he backed out into the corridor, followed by Caz. He looked at the key again to double check. An arrow pointing to the right indicated Apartments 520 - 525 and they found theirs immediately.

McCabe placed the card on the key pad and, with a click, the door was unlocked. He pressed down the handle, pushed the door open and stepped back to allow Caz to enter first. He followed her in, closed the door behind him and they left their luggage in the lobby and explored.

The apartment was modern. The lounge area was large with a marble tiled floor, a sofa, two armchairs, coffee table, TV and a large sliding door which led out onto a balcony the width of the apartment, overlooking the street. The balcony was equipped with two loungers, a table with three chairs, and waist high obscured glass panels topped with a hardwood handrail. They both stepped up to the handrail to look down at the street five floors below. McCabe went back into the lounge and then checked the rest of the apartment. A twin and a double bedroom, both with luxury bathrooms with bath and shower, a kitchen/diner with a table and four chairs, an electric cooker and a refrigerator fully stocked with wine, beer, milk, cheeses and other basics. On the worktop were two long, fresh baguettes still slightly warm from the boulangerie where they had been bought earlier.

He called out, "Are you hungry, Caz?"

"I certainly am," came her voice from behind him.

He turned, "Choose a bedroom, make yourself at home and I'll put a snack together."

Caz went to fetch her flight bag and he busied himself. In ten minutes he had arranged, on a large ornately decorated china platter, bread, a variety of cheeses, olives, cornichons, and put them, together with a bottle of Provencal Rosé and two wineglasses, on a large tray which he had found. He carried the tray through the apartment and out onto the balcony and placed it on the table. Caz was already reclining on one of the loungers in a turquoise micro bikini. She stood as McCabe stepped onto the balcony and he appraised her perfect, petite, tanned figure, not for the first time, but this time openly admiring her.

"You're looking good, Caz."

"Thank you," she said, smiling, and sat at the table. "This looks good, as well. And you managed to find some Rosé."

He poured and she took the glass appreciatively as he sat at the table opposite her.

"Cheers," she said and he felt a stirring as she gazed at him over the top of the glass, unblinking with her wide green eyes, the sun highlighting her auburn hair.

"Did you choose a bedroom?" he asked.

Still gazing at him, with the hint of a smile she replied, "I've put my things in the twin bedroom but I'll decide where to sleep later, Chad."

Chapter Fifty One

Quietus enjoyed his flight. It took off on time and he allowed himself the opportunity to sit back, relax and behave like any of the other passengers: business people, returning residents and holidaymakers flying south to the sun. He even allowed himself two small airline bottles of whisky to top up the half bottle of Moët that he had consumed with his lunch at Gatwick Airport. Not drunk but pleasantly mellow he allowed his imagination free rein to address the problem of killing McCabe. He always carried a passport with him, albeit a false one, and it was an unexpected bonus to be able to spend a couple of days in the South of France. Not what he had expected when he left his room at The Tower Hotel this morning with its view over St Katharine Docks and McCabe's boat. He would have checked out if he had known that he was going to France but, never mind, he could go back there tomorrow or the next day after he had dealt with McCabe. Maybe have a few days off and take advantage of everything that London had to offer as a reward for a job well done. That set him thinking about Bishop again but he would deal with it. He doubted that Bishop would carry out his threat and he still expected to be paid in full for the McCabe job, but he also knew that if Bishop welched on the deal and didn't pay, or if he tried to have Quietus killed, then Bishop's own end would be swift. As it was, he couldn't ignore Bishop's threat and he would terminate him anyway once he had finished with McCabe and been paid.

The aircraft had started its descent into Nice and Quietus looked out through the cloudless air towards the horizon 170 miles away but invisible in the distant ground haze, and then down at the fields and vineyards of France four miles below. He could deal with McCabe easily now. An accident was not necessary in France. Quietus wasn't known to the French police. He would hire a car and in the morning his contact in Nice would supply him with a handgun and tell him where McCabe was. After that it would be a simple job to shoot McCabe and leave the country. Assuming that McCabe was still in Nice when he shot him, it was a five hour drive to Lyon-Saint Exupéry Airport and, from there, he could catch a flight to London City Airport only twenty minutes by taxi from the Tower Hotel. Very neat he told himself.

His plan completed in his mind, Quietus sat back, closed his eyes and smiled to himself at the thought of finally completing the contract. Seventeen minutes later, EZY8357 landed at Nice Côte d'Azur Airport five hours behind McCabe and Caz's flight and taxied to the same stand at Terminal 2.

Chapter Fifty Two

"I've never appeared in a porn film! What gave you that idea?" Other diners turned to look as Caz flared up and she lowered her voice, "I would never do that."

McCabe looked confused and she frowned at him across the dinner table.

"I thought that's what you do for a living."

They had spent the afternoon sunbathing on the balcony and, when the day was beginning to lose its heat, they showered and dressed then left the apartment and strolled along the Promenade des Anglais arm in arm, enjoying each other's company as millions of couples before them had done. McCabe dressed in chinos, a casual light blue shirt and deck shoes, Caz in a white halter necked dress, stilettos, turning heads as passers-by took a second look at her mass of auburn hair and tanned features: the calm Mediterranean Sea, the palm trees, the beach, French cafe music from a beach bar all combined to create Nice's unique atmosphere. They had turned back before reaching Vieux Nice, the Old Town, and retraced their steps, stopping at the Blue Beach Restaurant not far from their apartment. There, facing the sea and warmed by an almost imperceptible breeze, they drank Pastis and both ordered the same meal from the menu, Salade Blue Beach followed by Scampis à la Provençale accompanied by a bottle of Château Pigoudet rosé. Now, having finished their meal, they had ordered coffee and Caz was sipping at a glass of Armagnac while McCabe swirled Rémy Martin around a brandy bowl and warmed it with his hands.

"Of course not," she said, still looking angrily at him, and then she smiled and laughed out loud and

McCabe felt a surge of relief flow over him. What she thought of him had suddenly become important.

"I make them, Chad. I don't appear in them."

"Sorry, I misunderstood."

"The business has been good to me. I've done well out of it: producing, directing, marketing, but I've had enough of it."

"What are you going to do instead?" asked McCabe.

"I don't know. I'm still deciding. I've had an offer from a rival production company. I might sell it to them. Have you seen any of my films?"

"I don't think so."

"You're not prudish are you, Chad?"

He smiled, "Not at all."

"I'm quite proud of my films. Lots of graphic sex but always with a story line. Not tacky. Erotica rather than sex for the sake of it. I've made quite a niche for myself but I never saw myself doing it forever." She gazed out to sea, lost in her thoughts for a minute until she said quietly, almost to herself, "I feel guilty sitting here enjoying myself while my sister is in danger."

"So do I."

"I'm not going to sit around tomorrow doing nothing to help her, Chad."

"According to our Monsieur Gravier today, she's safe and the police have them under observation."

"That still doesn't mean we shouldn't be worried about her. Remind me where they said she is?"

"In a village called Tende. I looked it up on Google Maps this afternoon. It's in the mountains, about 30 miles from here."

"Well I'm going there tomorrow. At least I'll be near her."

"I knew you'd say that," said McCabe, "so I looked up how to get there. A train from Nice Station in the morning goes straight there."

"And you're not going to try to stop me?"

"No. I'm coming with you."

It was getting dark. McCabe asked the waiter for the bill and paid with an American Express card adding a decent tip, and they finished their drinks. They crossed the Promenade and strolled the quarter of a mile to their apartment and again she put her arm through his. As they went through the lobby to the lift, the receptionist acknowledged them with a polite, "Bonne nuit monsieur et madame," and they returned the greeting. The receptionist smiled as they entered the lift. He recognised lovers when he saw them.

The little lift took them slowly to the fifth floor and, at the door to the apartment, McCabe placed the room card on the keypad. He pushed the door open and followed Caz in. She turned to look at him as he closed the door behind them.

"I've decided where I'm going to sleep, Chad."

"Where?"

She smiled at him, "With you."

Chapter Fifty Three

Tricia took Klaus Stritter by surprise; after 24 hours of the same routine he had let his guard drop. As he opened the door and entered Tricia's room, holding her dinner tray in one hand and returning the key to his pocket with the other, she launched herself at him. Although she was small, the sheer force of her attack knocked him back and he fell into the corridor with a crash of tray, plates, cup, saucer, spoon, knife and fork and he lay on his back for a moment, winded. It was enough. Tricia jumped over him and was away along the corridor, her goal in sight, the heavy oak front door. She got to the door in seconds and saw that the bolts were drawn open and she reached for the old fashioned iron door handle which operated a heavy iron rim lock. She forced the handle down and pulled at the door but it stayed tightly shut. She quickly examined the lock and saw a small lever on it. She pushed the lever down but it wouldn't move. She pushed the lever up. It moved and she pressed down on the handle again and felt the cogs inside pull a thick deadbolt from out of the door frame. She pulled at the door frantically and it began to open as she felt Gunter Meise's powerful arms circle her chest and lift her off of the ground. Kicking and cursing she was swung around and carried back to the room. Stritter was on his feet now. He grabbed her legs and the two men carried the helpless woman into the room and forced her onto the bed pushing her down with the weight of their bodies. Now she feared the worst and carried on lashing out, biting, swearing until she suddenly realised that both men had stood up and were looking down at her. She stopped fighting and glared at them.

"Behave yourself," ordered Meise.

Tricia didn't reply but continued to glare at them until they turned and left the room, locking the door behind them. She lay there and stared up at the whitewashed ceiling as tears filled her eyes. For the first time since she had been taken she was losing heart. She knew that Chad and Caz would be trying to find her but how could they? Alone in a room in France, she was starting to think that she would never see them again.

Chapter Fifty Four

McCabe awoke to see the sun streaming through a chink in the curtains and listened to the morning sounds beginning to build in the street outside. The single sheet that had covered them was on the floor, not required in the Mediterranean heat. He was lying on his back and both arms were around Caz who was draped over him, breathing softly against his chest. Her left leg was bent at the knee and her thigh lay across his waist as she clung to him, holding him to her still in the position in which they had fallen asleep, exhausted, four hours before. He ran the palm of his right hand gently down her naked body until it stopped at the top of her thigh.

She stirred and murmured, "No more. I can't," and then fell asleep again.

He continued to hold her and let her sleep for another half an hour as he listened to the street noises and marvelled at the turn of events that had brought them together.

Eventually, the gnawing anxiety of what might be happening to Tricia stirred him into movement. He stroked the back of Caz's neck and she gradually woke up. She rolled onto her back and stared up at the ceiling while McCabe propped himself up on his left elbow and looked down at her. He smiled at her and she smiled back and, for a moment, they gazed at each other sharing the secret known only to them.

"Good morning."

"Good morning you," she replied and reached up with her right hand and touched his cheek. She smiled again, "What have we done?"

"Something I've wanted to do since I first met you over a year ago."

"What took you so long?"

He leaned forward and kissed her gently on the lips. Then he got up and stood by the bed, reluctant to tear himself away, unable to stop looking at her as she lay there still smiling up at him. A police car raced by in the street below with its sirens wailing and the spell which had been cast the evening before was broken.

"We've got a train to catch," he said.

They showered together, taking longer than they needed to, and then raided the fridge for some cheese, eating it with the remains of the baguettes from the day before which were dry but, with butter, still edible. Several cups of coffee helped to drive away the tiredness that they both felt and McCabe phoned the taxi company which he had used before in Nice. At a few minutes before 9am he was paying off the taxi driver at Nice-Ville Railway Station. They stood on the pavement looking up at the white stone frontage and the three arches which make up the main station building, its ornate Arles stone sculptures and strangely contrasting steel roof all still as originally built in 1864. Crossing the wide pavement they went to the left of the main building and entered the ticket office, which looked more like a Victorian bank than anything to do with a railway system. There they joined a short queue and, within a couple of minutes, they were called forward to the counter behind which sat an attractive, dark haired, French woman in her late twenties.

"Bonjour."

"Bonjour," replied McCabe. "Do you speak English?"

"Of course, monsieur."

"Thank you." He was conscious of the fact that he should try harder with the French language. "I speak some French but it gets difficult with train times."

The woman smiled and graciously bowed her head slightly, "I understand, monsieur."

"We would like to go to Tende. What is the best way?"

"You must travel on Le Train des Merveilles, monsieur."

"The Train of Marvels?"

"Exactly, monsieur. It will leave here at 0917 and will arrive at Tende at 1124. Would you like two return tickets?"

"Yes please," replied McCabe.

"Then I can do a special deal for you, monsieur. I can sell you a Day Pass Alpes-Maritimes which will allow you to travel anywhere on this network for sixteen euros and, because you are together, your charming companion can travel all day for ten euros. Would you like that?"

"Yes, that would be perfect," replied McCabe glancing at his watch.

"Oui monsieur, you will need to be quick but you still have ten minutes."

The tickets were printed, McCabe paid with a credit card and picked them up with a smile and a "Merci" to the woman behind the counter.

"Monsieur," she said. "When you come back from Tende, your ticket will still take you to Monaco if you would like. If you do that, and you win a million euros on the tables, will you come back and share it with me for giving you such a good deal?" and she winked at him.

"We will definitely do that," replied McCabe and smiled at her.

With eight minutes to spare, McCabe and Caz hurried out of the booking office and into the station in search of The Train of Marvels.

Chapter Fifty Five

At the same time as McCabe and Caz were booking their tickets at Nice-Ville railway station, on the west side of the city Quietus was driving his hired Citroen C3 across the pavement into a car workshop brightly lit with fluorescent strip lights. He parked the car in the only remaining space, alongside three other cars which were all being worked on, popped the bonnet and stepped out closing the driver's door behind him. A waiting mechanic immediately came forward, lifted the bonnet and busied himself with the oil dipstick to make it look as though the car had a good reason to be there. Quietus was greeted with a nod from a muscular and darkly handsome man of about thirty, who knew him from previous visits and who was standing in front of a door set flush in the back wall of the workshop. The man opened the door and stepped aside as Quietus approached and closed it after him. He was in a short narrow passageway at the end of which was another door. As he reached the door it was opened, which suggested that a camera was watching the corridor although he hadn't seen one, and he walked into a room which was a comfortable and spacious office. On each side of the door through which he had just walked stood two men, handsome and similar in appearance to their brother who had met him in the workshop. He knew that they were the sons of the man he had telephoned from Gatwick Airport the day before; the Corsican known to Quietus and everyone else that he dealt with as Le Facilitateur, who now greeted him,

"How are you, my old friend?"

He spoke perfect English, was probably in his early Sixties, jet black hair greying at the sides, tanned and as handsome as his three sons. Immaculately dressed in a lightweight, dark blue business suit with a white shirt and dark blue tie, he rose from a high backed, black leather swivel chair and came around to the front of his antique desk to shake hands, towering above Quietus by a good 40 centimetres, partly aided by his snakeskin Cuban heeled Chelsea boots.

"I am well thank you and it's good to see you," replied Quietus.

Le Facilitateur, who would not deal with anonymous clients hiding behind a pseudonym had, years ago, ordered a complete background check on Quietus and knew his real identity, his address and a great deal more about him than Quietus would have liked. He gestured to one of the two visitors' chairs in front of the desk, "Please be seated. Coffee?"

Quietus, who would have preferred to complete their transaction and leave, smiled, "Thank you. I would like that," and sat down.

Le Facilitateur returned to his side of the desk and sat down as one of the sons immediately stepped forward with a tray taken from a small table in the corner of the room and placed two espresso cups in their saucers on the desk. He filled them both with newly made hot, black coffee from a silver pot, made no offer of sugar, then returned the tray to the table and took up station by the door again.

"So my friend," said Le Facilitateur, "we have three matters to discuss. The movements of a dark haired man and an auburn haired woman, the provision of a weapon and an insurance policy. Which would you like to discuss first?"

"The man and woman. Where are they?"

"Yesterday afternoon they arrived at Nice Côte d'Azur Airport. They were met by two men, not known to us, and they were driven to an apartment in Nice and were left there. In the evening they went for a walk along the Promenade des Anglais and had dinner at the Blue Beach Restaurant then returned to the apartment. This morning they were collected by a taxi and were taken to la Gare de Nice-Ville, and I was told as you arrived that they have booked tickets to Tende in the Alpes-Maritimes. They are probably departing as we speak. Do you want us to continue to watch them?"

"No thank you. That won't be necessary."

"We have a man travelling on the train with them. We will tell him to return."

Both men sipped at their coffee. Quietus wanted to go after his target and was resisting the urge to tell Le Facilitateur to hurry up, because he knew that it would be a mistake to do so. Instead, without realising it, he put down the cup and saucer and drummed the fingers of his right hand on the desk.

"I see that you are in a hurry. There is no need. It is about eighty kilometres to Tende by road and you can easily drive there in a couple of hours. You will probably arrive at the same time as your subjects." Le Facilitateur was careful not to use the word targets although he was well aware of Quietus' intentions, "Tende is a small, quiet village and it will be easy to do whatever you have to do without witnesses."

Quietus had stopped drumming his fingers and picked up the cup and saucer again trying to appear relaxed, but Le Facilitateur, useful as he was and friendly as he appeared to be, made him feel uneasy. So much power and as ruthless as Quietus himself.

Le Facilitateur continued, "Following your instructions we are supplying you with a weapon suitable for your visit."

The other son moved to the desk and placed an object wrapped in soft black cloth in front of Quietus then returned to his station by the door.

Quietus unwrapped the cloth and revealed a brown leather harness and shoulder holster containing a handgun which he removed from the holster. It looked like a short, black bicycle pump with a crudely shaped pistol grip attached.

"A Welrod Mk IIA," said Le Facilitateur, "developed by the British SOE during World War II and dropped in their hundreds to resistance units all over Europe. Antique but still in use today by Special Forces for close range assassination purposes."

"Yes," said Quietus. "I'm familiar with it."

"Then you will know that it is the most efficiently silenced gun ever produced. It has been serviced and fitted with new rubber wipes and is preloaded with five rounds of Sellier & Bellot 0.32 ACP. Bolt action, so it has to be manually cocked after each shot. I trust that will be satisfactory"

"Very satisfactory."

Quietus had practiced with this weapon before, always with perfect results. The bolt action to reload made it clumsy if more than one shot was required, but one close up shot was all he would need.

"Then that just leaves the matter of the insurance policy. I understand that you want the policy to come into effect in the event of your death. That is to say, in the event of your death by any cause whatsoever."

"That's right," replied Quietus.

"Are you expecting that in the near future?"

"No, but my life has been threatened and I'm dealing with it."

"And, if anything happens to you in the meantime, who will the beneficiary be, please?"

He slid a sheet of paper and a rolled gold Cross pen across the desk.

Quietus wrote on the paper Bishop's name and the prison that he was currently located in and slid the paper and pen back to Le Facilitateur who glanced at the name and address.

"You can be assured that the beneficiary will be eliminated in the event of your death. All that remains is the payment. Do you wish to pay a single, one off premium or would you prefer to pay a recurring annual premium?"

Quietus intended to complete the contract on McCabe and obtain the rest of his fee from Bishop, then kill or have him killed soon afterwards, so replied, "A single premium will be sufficient, I think. I will only require cover for the first year."

Le Facilitateur swivelled his chair to face a laptop computer by his right elbow and spoke as he typed, "Surveillance for 24 hours, one Welrod and a single premium for your die to win insurance." He moved the mouse and clicked it, and on the other side of the office a printer started up.

The son who had served coffee walked to the printer and removed the invoice, then walked back to Quietus and placed it on the desk in front of him. Quietus took his phone from his pocket and opened a banking app on its screen. He already had Le Facilitateur's banking details but double checked them against the invoice then added in the invoice amount and pressed the Send icon. "Are you sure?" appeared on the screen. He confirmed with a password and thousands of dollars were transferred across the Internet to one of Le Facilitateur's many bank accounts, in this case on the other side of the world.

Quietus looked up at Le Facilitateur and said, "Paid."

Le Facilitateur turned back to the laptop, pressed some keys and replied, "Confirmed. Thank you my old friend. It is always a pleasure to do business with you."

Both men stood and shook hands. Le Facilitateur bowed slightly and said, "I hope that we can do business again soon."

To which Quietus replied, "I hope so too."

He left the invoice on the desk and was politely escorted out of the office by the son who had served him coffee, who also picked up the pistol from the desk. As soon as they entered the workshop, he gave Quietus a slight bow and handed him the Welrod and holster wrapped again in its black cloth.

The Citroen was waiting where he had left it and the bonnet was closed. Quietus got into the car and turned it around, driving carefully out onto the street still in the shadow cast by its tall buildings. At the end of the street he pulled over and stopped. He turned on the air conditioning, programmed the Sat Nav for Tende, tuned to Riviera Radio, then drove away to find the glorious Côte d'Azur sunshine and the road which would take him up into the Alpes-Maritimes. That was where he would shoot and kill Chad McCabe.

Chapter Fifty Six

The Train of Marvels climbed steadily upwards into the Alpes-Maritimes until, just over two hours after leaving Nice, they arrived at Tende Railway Station 823 metres above sea level. Tende is a mediaeval village of approximately 2,000 souls close to the Italian border and surrounded by mountains. It has changed nationality several times in the last thousand years. Prior to 1947 it was Italian for nearly 90 years but, as part of the penalty for choosing the wrong side in World War II and mounting a small opportunistic alpine invasion in 1940, the Italians were obliged to cede the village and surrounding mountains to France. Some of the inhabitants still speak a language called Tendasque, some speak Italian and all speak French. Tende's economy is based on farming and hydroelectric production and it also attracts climbers who are drawn to the via ferrata (iron way in Italian) above the village - a kind of "safe" climb, already prepared, with steel cables and ladders waiting to be clipped onto. The village has a public swimming pool, a museum notable for its huge collection of Bronze Age rock engravings, and a railway station.

McCabe held out his hand and helped Caz to step down from The Train of Marvels. They had found it easily enough at Nice Station, modern, streamlined, blue and silver and painted with images of rock carvings and village names. The train was made up of three carriages with the front carriage bearing the legend Train des Merveilles in stylish white lettering. They found seats in the middle carriage and the train left immediately, steadily lifting them into the mountains through a constantly changing landscape of small towns, lush greenery, high rock faces, viaducts and tunnels. An English commentary by a guide, in her mid-twenties and employed by the railway, made the journey even more interesting. By the time they reached Tende, Caz and McCabe had acquired a holiday feeling which quickly evaporated as the train stopped and they remembered why they were there.

They left the station and were standing in an expansive car park, dusty in the glaring sunshine and looking like the bottom of a quarry. In front of them towered high stone crags and, in front of the crags, ran a road from left to right. They walked between buildings a hundred metres to the road and looked along it in both directions. To the right the buildings petered out so they were clearly on the edge of town. They turned left onto an attractive street, which a sign proclaimed was the Avenue du 16 Septembre 1947, and strolled hand in hand towards the centre of the village quickly realising that they would never find Tricia just by wandering around aimlessly. They were also aware that they were not supposed to find her. McCabe wondered what Barnard would say if he knew that they had defied him and come to the place where Tricia was being held.

They had passed surprisingly few people as they walked and, like all small villages in France, the streets seemed to be almost deserted. Perhaps because it was nearly lunchtime. Agreeing that it would be good to eat and develop some sort of plan of action, they went back a short distance to a small restaurant which displayed a sign in the window offering "Cuisine familiale". There they were welcomed and led to a window table by a smiling waitress who made sure that they were comfortably seated and then brought them a carafe of water with two glasses. At the same time she gave them each a printed card with the day's lunch menu on it.

Glancing around, McCabe saw that there were half a dozen tables, all with checked tablecloths, and the other diners appeared to be single men sitting on their own and trying not to stare at Caz.

"Home cooking," said Caz, "exactly as it says on the window and exactly what I would like."

"Oui Madame, cuisine familiale," replied the waitress smiling again. "Would you like to order drinks?"

"I think I would just like water, thank you," answered McCabe, and Caz nodded and said, "Moi aussi, s'il vous plait."

The waitress smiled again and headed for the kitchen and they looked at the menu cards. No choice, just a statement of what they were about to be served; a plat du jour. There followed a simple but delicious meal beginning with egg mayonnaise and then pork chops in a white sauce with boiled potatoes and roasted celeriac.

As the waitress cleared their plates she asked if they would like a dessert, "It is not on the menu, but it is made with eggs and vanille and I don't know what you will call it in English, but I will fetch Madame."

The waitress went to the kitchen and returned with a mumsy lady who very much suited a restaurant that serves home cooking.

"Monsieur," she said, "The dessert, in France, we call it crème brûlée," and looked surprised when Caz laughed.

"That is what we call it in England, also," said McCabe. "Yes please." He looked at Caz who nodded, still smiling, "For two."

Madame, chuckling to herself, and the waitress, flustered at having wasted Madame's time, hurried back to the kitchen and Caz suddenly looked upset.

"It doesn't seem to be right to be laughing and enjoying ourselves when my sister is somewhere nearby putting up with God knows what."

"I know, but we'll have her back soon," he replied.

"Coming to Tende has made it worse somehow. If she's here we're so close."

McCabe reached across the table and put his hand on top of hers, "But Barnard and the French police who we met yesterday want us to be patient. I'm sure they won't let anything happen to her. Remember? They said that they're watching the place where she's being held."

The waitress arrived with the dessert and asked if they would like coffee, to which they both said yes.

McCabe paid the bill and, as they were finishing the coffee, Caz who had been gazing at the street through the wide plate glass window, suddenly started and exclaimed loudly, "It's him!"

The other diners stared at her as McCabe glanced up and saw, on the other side of the street, one of Fleischer's men. They had seen him on the Thames riverbank at Beale Park dragging Tricia back onto the Wilhelmina, and again at the house at Shiplake bundling Tricia into a car. Strolling past the restaurant was Klaus Stritter.

Excited, Caz jumped to her feet, almost knocking over the table and McCabe rose and stopped her from rushing out of the restaurant and confronting Stritter. Within twenty seconds they had said goodbye to Madame and the waitress, "Au revoir"ed the other diners, who had now had their thoughts about mad English confirmed, and they were outside and following

Stritter. They kept their distance in the sure knowledge that he was going to lead them to Tricia.

The street was still empty of people and only the occasional passing car disturbed the silence. They hung back until Stritter was a good hundred yards ahead of them and quietly followed as he led them away from the village centre and station, south along the narrow, steep sided valley carved out by the Roya River. Stritter was carrying a shopping bag with two long loaves sticking out of it and, as part of his shopping trip, he had visited two bars and drunk three beers. He strolled along in the sunshine swinging the bag, enjoying the walk and looking very unlike the criminal thug that he actually was.

For five minutes, taking care not to alert him, they followed Stritter as, oblivious and enjoying the after-effects of the beers, he ambled along the narrow road away from the village. After a quarter of a mile the houses on the left thinned out and they were following a low wall. On the other side of the wall was a short, steep drop to lawns, trees, more houses, the river, and beyond was a view of the mountain peaks in the near distance. At any other time they would have loitered and studied that view but now they walked on without speaking, intent on following Stritter. They passed two more houses on their left with front doors which opened onto the road, isolated, semi-detached, two storied, hanging on to the side of the hill and, like all of the buildings in Tende, ruggedly designed to withstand the alpine cold of winter. In front of them a line of cars was parked beside the wall they were following and, watching Stritter, they failed to notice Quietus sitting in one of them. He turned away in case they saw his face and then, as McCabe and Caz walked past him, he took the Welrod pistol from the glove compartment, got out of the car and after quietly closing its door he followed them. He reasoned that, apart from the man with the bread who had walked past him a minute before, the French were all in their houses either enjoying lunch or a postprandial nap. The streets were deserted and this was his opportunity to kill McCabe and the woman. A close up, silenced shot in the head, McCabe first, then the woman and he would push them over the wall and they would drop into the vegetation below. Back into his car and he would drive out of the village with no one even aware that anything had happened. He holstered the gun under his jacket and quietly followed, getting closer to them at each step. If McCabe had turned around he would have seen Quietus only a few yards behind and he would have recognised him and stopped, but neither he nor Caz looked back. In a silent procession they carried on, unaware that because they had ignored Jean-Louis Gravier's warning and come to Tende, someone would die this afternoon.

Chapter Fifty Seven

If Klaus Stritter had looked back he would have seen McCabe and Caz following him still one hundred metres behind but, in his pleasantly comfortable beer haze, he was concentrating on his destination only another thirty metres ahead. He was passing, on his left, a solitary three storey house built onto the high edge of the valley which dropped away steeply, immediately behind it. The front elevation of the house was built close up to the road with windows facing the line of houses opposite, each of which had an integral garage at ground level and wide-open windows on the upper levels facing across the valley. At the far end of the building Stritter suddenly turned left and disappeared from view. When McCabe and Caz reached the place where he had vanished Stritter was not there and they saw a short flight of concrete steps leading down to a small courtyard, two sides of which were formed by the L shape of the house. To their right the end of the courtyard was contained by a low wall, so Stritter must have gone into the house through the single door in front of them on the other side of the yard. Caz, impetuous as always, ran down the steps before McCabe could stop her, crossed the courtyard and began hammering on the door. He caught up with her and began to pull her away as Quietus reached the top of the steps. Seeing them both in the courtyard, he pulled the Welrod from its holster inside his jacket and started down the steps. The door was thrown open and Gunter Meise stood there. He saw Caz, he saw McCabe, then he saw Quietus twenty feet away with a gun in his hand. Reaching behind him Meise pulled a handgun from his waistband. Quietus, seeing the gun in Meise's hand, hastily fired at him and missed. McCabe pulled Caz to the ground and attempted to cover her with his body. As Quietus struggled to pull back the bolt to load another round into the chamber of the Welrod, Meise fired two shots at him hitting him in the chest and killing him instantly. A rifle shot, fired from an open first floor window of the building opposite, echoed around the valley and Meise, with a surprised look on his face fell dead in the doorway. There was silence for a few seconds that seemed to go on forever until the garage door set into the wall of the house where the rifle had been fired from was pushed out and upwards. Out of the garage came black clad men from the anti-terrorist unit RAID, weapons raised, racing across the narrow road. Four of the men simultaneously blew in the two ground floor windows with frame charges and swiftly climbed through them into the house. Four more charged down the steps into the courtyard. One of them grabbed McCabe and another grabbed Caz, hauling them to their feet as they turned then dragged and half carried them up the steps and across the road. The other two entered the house through the front door. McCabe thought he fleetingly saw George Lee, the Reinhardt's Bar Allstars' violin player, lying in the courtyard with the Welrod pistol in his hand. Shocked by the gunfire and the sound of the explosions, McCabe and Caz were manhandled through the still open garage door and pushed to the floor face down. Their hands were bound with cable ties and they were quickly searched for weapons. They looked into each other's eyes, Caz looking stunned, McCabe talking to her, "It's OK, they're police."

    Voices around them were speaking loudly in French and they were hauled to their feet again. The cable ties were cut. At the back of the garage was a line of six white plastic garden chairs side by side and they were frog marched to them and made to sit together in the two centre chairs. Two of the RAID men stood facing them to make sure that they stayed put. Now they could see the road through the open garage door and, in bright sunlight and framed by the door opening as if in a widescreen movie, the house opposite with its ground floor windows blown in. Police from the Gendarmerie Nationale with automatic weapons at the ready were standing guard beside what was left of the windows. The remains of the wooden window frames were gently smoking. The gendarme on the left faced up the road, the female gendarme on the right faced down. McCabe and Caz could see the top of the steps but not down into the courtyard. A policeman appeared at the top of the steps, followed by Tricia looking confused and helped by a woman in civilian clothes. They led Tricia to the garage and, as they entered, Caz unable to contain herself, leapt to her feet and, ignoring the men guarding them, rushed forward and stopped in front of her. Tricia, her eyes not yet adjusted to the gloom of the garage, stepped back and then, realising who it was, threw herself at Caz and the sisters hugged each other crying and laughing at the same time.

McCabe got to his feet and a voice beside him said quietly, "When I collected you from the airport, I asked you on no account to try to find Miss Knight's sister but to leave it to us. You have created something of a problem for us, Monsieur McCabe."

He was reminded of Arthur Barnard saying something similar to him on a patrol boat in the English Channel the previous year, and turning to the speaker he saw Jean-Louis Gravier.

Chapter Fifty Eight

Arthur Barnard sat back in the comfortable armchair and sipped a small cognac, "I've smoothed things over with Monsieur Gravier but he's not happy with the way his operation was blown. He's lost the chance to catch Ulrich Fleischer in the act."

They were back in the apartment in Nice: McCabe, Tricia, Caz, and Barnard who had joined them to discuss what had happened.

Events had moved quickly and they had been driven by police car from Tende to Nice and delivered to the apartment to find Barnard waiting for them. The building was now guarded by plain clothes police who had taken over the whole of the fifth floor. Perhaps they'd already controlled the fifth floor, thought McCabe. Perhaps the police owned the whole building.

The apartment had been serviced while they had been in Tende: the fridge restocked, the bedding changed, and the only evidence that Caz and McCabe had previously occupied the place was their luggage and clothes which were still where they had left them.

The two sisters, like excited teenagers, had gone into the twin bedroom and were chattering to each other while McCabe and Barnard were left on their own to talk.

Barnard continued, "When you get back to England I'm sure that Fleischer's people will be waiting for you and will still want Bronek Kowalski's memory stick."

He reached into an inside pocket of his jacket and produced the flash drive from his wallet, passing it to McCabe who recognised it as the one he had given to Barnard in Henley three days before.

"We've finished with it," said Barnard.

McCabe looked at him, puzzled, "What do you want me to do with it?"

"I want you to give it to Fleischer."

"There was nothing of interest on it then?"

"On the contrary," replied Barnard. "My people discovered that it contains the names and addresses of all of the dissidents on Kowalski's emailing list. Absolute gold dust to Fleischer's client and very useful for us. You are not to know that when Fleischer's people pick you up."

McCabe thought that any new meeting with Fleischer's men, now that they had Tricia back, was unnecessary and dangerous and he said so, "I have no intention of ever meeting them again."

"Unavoidable Chad. They still want the memory stick and they believe that you've got it. They'll hunt you until they have it. They might even kidnap Miss Knight again. Once they have it, I think they'll leave you alone. Especially if they think that you don't know what's on it. I have another request for you," Barnard paused.

"Go on," replied McCabe taking a sip at his glass of chilled rosé.

"In an obtrusive way you've been very helpful to me Chad, what with The Normandy Run last year and now Fleischer. I wonder if you would like to work for me in the future?"

McCabe smiled, "I'm very flattered but I don't need a job. I'm too busy sailing and making music."

"Not a job, Chad, but an informal arrangement. I have agents in many walks of life who are my eyes and ears. I would like you to be one of those. I can't pay you I'm afraid but you would be helping your country and I don't think that you would find it too onerous. You might be in the right place to check something out for me occasionally or you might let me know if you see something that you think I should know about. That sort of thing."

McCabe thought for a moment then said, "I could do that. I'd be glad to help if I can."

Barnard smiled and raised his glass towards McCabe, "Thank you. I knew you would be."

They clinked glasses and Barnard sealed the deal with, "This is solely between us of course."

"Of course," replied McCabe.

"Can I have your phone please, Chad. I'm going to give you my direct number so that you can contact me at any time."

McCabe found Barnard in the Contacts section and handed over his iPhone. Barnard quickly keyed the phone number in.

He handed the phone back to McCabe and said, "Good! So the first thing you can do for me will be to deliver that flash drive to Fleischer."

"Really?"

"Really."

"I'm puzzled," said McCabe. "Why do you want me to give Fleischer the email list?"

"Can't tell you yet but I will at some point. Better you don't know at this stage."

"OK. Fleischer was expecting it yesterday so he'll probably be getting pretty angry about it by now. At least he doesn't know where I am."

"I'm sure that he does," replied Barnard. "He has his agents the same as I do. He can't get to you in this building, so we'll have your meals sent in and give you a day to rest up here. On Monday we'll arrange an escort all the way onto the aircraft for you but, as soon as you're back in London, he'll find you. We'll keep an eye on you when he does."

"You're going to have me followed?"

"For your safety, yes, but once you've handed the memory stick over you should be safe enough, so it won't be necessary after that. Let's talk about something else - the gunman who was following you at Tende."

"Strange how your mind plays tricks," said McCabe. "I only had a brief glimpse of him but he looked like someone I know."

"Who is that?"

"A guy called George Lee. I last saw him when we played at a gig in London two days ago.

"You're correct," said Barnard. "It was George Lee your violin player."

McCabe looked shocked, "So it was him. That's crazy. What would George be doing in Tende with a gun?"

"We think he was there to kill you."

"But he's - was - a friend of mine. Why would he want to kill me and how do you know that he was the Allstars violin player?"

"We know all of your acquaintances, Chad. You've been thoroughly vetted. I wouldn't have asked you to work for me otherwise. The body has been fingerprinted and the prints were checked on various databases. There was a positive result on the FBI database - they matched an English tourist, George Lee, routinely fingerprinted as he entered America at Dallas Fort Worth International Airport. He was changing flights en route from London to Guatemala several years ago. That's all we had but you've just confirmed that you recognised him so we'll take it that George Lee is his true identity."

"But that doesn't mean that George would want to kill me," answered McCabe, refusing to believe that his friend George would do such a thing.

"Ah, but there's more to it than that," said Barnard. "Do you remember the officer who gave you your tickets at Gatwick?"

"Yes."

"She noticed George Lee watching you from a distance at the airport, so she and a couple of her colleagues took an interest in him. He followed you to the airline check-in desk and, after you went airside, he booked himself onto the next flight to Nice. When he went through immigration they got his passport details. Not George Lee, by the way, but a different name, so we know that he was travelling on a false passport. When he arrived at Nice Airport the French police watched him for us and, this morning, he visited a car workshop which is a front for a well known local fixer called Blanchet - someone who arranges things for out of town criminals. After the shooting at Tende the police visited the workshop and spoke to Blanchet but they didn't get anything out of him. We believe that he supplied Lee with the World War II pistol that he had when he was shot - a pistol designed specifically for close up assassination by the way - and all the signs are that George Lee was a hitman. Blanchet says that he didn't meet him but, according to his staff, Lee had visited them to enquire about the cost of a car service. When questioned and asked why would George Lee want a hire car serviced he replied that he didn't know but the English were strange people and often eccentric."

McCabe looked thoughtful and then looked at Barnard, "You know, I often wondered what George lived on. He had a champagne lifestyle and no visible means of support except playing the violin, and he didn't do that very often as far as I could tell. Why do you think that he would want to kill me?"

"Just another job," replied Barnard. "Probably nothing personal. At first we thought that he was working for Fleischer but, if he was, Fleischer's man at Tende wouldn't have shot him. Who do you think might want you dead?"

McCabe scanned his memory for anyone who had enough of a grudge against him to want him killed, "Frik Benniker, Graham Allerton, Ricky Bishop, Bishop's two sidekicks."

"Exactly," answered Barnard. "All in prison now because of your efforts to break up their rackets last year. You can discount Benniker because, however much he must hate you, he wouldn't have the money to pay a hitman; neither would Bishop's thugs. Allerton might have had the money but all of his assets have been seized under a proceeds of crime order. That leaves Ricky Bishop. His assets were seized, but I don't think all of them. He could afford it and he has plenty of reasons to want you dead."

A bedroom door flew open and Tricia and Caz burst into the room giggling at some private joke. They threw themselves onto the sofa and looked at Barnard and McCabe in turn.

"So serious," laughed Caz. "Come on, we've got my sister back. We should be celebrating."

McCabe smiled at them both, "So we should be, who'd like a drink?"

"I'll do them," answered Caz, jumping up and going to the fridge in the kitchen. She opened another bottle of rosé and, returning to the group, topped up McCabe's glass without asking whether she should, then poured a glass for herself and Tricia. "Mr Barnard, can I top up your brandy?"

He smiled at her, "No thank you. I have to work later."

Caz sat next her sister again and Barnard turned to speak to them.

"Before I go, I wonder if you can tell me anything about the house at Shiplake." He looked directly at Tricia.

"Not very much I don't think. I didn't see a lot of it. They took me there after they grabbed me at Sonning. At first they kept me in the house, guarded all the time. I didn't know that I was in Shiplake but Caz has just told me that's where it was. For an hour every day they let me walk in the garden by the river with one of them guarding me. It was a beautiful place.

"Did you see any movement?" asked Barnard. "Anyone arriving or leaving?"

"On one of those airings I was walking on the lawn and I saw a boat arrive. They moored it in the boathouse. It had the name Fenland Princess on it. It was like one of those hire boats you see on the Norfolk Broads with a sliding roof for sunny days. As we crossed the lawn three men were pushing a trolley along the path to the boathouse. It had a tarpaulin over it but the wind was flapping it about and I could see that there was a large metal cylinder on it. I don't think I was supposed to see it because the one in charge - he was called Ernst - came roaring across, after the boat was in the boathouse, shouting at them to get whatever it was out of sight and get it loaded onto the boat. He was really angry and bawling them out, so they put me back in the main house."

"Did you recognise what it was?" asked Barnard.

"It looked like a big oil drum."

"OK. I'm sorry to interrupt," said Barnard.

"One morning," continued Tricia, "they put me back on the big boat and took me to meet Chad and Caz out in the country. I don't know where that was."

"Beale Park," said McCabe. "Near Pangbourne."

None the wiser, Tricia continued, "Then they took me back in their boat. It had the name Wilhelmina on it, and they put me in the house again. That's it really. They kept me locked in the house and that evening I thought I saw Caz looking down at me through the window. I thought I might escape through that window but it was too high up and had a steel grille outside it. Then they came in and dragged me out of the room and put me in a car and drove to an airport. I don't remember much after that until I woke up and realised we were in France."

"The cylinder you saw," asked Barnard. "Can you describe it?"

"Grey, like an oil drum," she repeated. "Heavy I think because they were working hard to push it and it had writing and numbers on it."

"Can you remember what the writing said?" asked Barnard.

"No, it was too far away to read it."

"Did you overhear any conversations about it?" asked Barnard.

"No. They were usually silent when I was around and when they did speak to each other it was in German, which I recognise but don't understand."

Barnard thought for a moment and then said, "I'll pass that information on but it was probably just a fuel drum, as you say. Anyway, if you'll excuse me, I must be going."

McCabe rose at the same time as Barnard did and said, "I'll see you to the door."

Caz and Tricia smiled at Barnard as he turned to them with a slight nod of his head, "Goodbye Ladies."

"Sorry you have to go," said Tricia.

"Bye," said Caz.

McCabe followed him and Barnard turned as he reached the apartment's front door, "There's something else I must tell you Chad."

They both stepped into the corridor, the sole occupant of which was a uniformed policeman standing by the lift and out of earshot.

Barnard looked at McCabe and said quietly, "Apart from trying to close down Bronek Kowalski's dissident group, we know that Fleischer is working for a terrorist group that wants to cause some mayhem. We don't know where or when but we expect it to be something catastrophic. I'd like you to keep an eye out for anything that might lead us to whatever it is."

"Why can't you just arrest him next time he's in the UK and ask him?"

"We don't have any grounds to. Fleischer keeps the illegal side of his business at arm's length, which is why the French wanted to catch him in the act at Tende. On the face of it he's a perfectly harmless businessman and no threat to anyone."

"Can't you arrest him for kidnapping Tricia?"

"I'd like to but, as she's escaped, we want to get him for something more serious. Kidnapping is serious enough but I think, if he was pushed, Fleischer would argue that she was in France of her own accord. As for Tende, he wasn't there and we can't link him to it."

"OK," replied McCabe. "I'll let you know if I see anything."

"In the meantime, we'll be watching when Fleischer's people contact you but I think your biggest threat is Ricky Bishop now that his hitman has failed to get you."

McCabe thought of the last time that he had seen Bishop, writhing in the car headlights. Yes, he thought. Bishop would certainly want his revenge. He looked at Barnard, "He'll come after me again won't he?"

"I think he will," replied Barnard.

Chapter Fifty Nine

Nice Côte d'Azur Airport,
1125 CEST Monday 6th August

True to his word, Barnard had arranged a police escort for the three friends. On arrival at the airport they were walked, no questions asked, through security and passport control by two tough looking officers who delivered them to the door of easyJet flight EZY8352 twenty minutes before its scheduled departure time of twelve noon. McCabe was left with the feeling that their escort, although polite, was not so much a matter of courtesy but to make sure that they left the country.

Tricia and Caz had shared the twin bedded room for their short stay in the apartment, leaving the double bedded room to McCabe and he had been unable to speak to either of them on their own. Apart from the time that the three of them spent together to enjoy a lunch and two splendid dinners prepared by a nearby hotel and sent in by the French police, the two women were either sunbathing together on the roof terrace of the apartment block, drinking wine together on the balcony or were in their bedroom. Yesterday evening Tricia had tried on clothes, delivered by a female police officer, to select an outfit to travel home in, and they were still talking to each other when McCabe had said good night to them both and retired to the silence of his bedroom where he immediately fell asleep. They chatted non-stop on the flight from Nice to Gatwick and McCabe sat back, quietly looking out of the window at France passing beneath them, and wondered how Tricia was going to react when she found out about him and Caz.

At 1304 UK time their flight touched down at Gatwick Airport and, after what seemed an age as the aircraft trundled its cumbersome way to the terminal, they disembarked and joined the throng of passengers waiting at the carousel for their luggage to arrive. After collecting McCabe's rucksack and Caz's suitcase, they passed speedily through immigration and customs and made their way across the busy concourse to the train station, stopping at the ticket office.

"I'm going to stay in Brighton with Caz," said Tricia turning to face him. "I hope you don't mind me not coming to the boat with you. I think I've had enough travelling for a while."

He'd been wondering what Tricia would want to do and this would give them space before explanations became necessary.

"Of course I don't mind. You need a rest and time to think," he said. Would Caz want her sister to know that she had slept with him the night before her rescue? he wondered. Would she want anything more to do with him? Perhaps it was just a fling brought on by being in Nice, like a holiday romance.

They bought their tickets, McCabe for London and the two sisters for Brighton. When they were through the ticket barrier they stopped to say goodbye before they went to their separate platforms.

Tricia stepped forward, hugged him and kissed him on the cheek. She stepped back looking up at him, "Thank you for rescuing me, Chad," she said smiling.

Caz stepped forward, put her arms around him and kissed him on the lips. The smell of her perfume and the feel of her against him made him dizzy as she said quietly, "Don't worry Chad, I'll explain it to Tricia. I'm sure she'll understand." She snuggled her cheek against his and whispered, "I want to see you again. Very soon."

"Me too," was all he could think of in reply.

She stepped back, smiling at him, then both women turned and walked away. He watched until, just before they were lost from his sight, they turned again and waved at him. McCabe waved back and when they had gone, feeling heady like a teenage boy after his first kiss, he made his way to the London platform followed at a discreet distance by Fleischer's man Stefan Merk.

*****

McCabe left the Gatwick Express at Victoria Station and was crossing the busy concourse when Ernst Kegel and Stefan Merk closed in. One on either side of him, they steered him to a glass door on the west side of the station which was the discreet and little used entrance leading directly into The Grosvenor Hotel. They stopped in the deserted, narrow, marbled passageway as soon as they had passed through the door and Merk pushed him so that his back was against the wall. McCabe had a sudden mental image of the many occasions that he had entered the hotel through this same entrance and had a drink at the bar while waiting for a train, or coffee in the hotel lounge at an arranged meeting. He was brought quickly back to the present by the sight of Ernst Kegel standing in front of him angry and menacing, his lower lip with stitches in it.

"We gave you until Friday to get what we wanted," he snarled. "You're three days late. Where is it?"

"If you mean Bronek's memory stick it's in my pocket."

Stefan Merk roughly searched McCabe's jacket pockets, found the memory stick and passed it to Ernst.

Ernst grabbed the front of McCabe's jacket with both hands and pulled it towards him so that his and McCabe's faces were only inches apart. "If you are trying to trick me, McCabe, I will find you and put an end to you. Understand?"

"No trick. You haven't even told me what you want but I found that in Bronek's guitar case."

"Have you looked at it?" hissed Ernst.

"I have but the files on it are encrypted, so I've no idea what they're about."

Ernst Kegel, satisfied, stepped back and pocketed the memory stick. "Stay there until we've gone," he ordered and Merk pulled open the glass door and they left.

McCabe watched until they mingled with the crowds on the station concourse and then he turned and headed for the hotel bar, hoping that he would never see them again.

Chapter Sixty

White towels, green towels, grey socks, blue jeans, t-shirts, polo shirts, kitchen whites, green bed sheets. Pile after never ending pile of washing cast off by hundreds of male prisoners and this was Ricky Bishop's life now, the price he had to pay for a lifetime of crime. Bishop, who for years had controlled the wholesale supply of hard drugs to a pyramid of dealers and lived a life of comfortable luxury, now worked in the prison laundry. A large part, but by no means all, of his assets had been seized by the justice system and what was left was hardly of any use to him while he was incarcerated. Now he was paid a pittance which, in the outside world, would not have kept him in his favourite perfume. At least, he thought, I have the satisfaction of knowing that Chad McCabe, the man responsible for my being here, will soon be dead when Quietus catches up with him.

Every day, Bishop and three other prisoners came to the laundry and for hour after hour they fed the huge industrial washing machines and driers. Not only with prison laundry but with tablecloths and napkins from local restaurants, washed and pressed as part of the prison's various commercial contracts with outside concerns. The restaurants' linen was processed in the same machines as the prisoners' bedding and clothes which were stained with urine, with blood from open sores and with faeces and semen. It would have killed the restaurants' businesses stone dead if their customers ever got to know about it. Every day the same monotony, but today was going to be different.

It wasn't until he stepped away from the drier which he had been feeding that Bishop noticed that his three co-workers had left the room. At the same time, a thin noose was slipped quickly over his head from behind and tightened around his neck. He had no time to shout or identify the man who was strangling him or even to struggle much as, within ten seconds, the laundry began to fade away and he blacked out as the blood supply through the arteries in his neck was restricted. The strangler and an accomplice lifted the unconscious Ricky Bishop up until his feet were no longer touching the floor. One of the men tied the end of the short rope, which formed the noose, to a water pipe which ran horizontally along the wall, and they left. The noose tightened further with the weight of Bishop's body and closed his trachea, completely cutting off his air supply until, after another four minutes, he could be considered brain dead.

There had been no need for a violent, bloody stabbing carried out as a warning to others; Bishop's strangulation had been a quiet matter, a straightforward business transaction. Blanchet, the facilitator in France, had paid out on the single premium insurance policy which George Lee, aka Quietus, had bought and the matter was now closed. Bishop's killers returned to their prison duties, both three thousand pounds richer.

Chapter Sixty One

Queenborough - 1929 BST Monday 13th August

"Do you want your fry up swimming in grease or would you like the grease poured on after?" called Zac from the galley.

"Any way it comes Zac," answered McCabe, smiling to himself at the same joke that Zac always made when he was cooking.

A week had passed during which McCabe and Zac had stayed at St Katharine Docks and, even though they both knew London well, they had adopted tourist mode and visited HMS Belfast the World War II cruiser moored in the Pool of London, the National Maritime Museum at Greenwich and some of their favourite pubs. Yesterday they had used the ebb tide and moved Honeysuckle Rose, without incident, down the Thames to Queenborough arriving just before midnight. They were not in a hurry, so today they had rested and now it was two hours before low water. Moored to exactly the same buoy that McCabe had tied up to with Tricia on the way to London three weeks before, they would wait for high water in eight hours' time when the tide would again turn in their favour.

The weather was a fine drizzle with visibility of, perhaps, half a mile. There was no wind for sailing at the moment but the forecast promised a steady south westerly force 4 to 5 later. If the forecast was correct, although the wind would kick up the waves and make for a bumpy passage once they left the shelter of the Kent coast, it would get them out of the Thames Estuary and around the North Foreland in quick time. That, coupled with a spring tide which would be ebbing out into the North Sea, would give them a good start on the next leg of their journey. Whether they would then put into Ramsgate Harbour or continue on to Brighton would depend on the tides and the wind strength against them.

Two hundred yards away, moored to a buoy, was a Broads cruiser with a sliding roof, which matched the description of the vessel which Tricia had seen at the house at Shiplake - the boat with the metal cylinder in it. McCabe had phoned Tricia this afternoon to ask her to describe the vessel again and it matched exactly. He had also spoken to Caz and the conversation created a sudden need in him to get to Brighton so that he could see her again. Now it was an hour before sunset, although the sun wasn't visible, and he was sitting in Rose's cockpit discreetly watching the cruiser through binoculars. She appeared to be about 35 feet long, two male crew on board and designed for the relative calm of the inland waters of the Norfolk Broads, not for going to sea. As she swung on the mooring buoy McCabe could see clearly through the binoculars the name on her bow - Fenland Princess. Attached to the stern on a short painter was a black inflatable with what looked like a powerful outboard motor. McCabe took his phone from his pocket and called Arthur Barnard to report what he'd seen. Barnard thanked him and told him that he would inform the relevant authorities and wished him a good trip.

Zac called him down to the saloon and they each tucked into a double sized helping of bacon, eggs, sausages and toast on the basis that, when you're sailing, it's always wise to eat well before you start because you don't know when you will get your next meal. McCabe was pleased to note that, contrary to

Zac's joke, the meal was mainly grease free and, as they ate and drank mugs of tea, they discussed the forthcoming trip.

"Looking forward to this, Chad. I haven't sailed this route for years."

"It's an interesting one, isn't it?" replied McCabe. "All sorts of hazards: sandbanks, adverse tides, shipping, wrecks. Nothing we haven't handled countless times before. We'll just have to keep our wits about us."

"What about that wreck we saw last night when we were coming in?" asked Zac. "It's been there all my life and they still haven't done anything about it."

"The SS Richard Montgomery, American liberty ship sunk there in a storm in 1944. Devastating if it ever blew up," replied McCabe. "I was telling Tricia about it when we were here three weeks ago. If it does ever explode it could send a wave up river into central London and cause a huge amount of damage to all the surrounding areas, including the gas tanks on the Isle of Grain."

"You'd think that the Authorities would have dealt with it by now," said Zac. "Why don't they?"

"Too dangerous, I think. There's talk of removing the three masts that show above the water all the time, because they're rusting. If one of them collapses it could set off the cargo."

"Bombs," said Zac.

"Bombs," replied McCabe. "1,400 tons of them. To put that in perspective, when the Germans were bombing London in 1940, a 500 bomber raid would drop 450 tons of bombs in a single night. If the SS Richard Montgomery blows up it will go up with the equivalent force of three nights of the Blitz with every bomb dropped on the same spot at the same time."

*****

At 0300 Zac and McCabe were on deck getting ready to slip their mooring and start out towards the estuary. They saw the Fenland Princess's forward facing red and green navigation lights flick on, then, as she swung away from them, the red and green were no longer visible and her white stern light came into view as she quickly disappeared into the drizzle.

"I wonder where she's going?" mused Zac. "Can't be going out to sea in a boat like that but they've picked the wrong time to go up river against the tide."

They had briefly discussed the Fenland Princess while they were eating and Zac had remarked that she seemed out of place in Queenborough. McCabe didn't tell Zac the background to it but he did wonder now whether he should call Barnard again and tell him that she had left. With enough to do to stow things away and get Rose started on her journey he decided to call him when they were under way.

The mainsail and genoa were readied for use but, with so little wind contrary to the forecast, they were not raised and ten minutes later McCabe started the engine and switched the navigation lights on. Zac went forward and slipped the bow line which was securing them to the mooring buoy. McCabe turned the wheel as Zac returned to the cockpit and swung Rose back towards the River Medway. Once there they would turn to starboard and head out into the Thames Estuary in a reverse of the trip he had done with Tricia. The two friends hunched their shoulders and drew their necks further down into the high collars of their sailing jackets as they motored at a steady 5 knots into the drizzle and blackness.

Thirty minutes passed while they pushed on into the darkness, Rose's 200,000 Lumen spotlight shining ahead to pick out any possible obstacles. McCabe had made sure that the spotlight, fixed in its bracket on the coachroof, was angled slightly to port to avoid the otherwise dazzling white light being reflected back at them from the sheet of drizzle in front. Zac had taken over the wheel and was following a carefully calculated compass course to clear the half mile gap between the Isle of Grain and Sheerness on the correct side of the channel. McCabe was below at the saloon table with Admiralty Chart 1183 spread out in front of him. It showed the Thames Estuary with a large part of the East Coast of Essex mid and top left and the North Coast of Kent along the bottom. The land was shown in yellow and the estuary and sea shown in blue for the shallows and white for the deeper water and channels. The hazardous sandbanks and flats, of which there are many, were shown in green. In the lower left corner of the chart were the River Medway and the Isle of Sheppey. He left Zac at the wheel as they cleared Garrison Point at the exit from the River Medway and they were now entering the Thames. McCabe referred to his passage plan, which he knew by heart but would still double check as they went along. It showed that after entering the Thames they would proceed in a north easterly direction following the Medway Approach Channel to keep clear of the wreck of the SS Richard Montgomery and, once they were level with the yellow flashing buoys on their port side, which mark the exclusion zone around the wreck, they would turn to starboard and motor east south east. This would keep them clear of the Cheyney Spit and, once they had turned, they would head towards the flashing green light of the Spile buoy and the entrance to the Four Fathoms Channel five miles away. Coastal passage making is navigated from one mark to the next, so the first thing to be done now was to steer north east and look for the lights around the Montgomery and its lethal cargo two miles away. McCabe returned to the cockpit, gave Zac the new compass course to steer and they both peered ahead into the murk waiting for the lights to appear in approximately twenty five minutes time. Five minutes later, Rose's searchlight picked out Fenland Princess's inflatable as it roared towards them from directly ahead. It flashed past them at high speed on their port side and they could see its two occupants, their faces obscured by the hoods of their sailing jackets, as it sped past them and disappeared into the darkness, bouncing as it planed across the water in a flurry of spray, heading back towards the River Medway.

"That was the inflatable from that Broads cruiser!"

"It was, Zac."

"Well I only saw two crew on the boat when it was on the buoy at Queenborough, so who's in charge of the cruiser? What was it called …?"

"It's called the Fenland Princess," replied McCabe. "Tricia saw it on the non-tidal Thames a couple of weeks ago and it's a bit of a mystery boat."

"Well I didn't hear any Mayday," said Zac, "and we've had the radio on Channel 16 ever since we left Queenborough."

"OK," replied McCabe. "Look, you carry on. I'm going below to make a phone call. Keep your eyes peeled though in case it's drifting somewhere ahead of us."

"Will do," replied Zac and McCabe went below knowing that Honeysuckle Rose was in safe hands.

He sat at the saloon table, took his phone from his jacket pocket and dialled Barnard's number.

"Hello?" Barnard answered the phone immediately.

"An update on my earlier call," said McCabe. "We've just seen the two crew members of the Fenland Princess come tearing past us in an inflatable and we think they may have abandoned ship and left it drifting. Either that or it's sunk."

"Where are you?" asked Barnard.

"We're about a mile from the mouth of the Medway and heading North East."

"Did you hear any Mayday?"

"No, and we've been keeping a listening watch as we always do."

Barnard was silent for a moment and then he said, "OK. I know exactly where you are. What's your passage plan?"

"To follow this course until we find a wreck and then turn East South East."

"Do you mean the wreck of the SS Richard Montgomery?" asked Barnard.

McCabe, impressed by Barnard's knowledge of the Thames Estuary replied, "Yes."

"OK. That's good," said Barnard. "If you come across anything odd that warrants it, don't call me but send a Mayday straight away, will you?"

"OK," replied McCabe intrigued now by Barnard's reaction. Did he, as usual, know more than he was saying?

"Good. Thank you Chad. You'd better keep a good lookout. Good luck. I have some calls to make," and Barnard switched off his phone leaving McCabe wondering what he was up to.

Realising that it was useless to speculate he put the phone away and climbed the saloon steps to rejoin Zac and, without speaking, they peered ahead through the drizzle, waiting to get a glimpse of the lights around the Montgomery.

The drizzle was slowly clearing and the visibility gradually improved as soon, to their starboard, appeared the continuously flashing white light of the Number 10 North Cardinal buoy marking the edge of the channel. Opposite, on their port side, the green light of Number 9 Buoy flashed every five seconds confirming that they were still following the channel correctly.

A few minutes later Zac suddenly called out, "There!" and he pointed at something off of the port bow.

McCabe stood up to get a better look and then he could see it; a yellow light flashing once every five seconds. It was the buoy marking the southern corner of the exclusion zone around the Montgomery. He swung the spotlight to get a better look at it and the beam cut through what was left of the rain and picked out a shape a hundred yards or so beyond it. McCabe rubbed his eyes with the back of his hand to clear some of the raindrops away and looked again.

"Zac! There's a boat inside the exclusion zone!"

"Can't be," replied Zac. "Who'd be crazy enough to go in there?" And he peered into the gloom. "Yes, I see it! Do you think we should have a look?"

"It might be an official boat - Coastguard, something like that - but I think we ought to go over there. At least as far as the buoy."

Zac changed course and they headed towards it. When they reached the edge of the exclusion zone they slowed to one knot while McCabe picked out the mystery vessel with binoculars. Its white hull shone bright in the spotlight, contrasting with the three black masts of the sunken Richard Montgomery still showing above the water.

"It's the Fenland Princess, Zac and she seems to be drifting. There doesn't appear to be anyone on board. No lights. They've just abandoned it."

"Should we go in there and tow it out do you think?" asked Zac.

"I don't think so. The reason for the exclusion zone is in case any disturbance sets off all the explosives. It wouldn't help if we go lumbering in there. Do you agree?"

"I suppose so Chad. We need to report it though."

McCabe remembered Barnard's words earlier on, "If you come across anything odd that warrants it don't call me but send a Mayday straight away, will you?" as if he knew that something like this was going to happen.

"You're right. I'll send out a Mayday. Keep your eye on her."

McCabe went down the steps into the saloon and picked up the VHF radio microphone. He checked that the ancient radio set was still tuned to Channel 16, turned up the transmission power to 25 watts, pressed the button on the mic with his thumb and he spoke:

"Mayday relay, mayday relay, mayday relay. This is sailing yacht Honeysuckle Rose, Honeysuckle Rose, Honeysuckle Rose. My position is two miles north of Sheerness on the edge of the SS Richard Montgomery exclusion zone. There is a boat drifting in the exclusion zone, apparently without any crew on board. Mayday relay, Honeysuckle Rose. Over."

Within seconds a female voice replied, "Mayday relay, Honeysuckle Rose, this is Thames Coastguard. I understand that there is a vessel floating unmanned in the Montgomery exclusion zone. Is that correct?"

McCabe replied, "Correct. Over."

"Standby please."

Some unintelligible chatter came over the radio, presumably from another vessel and the Coastguard came back with the command, "Seelonce Mayday!" demanding silence.

The airwaves went quiet and then the Coastguard came back again, "Honeysuckle Rose can you describe the vessel that's drifting?"

"It's a Norfolk Broads cruiser: fibreglass, white hull, sliding roof about thirty five feet long."

"Thank you, standby please."

A minute went by and then the Coastguard said, "Honeysuckle Rose, we are sending assistance. Keep a listening watch please. Over."

"Will do," replied McCabe. "Over."

He hung the mic on its cradle and went back into the cockpit. Glancing around, he could see the navigation lights of several ships in the distance but none close to them.

"Help is on the way, Zac."

Repositioning the spotlight onto the Fenland Princess he picked up the binoculars and had another look at her. They were closer now and he could see her clearly. She was lower in the water than before. He scanned the binoculars along the waterline and stopped at the bow. A chain was leading from the bow roller straight down into the water.

"She's anchored on the wreck, Zac, and she's sinking!"

Chapter Sixty Two

"We'd better do something," said McCabe. "If it sinks and hits the wreck it could set the explosives off."

"But if we go into the exclusion zone we could cause a problem ourselves," replied Zac.

"Well we can't just wait here and let it sink."

"What assistance are they sending?" asked Zac.

"They didn't say. I presume a lifeboat."

"So," replied Zac, "the nearest lifeboats are Sheerness a couple of miles away, and Southend on the other side of the Estuary, even further. Taking into account the time it'll take to crew them and launch, that boat'll be sunk before they get here. It's going down fast."

"You're right," said McCabe. "We've got to get in there and stop it from sinking until help arrives. Can you steer us over there and I'll try to get some lines onto her. At least we can keep her afloat if we lash her alongside."

Without further discussion Zac turned Rose towards the Fenland Princess and, in less than a minute, they were alongside her. Skilfully, he held Rose stationary while McCabe easily stepped onto the sinking boat with Rose's stern line in his hand. He lashed it to the Fenland Princess's stern cleat but he was concerned that it would break if too much strain was put on it. He got back onto Rose and quickly went through his rope locker until he found the spare anchor warp, thick rope used to add length to his anchor chain if required. He went forward and lashed the rope to Fenland Princess's bow roller at one end and secured it to Rose's anchor winch at the other. He stopped to take stock and was only then aware of the Richard

Montgomery's three huge masts, much larger then he had ever realised now that he was close to them for the first time, the nearest two towering above him and almost close enough to touch. He looked back along Rose's deck towards Zac, who was still at the wheel with the engine in neutral, and he could see that Honeysuckle Rose was already beginning to heel towards the cruiser as the weight of water inside the sinking vessel increased. He had to stop that heeling or both boats would go under, and there was no time to lose. McCabe rushed to the mast to release a spare halyard. He unwound the halyard's figure of eight from its cleat at the bottom of the mast, allowing it to run free and released the shackle securing the other end of the halyard to the bottom of the mast. He climbed over the rails and boarded the sinking boat taking the shackle end of the halyard with him. He crossed the Princess's low coach roof and reached the side deck farthest away from Honeysuckle Rose. As he clambered across he saw that the Princess's long sliding roof had been left wide open and the forward part of the interior was open to the elements. McCabe reached the steel handrail running along the outer edge of the Princess's deck and wrapped the shackle end of the halyard around it twice then tied it off with a double rolling hitch. Whether the one and a quarter inch diameter chromium plated tubular rail would hold was a chance he had to take. He had created a right angled triangle, the rope halyard forming the hypotenuse rising from Fenland Princess's rail over and above her deck to the top of Rose's mast. The mast formed the vertical side of the triangle and the decks of the two boats formed the base. He quickly returned to Honeysuckle Rose and wound the free end of the halyard around a winch on the mast. Using a handle he quickly ratcheted up the winch until the halyard was taught and taking some of the load of the sinking vessel. There was nothing more he could do with that. Now he needed to find out why the Fenland Princess was sinking.

"Are you OK there Zac?"

"No problem, Chad. Do you want any help?"

"Best you stay at the wheel, I think, Zac. Have you got a sharp knife on you?"

"I've always got one when we're sailing."

"Well keep it handy in case you have to cut the stern line free. I'm going to see why she's sinking. Can you angle the spotlight directly into that opening in her roof?"

While McCabe boarded the Fenland Princess again and worked his way along the side deck, Zac realigned the spotlight. Its direct glare shone down through the gap in the coach roof and illuminated the interior. As he looked down into the vessel he saw the metal cylinder that Tricia had described seeing when she was a prisoner at Shiplake. The cylinder was partly submerged in the black water and reflected the light of the spotlight back to faintly illuminate the rest of the interior. McCabe lowered himself into the water and began to wade further into the boat until he realised how futile and dangerous that was. He stood still and listened, hoping to hear running water, but all that he could hear was a gentle slap slap as the stricken cruiser rocked slowly and the water moved from side to side. What had the crew done? Made a hole in the boat or just opened a seacock somewhere? Whatever it was he wasn't going to find it by wading about in the water. He had to hope that being lashed to Honeysuckle Rose would stop her from sinking until a lifeboat arrived with pumps.

McCabe turned his attention back to the cylinder lying fore and aft on the saloon floor.

He felt around the cylinder under the water and found that it was in a cradle to stop it rolling. It was grey and exactly as Tricia had described. About the size of a large oil drum, the only writing that he could see on it was a stencilled Mark 6 in white painted letters. On one end of the cylinder was a dial with a pointer and a circle of numbers. At the top of the circle was the word SAFE. Around the rest of the circle were the numbers 30, 50, 75, 100, 150, 200, 250, and 300. The pointer was lined up with the 30. McCabe had seen enough black and white war films to know that this was a depth charge and that it was set to explode when it had 30 feet of water over it. So this was Fleischer's plan - to sink the Fenland Princess on the SS Richard Montgomery at a high spring tide and, as soon as the water over the boat reached a depth of 30 feet, the depth charge would explode and detonate the Montgomery's unstable cargo of explosives. He looked up at Honeysuckle Rose's mast which was now leaning over him as the Fenland Princess continued to fill with water trying to take Rose with her to settle on the seabed and be blown to pieces with the Richard Montgomery. He had to think fast. Make the depth charge safe and cut the ropes to release Rose so that he and Zac could escape and an explosion be avoided. And it had to be done quickly. Make it safe. It had the word SAFE written on the dial to the left of the 30. He crouched and studied the dial more closely.

Zac called out to him, "We're heeling badly Chad."

McCabe stood up and looked out at Zac, "Give me a bit longer, Zac. I'm just trying to sort something out."

He looked back at the depth charge. In the short time that he'd been on board the Fenland Princess the water inside her had risen by at least a foot. He crouched down again and studied the depth charge more closely.

"There's a boat coming," shouted Zac. "A fast RIB of some sort with a flashing blue light."

Concentrating on the dial on the end of the depth charge, McCabe studied the settings again. The word SAFE and the numbers 30, 50, 75, 100, 150, 200, 250, and 300 with the pointer on the number 30. The word SAFE was to the left of 30 so, if he turned the dial to the left and set the pointer on the word SAFE that should do what it said, make the depth charge safe, or so he hoped. He reached out, grasped the dial and tried to turn it to the left but it didn't move. He tried again, with more pressure this time. Nothing. He tried again and felt the boat lurch as he did so. Again the dial wouldn't turn. He looked up and could see Rose's mast at a 45 degree angle above him as she heeled almost to the point of capsize and, at the same time, he saw that her mast and shrouds were being bathed in an eerie blue light which flashed quickly on and off. He turned his attention back to the dial and tried once more and, at the same time, he heard footsteps on the Princess's deck, but he ignored that. He had to make the depth charge safe. Now! The Princess was going to sink completely at any moment. A torch shone down on him from above and a figure dropped into the water next to him, landing feet first with a splash and sending water surging around the cabin. McCabe had time to register a camouflage uniform in the torchlight and then the torch was directed onto the depth charge dial.

"Get back," a voice ordered as the figure reached towards the dial and twisted it to the right.

The pointer on the dial passed the 50 the 75 and went through the rest of the numbers clockwise until it reached SAFE and stopped.

"Come on, we've got to get out of here," the voice ordered and its owner hauled himself out of the cabin onto the deck and reached back to help McCabe.

He grasped the man's right wrist with his right hand, the man grasped McCabe's wrist and hauled him out onto the Fenland Princess's deck.

"Get your boat clear," the voice ordered.

McCabe scrambled over the side rails and boarded Honeysuckle Rose now leaning at an impossible angle with her mast nearly horizontal to the water as the Princess dragged her down. Lit by the flashing blue light, he saw the man jump into the RIB at the Princess's stern and the RIB quickly pulling away to safety.

He shouted at Zac who he could see hanging on precariously in Rose's cockpit, "Cut the stern line Zac!" and he saw his friend start towards the stern with his feet against the almost horizontal toe rail.

McCabe hauled himself up to the base of the mast and released the halyard then turned and clawed his way towards Honeysuckle Rose's bow, trying to reach the anchor winch and the heavy rope that attached them to the Princess. There was a sudden lurch as Zac cut the stern line and Rose, still attached at the bow, swung away from the other boat and her mast swung violently upwards and seesawed sickeningly from side to side for a good minute until the motion slowed and settled. For that minute neither Zac or McCabe could do anything but cling to Rose's side rails while the Fenland Princess, her deck awash began to pull Rose's bow down into the water. McCabe let go of the side rail and slid down the now sloping foredeck crashing hard into the anchor winch which stopped him from sliding through the pulpit, the curved rail on the bow which was already pointing downwards, and into the water. As the Princess sank further McCabe was suddenly up to his waist in water and he realised that releasing the rope from the winch was going to be impossible. He looked back along Rose's deck and saw the stern rising out of the water already ten feet in the air. He saw Zac, in the pulsating blue light, jump from the stern and crash down into the water. His mind raced to find a way to save his precious boat. He felt in his pockets for the folding knife that he normally carried with him so that he could cut the rope, but he couldn't find it, and then the RIB was nosing into the bow and a voice was shouting at him.

"Jump man! Jump!"

And self-preservation took over and McCabe forced himself forward, half wading and half swimming and dragged himself into the RIB which rapidly reversed away as he slipped and fell against its side tubes and landed on his backside among some bags of equipment. He found a handgrip as the RIB slowed then lurched forward and saw that there were two men in the boat with him. The RIB suddenly stopped and he watched as the men leaned over the side tubes and hauled Zac on board. McCabe struggled to his knees and clung to the handgrip as one of the figures took the wheel and steered them away at speed from the two stricken vessels. The RIB stopped again, dead in the water, when it was a hundred yards away and shone a powerful searchlight back at the wreck. They watched as the Fenland Princess disappeared slowly beneath the water and, in slow motion, Honeysuckle Rose was dragged bow down and stern up, sliding slowly below the surface until the water reached her cockpit. Then it was over fast as her saloon filled with water and she was gone. He choked back tears of frustration at the loss of his beautiful boat, his home and his possessions. He cursed his decision to secure her bow with the thick anchor warp instead of her normal bow line which would probably have snapped under the strain and Rose would have remained floating. But she had gone and there was nothing that he could do about it.

He pulled himself up until he was sitting on the side tube of the inflatable and took stock of their situation. Zac was sitting near the stern of the boat wrapped in a space blanket to keep him warm after his sudden immersion in the water. The blue light was still flashing and he could see that the boat was a Delta RIB about 7 metres long of the type used by the military all over the world. As he had jumped aboard he had seen a sign at the stern, black with white letters, RN BOMB DISPOSAL. So, they had been rescued by the Royal Navy. The boat was so full of equipment that there was just about enough room for the two man crew and little else. Both men were wearing camouflage clothing and berets; one of the men was a naval officer and the other was a rating. The officer, who had been reporting the situation to the Coastguard, replaced the mic in its cradle, turned to McCabe and spoke.

"Sorry about your boat."

It was the voice of the figure who had boarded the Fenland Princess and made safe the depth charge.

"It was my fault," answered McCabe. "I couldn't get the bow line free."

"Not your fault at all. If you hadn't supported that sinking boat for as long as you did I wouldn't have been able to get on board in time to make the weapon safe. Pretty primitive stuff but typical for terrorist attacks."

"What was it?" asked McCabe. "I saw the words US Mark 6 on it."

"It was an obsolete World War II Mark 6 depth charge. Set the depth, drop it in the water and bang, the pressure wave cracks open anything near to it, usually a submarine. You know that's the wreck of the SS Richard Montgomery full of unstable explosives?"

"I do."

"Then you'll know that, if it had gone off, it would have likely blown the whole thing sky high and done untold damage for miles around. You and your friend have performed a great service in alerting us and giving us time to act."

McCabe looked over to his friend, "You OK, Zac?"

"OK Chad," Zac as unflappable as ever.

McCabe turned back to the officer, "How did you get here so quickly?"

"We were put on standby at Sheerness earlier this evening. Only two miles away so, when you broadcast your Mayday, we made straight for you - only five minutes in this boat. And Sheerness is where we're going to take you now."

The officer took the wheel and pushed the throttle forward and the RIB surged forward lifting half out of the water as it headed in a straight line for Sheerness and safety. As they skimmed across the still calm sea, McCabe looked back at the winking yellow lights around the exclusion zone and thought of the two new wrecks tied together on the seabed with another container of explosive to add to the SS Richard Montgomery's lethal inventory.

Chapter Sixty Three

Brighton - 1150 BST Thursday 16th August

Caz and Tricia had gone into the town together. McCabe and Arthur Barnard were sitting at the kitchen table talking and drinking coffee in Caz's flat near Brighton Station.

"I've got to thank you, Chad. It's quite remarkable what you did."

"I felt quite useless to be honest. It was the Royal Navy officer who saved the day. I didn't know what I was doing."

"I've spoken to him," said Barnard, "and he tells me that if you hadn't stopped that boat from sinking for as long as you did, he wouldn't have been there in time to make the depth charge safe. So we owe you a great deal. Without your intervention the damage to people and property for miles around would have been appalling. I'm sorry you lost your boat because of it."

"Not just my boat but my possessions as well. Clothes, guitars, laptop and everything else that was on board. I've spoken to the insurance company about a claim but what view they'll take I don't know. Are you covered by insurance when you deliberately put your boat in harm's way?"

"I don't know," replied Barnard, "but if there's anything I can do, please let me know. We can discreetly talk to them for you and explain that you had good reason to do it and point out to them what the insurance claims would have been if the Montgomery had blown up."

"What about Fleischer?" asked McCabe.

"Not even in the country when his men scuttled the boat, but we know from what Tricia told us that it was moored at the house at Shiplake. That links him to the attempt to blow up the Montgomery but it's not enough to make a case against him personally. He can claim that he knew nothing about it. To be honest, we don't even know where he is at the moment. He flew back to Geneva from Luton a week ago and, from there, he could be anywhere? We don't have the resources to constantly watch him."

McCabe frowned, "But what was the point of it all?"

"We believe now that Fleischer was acting for a hostile government. If the attack had been successful, there would have been a false claim of responsibility in the name of one of the many Islamic terrorist groups. The purpose of this false claim would have been an attempt to start civil unrest, particularly in London where there is a huge immigrant population. They would hope that, if the indigenous population could be encouraged to start attacking the ethnic groups that they held responsible for the devastation, then that in turn would spark an uprising when the Government intervened to put a stop to it. The resulting anarchy could go on for decades and seriously weaken the UK. Fortunately you stopped it but there'll be another attempt and we must be vigilant. Of course, like so many of these incidents, the British public will never hear about it and I trust you to be discreet."

"What about Bronek's memory stick," asked McCabe. "Why did you tell me to give it to Fleischer's people?"

"We analysed it and, as we thought, it contained a mailing list - the names and email addresses of hundreds of dissidents in Bronek Kowalski's home country. We removed the mailing list and replaced it with the names and addresses of party faithful who support the regime. They'll have a lot of explaining to do when their secret police round them up and interview them. The object is to sow discord amongst the upper echelons of the ruling party. Dirty tricks department."

"Dirty tricks indeed!" said McCabe.

They heard the street door being opened and Barnard stood up, "Time I went, Chad. Everything I've told you is in the strictest confidence of course."

"Of course."

As they stood up and shook hands, Caz entered the room smiling and looking gorgeous in a saffron coloured summer dress.

"Are you going?" she asked.

"I have to I'm afraid," replied Barnard. "I have a car waiting for me and two more meetings today." He turned to McCabe, "Don't lose touch Chad. I'll let myself out. Goodbye Caz. I hope we meet again," he said, shaking hands with her.

Barnard left the room and Caz followed him, waiting at the top as he descended the stairs and let himself out of the street door. She returned to the kitchen and threw herself at McCabe, arms around him, pulling him to her and pressing her cheek to his chest, "I've missed you so much!"

He laughed, "You've only been gone for two hours."

"I know but I still missed you."

"What have you done with Tricia?"

"We met a couple of her friends and she's gone off to have lunch with them."

"Right. Well I think we should do the same. Are you hungry?"

"I will be in an hour or so," she replied.

"OK. Well I've got something to show you first. Come on," he took her hand and headed for the stairs.

"Where are we going?" she asked.

"It's a surprise. "

They left the flat and crossed the road to Brighton Station where they got into the first in line of the waiting taxis.

"Where to?" asked the driver.

"Brighton Marina please," replied McCabe.

They sat back and held hands, comfortable and easy with each other, as the taxi drove through Brighton and then turned east along Marine Parade which shone brilliant in the sunlight reflected from the white facades of the seafront buildings. Caz looked out of the taxi's window at the sea and the horizon with its distant line of tiny ships, without really seeing anything. She thought about the events of the last few weeks and how, ever since their time in Nice they had become so close. The last two days in particular had intensified her feelings towards Chad, perhaps because they had been living at her flat together, and she knew that her longing for him was real and not just something brought about by being in the South of France with him. She felt vulnerable. Caz had never in her life felt this way about a man and it made her happy and sad at the same time. Happy because she was experiencing love and he was with her, but sad because she knew that he would have to leave. Not because he didn't want her but because his life was nomadic. At the moment Chad had lost everything: his boat, his guitars, his way of life and all that was important to him, but Caz knew that these things could be replaced and, as soon as he was able to, he would go. And what would she do then?

They reached Brighton Marina and the taxi stopped by the West Jetty. McCabe paid for the ride and, hand in hand, they walked along the concrete ramp to the security gates. He took his keys from his pocket and pressed the security fob to the pad which unlocked the gate and allowed them through.

"Where are we going?" asked Caz again.

"Nearly there."

McCabe led her past the scores of moored boats to the end of the jetty and stopped by an imposing 51 foot, white fibreglass sailing yacht.

"What do you think?"

"About what?" she asked.

"About the boat."

"Which boat?"

"This boat?"

She looked at it with more interest, "It's very nice. Why?"

"Because I've made an offer on it, subject to survey."

Caz looked at the boat again, concern on her face, "Really?"

"Really."

"Are you going to live on her?" she asked.

"For a while at least. I'd like to go travelling in her."

"Where to this time?"

"I think the Med again, but this time I rather fancy the Greek Islands. Would you like to come?"

She reached out, took both of his hands in hers and looked up at him. Tears began to form in her beautiful green eyes and she answered, "With you Chad, I'll go anywhere."

THE END

Afterword

This book is a work of fiction but the wreck of the SS Richard Montgomery is real and continues to be a danger to life and property. Successive British governments have studied, debated and prepared reports on the problem of what to do with it but nothing happens. It may have reached the point now where it is just too dangerous to tamper with the wreck's contents and the threat that it poses will continue to exist unchallenged.

The easyJet flight numbers for the Gatwick-Nice-Gatwick route are the ones that were in use at the time in which the story is set. However, at the time of publication the flight numbers have been changed and the numbers referred to in the book are now being used on a different route.

Brett Hoskins
April 2024

Also available in this series:

The Normandy Run